Turn On Your Radios, San Diego
Let Dillon Danvers Turn You On...

WXNT, San Diego, proudly invites you to tune in to Dillon Danvers's nightly radio program, "Dillon After Dark." Discover what so many loyal listeners already know, that Dillon has what it takes to heat up the airwaves. He's erotic and hypnotic, an enigma to all of San Diego. Whether you thirst for intelligent conversation or an intimate consultation, Dillon's telephone lines are open. Call now....

MEN at WORK

—MILLIONAIRE'S CLUB   —BOARDROOM BOYS   —MAGNIFICENT MEN

—TALL, DARK & SMART   —DOCTOR, DOCTOR   —MEN OF THE WEST

—MEN OF STEEL   —MEN IN UNIFORM

MEN *at* WORK

LEANDRA LOGAN

DILLON AFTER DARK

MAGNIFICENT
MEN

Harlequin Books

TORONTO • NEW YORK • LONDON
AMSTERDAM • PARIS • SYDNEY • HAMBURG
STOCKHOLM • ATHENS • TOKYO • MILAN
MADRID • WARSAW • BUDAPEST • AUCKLAND

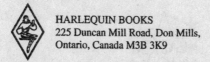

HARLEQUIN BOOKS
225 Duncan Mill Road, Don Mills,
Ontario, Canada M3B 3K9

ISBN 0-373-81052-0

DILLON AFTER DARK

Dear Reader,

Time has flown by since I came up with the concept for *Dillon After Dark*. My children were young, and I was relatively new to Harlequin. Since then I've written many romance novels for the company, and learned through personal experience that teenagers do indeed behave very much like my fictional creation Julianne Jordan!

As for my heroes, they've remained deliciously similar in temperament through the years—rough around the edges, but pliable in the right woman's arms. Dillon Danvers is just such a man. And his persona is one I still fantasize about: California surfer by day, seductive radio personality by night.

I recall my editor Dominique calling me soon after receiving the original manuscript and saying in her delightful French accent, "Thank you for Dillon...."

I hope you feel the same way.

Leandra Logan

To Gene, who makes all my nights special...

"GOOD EVENING. Once again it's the tenth hour here at WXNT. This is the 'Dillon After Dark' program, 103.9 on your FM dial. I'm Dillon, your host for the next three hours. Whether you're an old friend, a new listener, or an accidental eavesdropper flipping through stations, welcome to nighttime radio. It's Sunday, the fifth of March. The current temperature here at our home base of San Diego is a comfortable sixty-five degrees. For our more adventurous souls, Paris is reporting a Fahrenheit reading of forty-six, Honolulu a mild seventy-two.

"Surfing was excellent along the coastline today. Santa Cruz carvers were reporting eight-foot faces while Ventura varied between five and eight. Tomorrow promises much of the same. I'll be with you listeners in spirit at dawn while I enjoy my slice of surf with all you early risers.

"Moving onto other interests—as promised, my guest for the second half of the program will be author Verda Fitzsimmons, creator of the popular Kelly Madigan detective series. Prepare your questions for her. We'll also look in on WXNT's own entertainment critic Doug Fairmont, who is on location at one of San Diego's trendy new nightspots. All that and more coming up in our second segment. But first things first. Time to relax. That's right—slip it out of high gear into neutral. Let's enjoy some soft music, share some mellow musings on the human condition. I see my telephone lines are already blinking—

"Dillon here."

"Hello?"

"You're on the air."

"Dillon, this is Julianne."

"Julianne from Coronado, I presume."

"You know it is! It says so, right on your monitor."

"So true. I'm glad you called, Julianne. I always like to keep up with my regular listeners. So what's on your mind tonight?"

"I want you to know I entered your poetry contest."

"I'm glad to hear it. But you know I'm not at liberty to discuss the contest with my listeners. Each poem will be judged anonymously."

"Oh, sure, I know. But I just had to tell you I plan to win."

"So, how have you been, Julianne?"

"Okay, I guess..."

"You sound troubled."

"You always know what I'm feeling, Dillon. You always understand."

"That's what I'm here for. Now tell me all about it."

"It's still my mother."

"Ah, yes... As I recall she was continually invading your privacy."

"A constant battle, Dillon. Day after day after day—"

"I get the picture, Julianne. Any progress yet in setting her straight?"

"No. I followed your advice—you know, about being more vague about my personal business."

"Yes, of course. I figured if the poor thing had less information, she'd have less to pick apart."

"Well, the old girl saw right through that! Got bent out of shape. Wondered where I got the idea in the first place."

"Oh."

"Don't worry, I didn't tell her about you."

"You could have, Julianne. Perhaps she'd like to call me herself."

"No! You're one thing that's all mine. I mean, I—"

"I know what you mean. I understand."

"Yes, Dillon. You do understand. No wonder all the ladies love you."

"Well, I wouldn't go that far..."

"Anyway, I was wondering if you have any more ideas, any other ways I can handle my mother."

"Hmm... Perhaps if you could steer her in another direction, draw her away from you. Does she have any social life of her own—other things to think about?"

"She goes out once in a while. But mostly she spends her time poking into other people's problems. It's pretty much all she does, come to think of it, Dillon. She gets such a charge out of giving people the third degree. Always asking them what they do and why. And if they're going to do it again. The questions can go on forever!"

"Sounds like a terrible existence. Even for the infirm. Is she mobile?"

"Oh, of course. She drives and everything."

"You did say last week that it would be impossible to find her another residence, didn't you?"

"Uh-huh. She's hangin' tough right where she is."

"Julianne, there are so many facilities now that provide excellent care for those in their twilight years."

"Like a nursing home? Gee, she's not ready for a nursing home!"

"No, no. I'm talking about communities designed for older folks who aren't as spry as they once were. They live independently, but help is just a phone call away. There aren't a lot of stairs to climb at these places. Outdoor work is taken care of, building maintenance, too. There are peers on hand to play cards with. Field trips are planned. Sounds pretty wonderful, doesn't it?"

"It does sound nice..."

"You sound rather doubtful, Julianne. Isn't there any chance your mother would be interested?"

"I don't think so, Dillon. She's pretty crazy about our house. And there is her father—my poor old grandfather—to consider in this, too, you know. Remember, the retired admiral?"

"Oh, yes, he lives with you, too."

"He's such an old sweetie. And such a help around the house. Cooks, cleans. My mother has it made."

"It sounds rather cushy for your mother. Extended family

situations can be difficult when some members don't share the load."

"The worst part is my mother won't let me grow up!"

"I imagine you'll always be a youngster in her eyes. It does happen."

"Exactly! I'm still a child in her eyes. You're so wise, Dillon. I hope your family appreciates you."

"My listeners are my family, Julianne."

"I guess I've kept you long enough, Dillon."

"All my lines are blinking, so I should go on to the next caller. Hang in there, Julianne. You are to be congratulated for keeping the family under one roof."

"Thanks, Dillon. That means so much coming from a wonderful hunk—I mean, a wonderful talk-show host like you."

"I sincerely mean it, Julianne. Many young women shun the older folks, but you're handling two generations of parents. Commendable."

"I try, Dillon. I really try."

"Well, keep in touch, Julianne."

"I will. And I'll try to get Mother out of the house—back into the world!"

"Start with something small, perhaps a movie or a play."

"Maybe I can find her a man of her own."

"Ah, perhaps a platonic checker partner would be a more practical beginning. But I admire your spirit. Bye for now, Julianne. Remember this, listeners—we're all one big family here on WXNT on the 'Dillon After Dark' program. Dillon cares. He cares about you."

JULIANNE JORDAN shifted position on her bed and set her hot-pink telephone back on her nightstand. Dillon's voice emanated from the boom box on her maple dresser, filling the lamplit room with husky, velvety tones. It was always hard to hang up. Always hard to let him go. He was talking to another caller now, laughing with a deep sexy richness that made her tingle all the way down to her painted toenails.

She reached over to her nightstand once again, this time to retrieve a blue ceramic plate holding a thick slice of apple pie. She leaned back on the two plump pillows propped against her brass headboard and drew her knees up against her chest to hold the plate.

Dillon and dessert at night. Mmm... Life could be awesomely excellent at times like this. The house was blissfully quiet; Mom and Grandpop were sound asleep. It was like she was out on her own and Dillon was her special dream man. With a movement honed by nights of practice, Julianne gathered her long flyaway black hair in one hand and tossed it over her shoulder, clearing the path between pie and mouth. She then dug into the pie with gusto, savoring the tangy apple-cinnamon taste.

When Julianne was old enough to have her own apartment, there would be late-night sweets every night—right out in the open! She could listen to Dillon in her very own living room on a huge stereo with Dolby sound!

As it was, she was stuck with Mom's rules. Whew, would Mom freak if she knew about Dillon and the pie. Neither one should be ingested so late, Kristina Jordan would say. No way José.

So many little things seemed to bother the woman, Julianne lamented, chomping away in frustration. Julianne was too young to date at fourteen, too old to leave her room messy, too old to whine about taking out the garbage. Julianne could hardly keep all the rules straight. And so what if she collected dessert plates under her bed from time to time? After all, she couldn't very well return them to the kitchen in the dead of night! What if there was a burglar downstairs looting the study? What if one of Mom's crazy patients came for a surprise nighttime visit? What if she tripped on the stairs while she was carrying a stack of dishes, knocked herself out, and no one found her until morning?

There were a million reasons why she was much better off shoving the plates under her bed for the time being, until she had a free moment in the daytime to bring them downstairs. And she would get around to it, she vowed, pressing the last crumbs onto her fork. Lately it seemed that whenever she was in her bedroom she was just too busy—too busy thinking about life and things.

The mattress squeaked as Julianne leaned over to shove the plate and fork beneath the bed. She winced as ceramic hit ceramic. Oops! She carefully fluffed the ruffled hem of her bedspread to conceal the last of her growing crockery collection, then fell back against her pillow with a sigh.

No doubt about it. Mom simply expected too much from her. And her rules were prehistoric! Mom would be searching the house for her dishes pretty soon and probably make *her* wash them—by hand because they're the good ones. Then there was the lights-out rule of ten-thirty on school nights. Whew, was she ever living in the Stone Age! Look out, Wilma Flintstone! Brave Grandpop had been trying to loosen the rules a bit since he'd moved in. But he would only do so much and he was a little out of touch after all his years at sea...

Julianne's spirits brightened as her thoughts once again turned to Dillon. Julianne rarely missed his show and she was never disappointed in him. Dillon knew how to treat a lady and his advice was awesomely excellent. He sure understood her problems with her mother! True, Mom wouldn't go for one of those old folks residences he'd suggested, but she did need a social life—something to fill her time.

Get the old girl out and about, that was the answer! Dillon was so wise. He was one of those rare people over twenty-one who was in touch with the real world. Julianne wasn't sure exactly how old Dillon was. But he sure wasn't an ancient thirty-four like Mom!

Julianne reached over to the nightstand for her soft drink. He was probably a trendy twenty-three or so, she guessed confidently, tipping the aluminum can to her lips to wash down the pie. Old enough to have been around, but young enough to enjoy life. The perfect age for her. She wouldn't be fourteen forever. If she could just meet Dillon face-to-face... He'd see their love was meant to be. He'd be willing to wait!

Julianne reached under her pillows and produced her one

and only picture of her camera shy hero. It was only a small grainy photograph she'd clipped from the newspaper, but considering how private a man Dillon was, she felt herself lucky to have it.

She set the picture on her knee and gazed at it with intense longing. Did his eyes crinkle at the corners when he laughed? Did he have a dimple in his chin when he smiled? He wasn't smiling in the clipping. He looked downright sober. Downright sexy.

It wasn't enough! Listening to the velvet magic of his voice night after night, staring at a wrinkled piece of paper wasn't enough. She had to meet Dillon! She was going to meet him, Julianne assured herself with adolescent faith. The radio station's "Dillon After Dark" contest was the opportunity she'd been waiting for: write a poem about the reclusive, mysterious announcer and if you win the contest you spend a romantic evening as his date. She'd followed the rules to the letter. An eight and a half by eleven sheet of paper. Typed. Double-spaced.

Then there was the poem itself. The heart-wrenching masterpiece! Julianne nearly choked on her cola as she thought back on her brilliant work, the flowing verses of her labor of love. There had been so many sacrifices to endure! She'd missed a few of her favorite sitcoms, plus an interview with Tiffany on cable. Of course there were also a few less important snags—homework, for example. Math and biology had really suffered during the week-long burst of agonizing creativity. In truth, all her subjects had died a sudden, quite painless death. Of course, her sagging grades would catch up to Mom sooner or later, she realized with a resigned sigh. But the poem would pay off before then. No sense even thinking beyond her date with Dillon. Time would stop a week from Saturday night. Dillon would make all her dreams come true.

Julianne drained the pop can, tossed it into an open dresser drawer where it would have plenty of aluminum company, and snuggled under the covers.

She had to win the contest! It there was one single shred of fairness in the world, she would come out the winner with Dillon Danvers. After all, it was fate, and people weren't supposed to mess around with the stuff like that. No way José!

1

"GUESS WHAT, MOM! You'll never guess what!"

Dr. Kristina Jordan gasped in amazement behind her desk as her daughter Julianne dashed through her reception room with the agility of a long-legged doe, nearly colliding with her last patient of the day. For a brief uncomfortable moment Kristina watched her bubbly fourteen-year-old play a dodging dance in her office doorway with plump, nervous Mrs. Ellerbee.

"Ah, excuse me, ma'am," Julianne said breathlessly, her wide-set violet eyes round with excitement. "I'm sorta in a hurry."

Mrs. Ellerbee's hands fluttered in jerky movements. "See, Doctor, everybody's in a hurry," she trilled. "I'm making dinner for ten people tonight," she told Julianne.

Kristina rose from her desk with a cool efficient stride, her dainty features projecting patience. "I was just telling Mrs. Ellerbee to slow down a bit. Perhaps you could do the same, Julianne," she suggested, stilling her fidgety daughter so Mrs. Ellerbee could pass by without further hindrance.

For a second Kristina wondered if the calm approach she'd recommended for Mrs. Ellerbee would in fact benefit her daughter. Not a chance, she realized, eyeing her ever-moving elf, who was literally up on tiptoe she was so excited. Julianne didn't have a calm bone in her body.

"Loony-tune," Julianne murmured in wonder once the woman had departed in a flurry. Shaking her head, she jogged ahead into Kristina's hushed oak-panelled office.

"How many times have I warned you about calling my patients names like loony-tune and space cadet," Kristina scolded, following Julianne into the room with a disapproving frown.

"She didn't hear me," Julianne tossed back, her reply swiftly drawn from her brimming cache of retorts.

"Just be careful." Kristina insisted. Circling her gleaming hardwood desk, she sank into her velour-cushioned chair with a weary sigh. Mrs. Ellerbee's file was still open on the desktop, a reminder that she'd intended to make a few notations on her patient's progress before leaving for the day. She swiftly picked up her pen to scribble some observations before Julianne had the chance to launch into her latest scheme. It had to be big, Kristina realized, for the girl wasn't in the habit of popping downtown at the dinner hour.

"I'm sure you'll cure that jumpy lady, Mom," Julianne ventured confidently.

"Thanks for the vote of confidence," Kristina murmured as she wrote.

Julianne sighed impatiently and wandered over to Kristina's plant shelf near the window, picking the dead leaves off a large red azalea. "You're the best shrink—psychologist in San Diego. And your flowers get lots of love. Just like I do."

Kristina lifted her eyes from her work. "Hmm... Sounds like a buttering-up job to me." A skeptical, but not humorless expression crossed Kristina's face as she surveyed her one and only offspring. Julianne was so much like herself at fourteen—black tresses flowing freely over her small shoulders, violet eyes full of sparkling mischief. And of course the latest of fashion on her lithe, graceful shape—black denim jeans, oversized black cotton blouse, and satin floral vest.

Twenty years ago Kristina had been the grooviest in low-slung bell-bottom jeans and a poor-boy shirt. But those carefree days were naturally behind her now, she thought, unconsciously patting the glossy black knot of hair at her neck. Her skirted gray suit suited her just right. As did her maroon blouse with harmonizing gray pinstripes. She was a professional inside out. A dedicated psychologist whom her patients trusted and admired. Comfortable and capable. She'd attained both those goals after a long hard climb.

"I suppose you're wondering what I'm doing here," Julianne blurted out impatiently, scooting over to Kristina's desk.

"More to the point, I'm wondering just how you got here." Home was in Coronado, one heck of a hike from downtown San Diego.

"Oh, Grandpop dropped me off," she replied airily.

Kristina's thin black eyebrows arched with hope. "Is he parked downstairs? We could pick up a bite down the street."

Julianne shot her a pitying look. "You're dreamin', Mom. You know how Grandpop feels about restaurant food." To demonstrate, she clutched her throat and poked out her tongue.

"If it isn't Navy, it better be Howard's." Kristina wrinkled her nose in dissatisfaction as she proclaimed the well-worn phrase. Since Howard, her father, had come to live with them six months ago, he'd taken over the kitchen duties. There wasn't much she could say in complaint. As lousy a cook as he was, he was the gourmet of their threesome.

"He went back home to cook up a special celebration meal," Julianne gushed, clasping her heavily ringed hands together.

"What are we celebrating this time, Julianne?" Kristina coaxed, tapping her pen on the desk.

"I won a poetry contest!" she announced, lifting her chin higher with a smug grin.

"In composition class?" Kristina's face lit up, instantly thinking academic thoughts. This was wonderful news. Julianne had been showing so little initiative during her freshman year at Bellwood Girls Academy. Déjà vu. Kristina too had goofed off at the academy and had had to work like crazy in college to get back on the track. She'd hoped that with a little pressure, Julianne would put a bit more enthusiasm into her studies. Apparently she was finally getting a response.

"School?" Julianne balked at the notion with open-mouthed denial. "We're talking about a real-life contest here! My name in lights! Almost..."

What was it this time? Kristina wondered. A couple of months ago it had been some kind of ridiculous singing correspondence course—as if a person could learn a sing by mail with the aid of a plastic pitch pipe! She'd reported that little scam to the postal authorities. Last week it had been the false fingernail kit with rhinestone studs. Would she ever cease to find thumbnails everywhere from the sugar bowl to the bathtub?

"C'mon, Mom, take a guess," she challenged, rocking on her heels with a teasing grin that implied the task was impossible.

Kristina leaned back in her hair, tossing aside her pen. "It's been a long day, Julianne. Please spill it."

"Okay, okay," she placated, raising her palms. "Get this. I won the 'Date With Dillon' contest."

"What?" Kristina's voice escaped in a shriek, her heart lurching at the sound of that horrible four-letter word: *date*. Julianne was still a child! A typical kid who occasionally bounced her doll on her knee when she thought no one was looking and giggled her way through hokey forties monster movies. True, Julianne had attended a few dances and mixed parties. But no real dates—not yet.

"Isn't it the ultimate?"

"Who is Dillon?" Kristina demanded in a quieter tone, her eyes narrowing as she fought to suppress her panic.

"He's the late-night announcer at WXNT," Julianne gushed. "'Dillon After Dark.' It's the hottest show and he's the hottest hunk in town. Plus he's the sexiest, the sweetest—"

"It can't be true." With a moan, Kristina rested her face in her hands. Her head felt suddenly very heavy.

"Sure it's true," Julianne assured her matter-of-factly. "Just a minute, I have the telegram right here." Julianne took her long-strapped purse from her shoulder and dumped its contents onto the desktop.

Kristina grabbed Mrs. Ellerbee's file just in time to save it from being buried under a heap of scented junk. Dread gnawed her insides as she picked through the pile of cosmetics, candy, coins, and of course fingernails, to extract a crushed ball of paper. She smoothed the telegram flat and glared at it.

"It's all there between the lipstick stains," Julianne announced with pride.

Kristina absorbed the news with a sour look. In the opinion of WXNT's official judge, Julianne had written the most inspired poem about WXNT's Dillon After Dark. In appreciation, she was invited to an intimate dinner with the radio host. "Who would award such a prize to a little girl?" she muttered under her breath.

"I may have a young body, by my heart is ancient!" Julianne cried defensively. She picked a half-eaten candy bar from her pile of possessions and peeled back the wrapper. "This date is my destiny!" she said, biting into the chocolate. "Our two old hearts beating in one mind!"

"How old is his body?" Kristina asked bluntly.

"I'm not sure," she admitted between chews. "But he can't possibly be too old for me."

"Pack your stuff back into your purse, Grandma Moses," Kristina directed. "It's time to go home." Two hearts as one, she uttered inwardly. Did this Dillon say hokey things like that on the radio? What goo. With file folder in hand, Kristina pushed aside her chair with a disgruntled nudge and got to her feet.

"I'm not quitting on Dillon," Julianne warned as Kristina moved toward the bank of file cabinets against the wall.

Kristina turned to her daughter who was swallowing the last bite of her Milky Way bar in a defiant gulp. "Heartfelt unions are out of the question for you, Julianne. At least for five to ten years."

"That's like a prison sentence! I'm mature now!" she claimed, stomping her foot.

"You're a young lady," Kristina retorted, stuffing the file back into its rightful drawer. "A young lady who just dropped a candy wrapper on the floor," she added significantly.

Julianne swiftly bent to retrieve the wrapper and tossed it into the wastebasket. "Dillon understands me. And he understands you, too!"

Kristina eyed her daughter with keen suspicion. "How on earth could he understand us? He doesn't know us."

Julianne bit her lip. She'd almost blown everything with a slip of the tongue! Mom might not understand why she so counted on Dillon's advice, why she told him all sorts of secret things. She would have to handle Mom very carefully. Grandpop would help her out. He was darn good at it.

"Julianne, we have to talk about this contest. This date. This Dillon!"

"We can't talk about it until you get a grip on yourself," Julianne announced nobly. Hands on hips, she marched out to the reception area.

"I may not get a grip until you're married to a stockbroker or a lawyer," Kristina called after her. "I may never get a grip!"

It was Kristina's habit to use her after-work drive from her office in downtown San Diego to her home in Coronado as a buffer between business and home. Though the latest family trauma had already invaded her solitary time in the car, she decided to slip a mellow Anne Murray tape into the player and hope for peace. For whatever reason, Julianne was willing to discuss Dillon to the strains of Anne Murray. She quietly stared out the passenger window as Kristina guided her silver Camaro through the congested downtown traffic.

As usual, Kristina's spirits brightened as she crossed the San Diego-Coronado bridge. Coronado had always been her home, the only place she cared to live. The city was almost an island, sitting in the curve of the San Diego Bay. The seaside resort town was a world of its own with quiet, tree-lined streets and old-fashioned Victorian-style homes. Southern California was not a spot one might expect to find English-style mansions with peaked roofs and gabled windows. Its charm had left an indelible mark on Kristina over the years, as did the friendly people.

Though Kristina's parents had been married until the day her mother died three years ago, Kristina had often felt as though she was part of a single-parent family as Julianne now was. Kristina's father, Admiral Howard Hayward, had been a loyal navy man, absent for months on end. Living near the North Island Naval Air Station was as natural as breathing. Living with families in the same predicament was comforting. These surroundings were the best she could give her daughter.

Moments later their pale yellow Victorian mansion with its white wraparound porch on its huge corner lot came into view. Julianne spoke for the first time since entering the car.

"Look, Mom! Grandpa's torching something on the barbecue!"

Gray billows of smoke enveloped the Camaro as Kristina rolled up the narrow concrete driveway. "Must've gotten tired of preparing his five-alarm chili and fried chicken."

"And about time, too," Julianne added with a pained expression.

"Don't throw away the Rolaids just yet," Kristina whispered, shutting off the engine. "Pop?" she called, stepping out of the car into the charcoal-grease fog. "Are you out here?"

The back screen door creaked open, then slammed behind Admiral Howard Hayward. The large-framed man lumbered down off the porch with a long spatula in his hand. His thatch of mussed gray hair, baggy dungarees, and long white butcher's apron emblazoned in red with the slogan, Burn Baby Burn, belied the fact that he'd spent the last fifty years serving his country with gruff dignity.

"Hi, girls. Seems my fire flared up a bit." He wound a heavy muscular arm around Julianne and flipped some very black burgers on the Weber grill with the other.

"Everything under control, Pop?" Kristina asked dubiously.

"Searing in the juices is all," he claimed jovially.

"They look good and crunchy!" Julianne observed with an appreciative sniff.

"Thank you, kind lady," he replied magnanimously, sliding Kristina a wink. "So how was your day, Krissy?" he asked, the smile on his face a dazzler to be sure.

"I've had better, Pop. Julianne—"

"I have to dash," Julianne interrupted breathlessly. She stood on tiptoe to kiss her grandfather's wrinkled cheek and skipped off toward the house. "Surf's up!"

"But, Julianne!" Kristina raised her voice in protest.

"Grandpop needs a platter for the hamburgers," she called back over her shoulder before disappearing through the screen door.

"Aw, let her go," Howard advised with a carefree wave of his utensil. "She's probably ashamed of my apron." The thought made him bark with laughter. "Hardly seems fair, though. If I hid every time she wore those goofy clothes of hers in public, she'd be forced to take the bus everywhere but the bathroom!"

Kristina frowned, frustrated that her father's complaint was punctuated with glee. "Pop, you're entirely too lenient with Julianne."

"Oh, c'mon, honey. I'm just enjoying her, that's all. You can't imagine how much it means to hold the little sprite in my arms every single day. All those years of brief visits, watching her grow through photographs. Forgive me, Krissy. Forgive me for longing to see her face light up with pleasure." His bright face grew meek along with his tone.

"For Pete's sake, Pop!" Kristina folded her arms across her chest and paced back and forth in the smoky haze, trying to think of a comeback that would penetrate the admiral's thick skull. Her father was a tough one to debate. He was accustomed to giving orders to sailors. He was accustomed to having his own way. In the six short months since he'd retired and moved back into the family home, he managed to continually undermine Kristina's parental authority until she felt like the third wobbly wheel on a tricycle going downhill. Children couldn't be raised on sentiment alone! No matter how well-intentioned a grandpop was. Kids needed discipline—the sort of guidance Kristina's own passive mother hadn't applied to her. Kristina had been quite adept at manipulating her mother into letting her run wild. Julianne wasn't going to be given the same option.

Howard grew sober as his shrewd eyes followed Kristina in her soul-searching trip around and around the Weber grill. "You need a man around here, Krissy. And not one like that beach bum who calls himself Julianne's father. It's disgusting the way he ran off and left his family. The way he lives to ride a wooden board around on the water."

"I believe the boards are Fiberglas these days, Pop," Kristina interrupted.

"What's the difference?" Howard shook a large fist. "A bum on wood, a bum on plastic. He lives in a sugar shack in Hawaii, takes our Muffin for a couple of weeks a year and figures that's enough. You need a man with roots, honey. And Julianne needs a full-time father."

Kristina frowned with doubt. "It's hard to imagine it all, Pop."

"Your Mother needed more than I gave, God bless her soul." Wistfulness touched his gravelly voice. "I've come to wonder how she ever raised you without me at her side."

As always, her father was managing to talk circles around her. She walked in circles as he talked in circles. The trained psychologist in her could flatten him no doubt. But this wasn't an objective situation. She had to intervene as his daughter, let her own needs and memories wash over her professional point of view. Howard was her pop. The man she'd longed for over the years, the sailor who she'd desperately wished would go into dry dock, like a ship that had run its course and was back for good.

Well, she thought with a rueful smile, her wish had come true. Howard Hayward was finally home. She was thirty-four years old and he was back for good. Too bad it was so late. Kristina was now comfortably accustomed to raising Julianne without a permanent male fixture. "Pop, I know what's best for my daughter. I've had fourteen years of experience."

"I barely saw you when you were growing up," he cut in with a line of patter she could recite by heart. "I rarely bounced Julianne on my knee when she was a baby. But don't fret, Krissy. I'll be here to fill in until Mr. Right comes along. I'll enjoy each and every minute of it, too."

"It's like one big party, Pop. You give in to her every whim."

"Naw," he scoffed.

"Take today, for instance. You drove her downtown when I was within an hour of returning home." Kristina eyed him with a knowing lift of her chin.

"She wanted to show you the telegram right away. Guess I got caught up in the thrill of the moment. It's so much fun to share her childish enthusiasm over small pleasures. Does wonders for an old man's crusty outlook."

"How involved are you in this 'Dillon After Dark' thrill? Did you know she was entering this contest?" Kristina demanded suspiciously.

"No, no! It's not the sort of thing I'd approve of."

"Whew." A small smile of relief spread over her face. "There's no way I can deny Julianne this prize without your support." She reached over and adjusted the collar of her father's plaid shirt, her tone softer.

"Uh, honey..."

Looking up into her father's face, Kristina saw the age lines around his eyes deepen with doubt. Before she could question him further, the wooden swing on the front side of the porch creaked loudly and Julianne rounded the house.

"Everything set?" she called out cheerfully, propping her forearms on the white wooden rail with an expectant look.

"I'm a bit behind schedule, Muffin," Howard confessed.

"You haven't told her yet!" Julianne squealed in dismay. She clapped a hand to her mouth, her expression stricken. "Oops."

"What have you done now, Pop?" Kristina asked, though the question was rhetorical. She now understood why Julianne had been so quiet in the car, why she'd flown into the house. She wanted her grandpop to fire the last torpedo at her flank.

"I accepted the prize," Howard confessed quietly, with a helpless shrug. "It seemed cruel to yank a dream-come-true away. It would've been different had we known in advance—before she entered..." Howard trailed off, sheepish over the weakness of his alibi.

"The world won't end if you say no to your granddaughter on occasion," Kristina blurted out with exasperation. But one look at her father's contrite face told her that he really believed it would. How could she handle the two of them without losing her sanity? she wondered.

"He's a thirty-five-year-old man," Howard scoffed. Then lowering his voice he added, "He'll take no interest in our little beanpole gal. It would've been like you dining with Captain Kangaroo at her age."

Kristina shook her head with wry amusement. No doubt about it, the admiral had been at sea far too long! "Pop, teenage girls are dreaming of heroes a bit more sophisticated than the good Captain."

"It's all the same to these celebrities," Howard insisted, unfazed. "They're doing guest appearances all the time, mingling with all ages."

"Surely this prize was meant for a grown woman."

"You can't take Dillon away from me!" Julianne cried, darting off the porch and over to the barbecue. "He's mine, I tell you."

Kristina grasped Julianne by the shoulders as the girl stomped her foot in fury. "Julianne, you cannot go to dinner with a grown man."

"But I won him fair and square," she protested. "Two hearts—"

"Quit giving your heart to this man!" she huffed.

"There must be a way, Krissy," Howard interceded hopefully, raising a bushy gray eyebrow. "It's just a meal at some fancy hotel in San Diego. Perhaps a chaperon..."

"There will be plenty of people at the restaurant," Julianne pointed out.

"True, Krissy," Howard chimed in.

"So, what do you say, Mom?" Julianne pleaded, attempting to catch Kristina's eye as she stared into the horizon.

"Mmm...there's nothing else for it, is there," Kristina murmured thoughtfully, deep in her own thoughts.

"What do you mean?" Julianne asked, her mood brightening with her mother's hopeful look.

"I should've thought of it before. After all, I've become quite experienced at being the third wheel around here..."

Julianne backed away in horror. "Oh, no, Mom, you can't. Please!"

"What is it?" Howard asked, his puzzled eyes shifting from one female to the other.

Kristina grinned merrily. "Guess who's coming to dinner?"

WOULD JULIANNE ever lighten up about Kristina's plans to join her and Dillon at the restaurant? Kristina pondered the question as she prepared for bed later on that evening. She pulled her short white nightie over her head, tugging it straight over her slender shapely hips. Julianne had remained grim over their meal of black hamburgers, her young face set in a stony expression that would've made an intriguing fifth bust up on Mount Rushmore. But Kristina stood her ground. Julianne could either gracefully accept her mother's presence on the date or forget all about meeting Dillon. Julianne couldn't forget him. Dillon was dreamy, dreamy, dreamy. Awesomely dreamy.

Kristina wandered across the hall to the bathroom to brush her teeth. She squeezed some toothpaste on her brush and faced the cabinet mirror. Imagine Julianne being afraid she would embarrass her in front of Dillon. She claimed Kristina wouldn't know how to act, knew nothing of romantic sparks.

"Hah!" she mumbled, jamming her toothbrush into her mouth. Where did the kid think she'd come from? A mail-order catalog like her plastic pitch pipe?

Visions of her ex-husband Wade, Julianne's father, flooded her mind. They had been happy once, very much in love. But it had been a puppy love, fueled by the thrill of the sand, surf and continual beach parties. Married at eighteen, divorced at twenty-two. The marriage ended when Kristina realized that life wasn't supposed to be Beach Blanket Bingo.

The birth of Julianne had been the turning point in Kristina's life. She began to mature, accept the adult responsibilities of being a parent. She gradually grew from a rebellious teenager to a mother willing to work.

Unfortunately Wade saw things quite differently. He'd wanted Kristina to remain the wild sea nymph he'd married. When Kristina inherited a sizable sum of money from a favorite aunt around the time of Julianne's first birthday, it was the beginning of the end.

Wade saw the money as his stake on the pro surfing circuit. Kristina saw a college degree in her future. Wade hit the surf, Kristina hit the books. End of love story.

Perhaps Kristina didn't dwell on the magic of romance anymore. But where on earth was the time to daydream, to play out little games of seduction in her head? Life was a serious business. So was raising a teenager. Add to it all an interfering retired admiral, and she was booked solid!

It wasn't as if she no longer felt attractive... She rinsed her toothbrush and set it back in its holder, her gaze centering on the cabinet mirror. Her looks hadn't changed too much over the years. Her creamy complexion, delicate face, and upturned nose had always made the issue of her age a hard one to call. Her violet eyes were her most striking feature, shifting in shade with her emotions. Perhaps the eyes staring back at her didn't hold the same sparkle they once did, she surmised objectively. But she was happy enough.

With a weary sigh, Kristina moved her palm over the bathroom light switch and padded into the hardwood hallway in bare feet. She stopped in midstep on the way to her bedroom, certain she heard an unfamiliar hum. Further investigation led her to Julianne's closed bedroom door. Julianne had to be asleep by now, didn't she?

Kristina closed her hand over the knob and quietly opened the door. Faint strains of a popular Phil Collins tune—the one about two hearts in one mind filled the hushed lamplit room. The digital clock read 10:05 p.m.

"Dillon After Dark." What an appropriate theme song for a romantic radio host, she thought, easing her way through the doorway. And what an appropriate time to eavesdrop on Mr. Dreamy himself.

Julianne was fast asleep, she realized with relief, sprawled across her bed with her lime-green boom box clutched in her arms as if it were a newborn babe. Kristina picked her way through the messy room, stepping over discarded clothing, shoes, stuffed animals, and stacks of teen magazines. There was barely a trace of the peach-colored carpet visible beneath her feet!

It had been almost a month since Kristina had set foot in the sacred turf of her daughter's bedroom. Julianne had protested so strongly over her mother's weekly invasions with vacuum cleaner and feather duster, that Kristina had given up and passed the cleaning responsibilities directly to her.

A lot of good it had done either of them, she thought, pausing near the bed to gape at the colorful clutter. Julianne obviously hadn't lifted a finger in her own behalf since that day! She pulled a lacy purple anklet off the bedside lampshade with a huff of despair.

She gazed down at Julianne with a rush of irritation and tenderness. She looked so young and vulnerable lying in slumber. Her face was smooth, her long black lashes fanned her suntanned cheeks. Her thick hair was a tangled spray on her pillow. What would Dillon think if he saw his date-to-be now, her gangly form in a Garfield nightshirt?

Kristina leaned forward to disengage the boom box from her daughter's embrace, releasing an involuntary gasp as she stubbed her bare toe into a fork and plate under the bed. She dug her toe into the carpet, biting her lip to absorb the pain, then dropped to her knees for a look. She gaped at the sea of ceramic under the box spring. No wonder Pop was so intent on serving dinner on her old Melmac set. Julianne was obviously snacking during her late-night sojourns and he was covering for her. Again.

Luckily the girl was in a deep sleep, so Kristina's movements didn't awaken her. Kristina took the playing radio from her daughter's arms, gripping the handle firmly. It was heavier than she anticipated and she had to struggle for a few seconds to keep her balance. Once again surefooted, Kristina slowly moved back through the room in the company of Phil Collins. She paused at the doorway, reluctant to leave the dirty dishes under Julianne's bed. But she wasn't up to another tiptoe through the twilight zone, she realized, still clutching the radio.

She was about to switch it off when a luxurious male voice erupted from the twin speakers. "Good evening, everyone. It's a few minutes after ten. This is the 'Dillon After Dark' program on San Diego's WXNT. Settle back. Relax. Let's enjoy the mellow sounds of the night..."

The romantic wizard himself, the talk of the city. Kristina closed her eyes as the husky voice of Dillon temptingly coaxed her into a silken web of verbal seduction. With a deep sigh she tilted her head back against the door, first allowing, then eventually welcoming Dillon's rich, soothing tones to flow over her like sweet, succulent nectar. He tantalized and teased, stroking her as gently and slowly as the most ardent of lovers.

Time stood still for a while. The soothing hypnotic quality of his lingo froze Kristina in place. He was a master, effortlessly leaping from his fascinating anecdotes, to his glib advice for callers. Beneath the serene velvet cloak of late-night crooning, Kristina could sense a steely band of power. A persistent, pulling force, demanding a listener's complete emotional participation.

Obviously Dillon had a remarkable talent for control.

What a disturbing thought, to be so easily taken in on his romantic flight of fantasy. Over the years she'd spent many candlelit dinners in the company of men with whom there had been far less intimacy.

With an assertive thumb, she pressed the power button. In

a sense, Dillon's job was like hers—listening to people, helping then work through their heartaches, enjoy their triumphs. But there was one huge difference. While Kristina checked her emotions at the office door in order to deal with her patients more effectively, Dillon used his as a multipurposed tool. He was a professional seducer, using the airwaves to deliver his verbal caress. Dillon disturbed her, enticed her. All without laying a finger on her flesh!

Kristina's heart lurched as she thought of Julianne. Her baby was madly in love with this sensuous creature of the night! If only she hadn't already consented to the dinner date. She couldn't go back on her word now. But she could speak to this pied piper of passion before dinnertime next Saturday night. His seemingly insatiable appetite would have to be confined to items on the menu. She would see to it!

2

"IS THIS DILLON?"

"So who wants to know?"

It was Dillon all right, Kristina mused with startled irritation the following morning, rolling her executive's chair closer to her desk. The light of day did nothing for his disposition. It seemed he was indeed an "after dark" man.

"Who is on the line? How did you get this number, miss?"

"My name is Kristina Jordan. I'm calling about your contest."

The response on the wire was a groggy, animallike growl. "The contest is over. I regret to inform you that WXNT has a winner."

"But—"

"I cherish my privacy, Crystal Jordan, and I demand to know where you got this unlisted number!"

Kristina gripped the gray telephone receiver, her blood beginning to boil as she spoke in quiet even tones. "My name is Kristina Jordan. I know you have a winner. She is my daughter, Julianne Jordan. I got your number from Arnold Rodale, the station manager of WXNT, and furthermore—"

"Rodale had no right to release my number," he interrupted in harsh accusation. "A man has a right to his privacy."

"Your privacy is safe with me," she assured him bluntly. "When our conversation is over I will tear up the slip of paper bearing your phone number into tiny little pieces and burn them in my wastebasket. Then, I will stomp the ashes to dust."

The line was dead for a moment or two. Kristina stiffened, waiting for the dial tone to buzz in her ear. She doubted he was accustomed to women threatening to dispose of his phone number. Perhaps he was in shock. Kristina tried to steady her rapid-fire heartbeat while she waited for his response. She hadn't meant to go so far, but he was so grumpy. Despite her ability to see through his showmanship of the night before, she was disappointed in him. Disappointed that he sounded so human. So humanly rude.

"Exactly why are you calling me, ma'am?"

Kristina frowned in puzzlement. Dillon had yet another tone of voice. Now he was far more alert, less gruff. Called her ma'am this time instead of miss. Kristina couldn't quite pinpoint the swing in mood, but he sounded almost respectful.

"I didn't mean to wake you," Kristina began, glancing at her watch to find it was nearly nine-thirty, "but I have a busy day ahead."

"It's your nickel, ma'am."

"Yes. Well, as you may know, Julianne received your telegram yesterday, and my father accepted the prize on her behalf."

"So, what's the problem?"

"This dinner date can't proceed as it stands, Mr. Dillon."

"There really isn't anything for you to be concerned with, Mrs. Jordan. It is simply a meal downtown."

Kristina heard the creak of what sounded like a mattress in the background and shivered slightly. She had no body to pin on the seducer of late-night radio, but she couldn't help recalling how sexually inviting he'd sounded last night, as if he'd been talking from his bed then. But that was last night. The contrast between night and day was often stark.

"Perhaps this predicament seems simple to you," she continued briskly, running a finger across the top of Julianne's framed photograph on the corner of her desk, "but Julianne isn't accustomed to dining with men downtown. She's only—"

"I realize she's your only child," he interrupted in the throes of a huge yawn. "She's explained a lot of things to me over the past several months and I believe I understand how things are. I assure you, you have nothing to fear."

"She actually calls you on the air?" Kristina's question was a gasp.

"Yes, probably after you've gone to bed, Mrs. Jordan." He was stretching now. Kristina could tell by the deep-chested rumbles on the wire. She shifted uncomfortably as erotic images flooded her mind, three-dimensional pictures taking shape before her eyes. Strong limbs, miles of chest. A velvet touch to match the velvet voice. Her muscles began to soften with her overactive imagination, her body melting into her cushioned office chair.

"Mrs. Jordan? Are you there?"

"Yes," Kristina replied, catching her breath, willing her mind to get back on course. "You were saying that my daughter calls your show. What do you talk about?"

He inhaled haltingly. "We discuss all sorts of things on my program. My show is a blend of romance, heartfelt discussions. I encourage my listeners to confide in me. I try to help them out with their troubles."

Kristina clenched the phone, her body growing ramrod stiff with suspicion. She knew a dodge when she heard it. "Does my daughter call your show to discuss me?"

"Sometimes," he reluctantly admitted. "You sound irritated, so I hope I'm not speaking out of turn. Let me assure you, Mrs. Jordan, your name is never specifically mentioned on the air."

"I'm so grateful to hear it!" Kristina's heart pumped furiously as the situation came into focus. This man knew all sorts of personal things about her. She felt invaded in a most intimate way. He certainly had a lot of nerve grumbling over the fact that she had his phone number! "Like you, I am a very private person, Mr. Dillon. I don't appreciate your show, your hold on my daughter, or your 'heartfelt discussions' concerning me."

"Have you ever listened to the show?"

"Yes, last night was my first time."

"There is no reason to feel shy about the first time," he said silkily. "There's no sin in being lonely enough to reach out to Dillon." His voice continued to soften until his on-air persona was in full verbal bloom. "No sin to overprotect your daughter—though I advise you not to."

"You wish to advise me?" Kristina erupted in awe. His nerve was boundless.

"I'm on call to all my listeners," he intoned. "I believe I've helped Julianne and I think I can help you, too."

"What sort of advice have you given my daughter, Mr. Dillon?"

"You can drop the mister," he invited. "My full name is Dillon Danvers. Simply call me Dillon, as the others do."

"Very well, Dillon," Kristina obliged him through gritted teeth, her last thread of patience snapping. "Did you give her the green light on her messy room? Permission to stay awake all hours listening to you? Encouragement to inhale rich late-night snacks?"

"I've encouraged her independence, Mrs. Jordan," he responded mildly. "Those complaints of yours sound mighty picky to me. Maybe what you need is a change of habit. It sounds as if you've got lots of spare time to fill."

"I certainly do not! You have a lot of nerve."

"You called me, remember?" Dillon's reminder held a good-humored chiding. "Though I may sound nervy to you, ma'am, I'm accustomed to being asked my opinion."

"Well, doling out advice is something for professionals only."

"I'm trying to be patient with you, ma'am, because of the circumstances, but I don't care to be personally attacked."

"What circumstances?"

"Your place in life. Your age. I hate to cast stones, but if my information is correct, you waste away many an hour doling out advice yourself. A little discretion is in order when one spends hours sitting in the kitchen on the telephone, chatting with one friend, then another. Then another, until half the world's problems are analyzed."

"Is that what Julianne told you?" she growled, pounding a fist on her desktop.

"I drew a few of my own conclusions, but in a nutshell, yes she did. And what if her room is a bit untidy? So is mine on occasion. She's busy. So is your father—with the cooking and cleaning duties. Perhaps you should quit hanging on the phone day after day solving other people's problems and pitch in with some of the household chores."

"Anything else, Dillon?" she inquired, twisting his name over her tongue like a sour lemon slice.

"Well, it might do you a bit of good to get out and about more often," he answered with an infuriatingly patronizing tone.

"Oh, you think so, do you?"

"Never hurts. Get a card club together. Go for a picnic."

"Good thinking," Kristina said sweetly. "For starters, I believe I'll go to dinner with you and Julianne next Saturday night."

"Let's not be hasty," he protested with less polish. "Let me—"

"Let me, Dillon. Let me enlighten you on a couple of points that have escaped the dark side of your brain." Kristina's fury was loose now, her voice seething. "First of all, you can drop the Mrs. Simply call me Doctor, as the others do."

"Huh?"

"Julianne has mislead you. I am not a gossipy old biddy. I am a thirty-four-year old practicing psychologist. I do not sit around my kitchen all day long nosing out newsy tidbits. I've managed to acquire some office space in which to conduct business. I treat patients, Mr. Danvers. Patients who trust me as a trained professional to treat them with dignity."

"Oh, damn..."

"Beginning to see the light? Julianne is far more than my only child, she *is* a child! A fourteen-year-old girl who needs a parent's discipline."

"Believe me, I never suspected—"

"So you see, I'm not a doddering old lady looking for activities with which to fill my days."

"No, Doctor, obviously you're not."

"I would appreciate it if you'd stop advising Julianne on how to handle me."

"I most certainly will."

"And I hope you will gracefully accept my presence at the prizewinning date. You are her hero and she's counting on meeting you."

"I have no control over the contest rules, but I will discuss the matter with my station manager."

"Sorry to have interrupted your sleep, Mr. Di-Danvers."

"I think it's about time I get up anyhow, Doctor. Er, ah, good day."

"The very same to you, sir," Kristina returned bitingly, jamming the receiver back in place with force.

"THIS IS A CATASTROPHE!" Dillon Danver's fist landed on Arnold Rodale's desk an hour later with a tremendous slam, jiggling all the knickknacky items cluttering the surface.

The pudgy program director lunged forward in his plush chair and made a daring grab for a glassblown swan threatening to take flight. He cradled it in his padded palms with relief and leaned back with a sigh. "You act as though it's my fault," he grumbled, his round face a study in discontent.

"It is your fault, Arnie." Dillon growled, shaking his fist in the air. "The contest was your idiotic brainstorm."

"Hey, not all is lost. You've gone up several points in the ratings. And," he added with a proud sniff, "we've garnered a few very heavy-hitting sponsors. The kind you've always dreamed of. And they're behind the contest all the way."

"Are they now?" Dillon leaned over the huge desk with a murderous gleam in his blue eyes, his generous mouth thinned to a lethal line. "Sponsors for teething rings and jump ropes? Have you told the makers of Suncatcher Surf Supplies and His'n'Hers Musk that a child has won the contest? Have you told Roger Calhoun?" he asked pointedly.

The terrified look on Arnold's face told Dillon he hadn't warned the sponsors, nor his station-owner uncle. "Please sit down, man," Arnold suggested, his eyes darting nervously over his scattered possessions. "Having you hover over my delicate glass knickknacks rattles me."

Dillon ran a hand through his shaggy bleach-blond hair and obligingly dropped his large body into one of the chairs opposite Arnold, now content that he had the edge over the executive in his custom-tailored suit.

Having the edge meant everything to Dillon Danvers. It kept him on top with his program. It kept people at arm's length. He'd covered all the angles today, he decided, settling back in the cushioned chair, crossing his bare ankle over his knee. He too had dressed for power—not in fine wool like his co-worker, but in some of his trademark beach-bum clothing: green tank shirt, cutoff jeans, and leather sandals. Exhibiting his tanned, muscular physique threw his pudgy associate off balance every time. Hovering over all his glass stuff seemed to disrupt matters, too. "All right, Arnie. I'm out of slamming range. Let's sort this out."

"Good, good." Arnold gingerly replaced the glass swan in its rightful spot beside a china toothpick holder from the Orient. Dillon was so damn hard to figure out, he mused. Out of the goodness of his heart he'd brought the holder back from his Far East trip last year, nursing it through a month of travel. Now, in a flair of temper, he'd almost crushed it to pieces under his fist. Certainly hot-headed. But on occasion oddly warmhearted, as well. All show people were crazy, he rationalized. Crazy as bedbugs.

"I admit I should've been suspicious when the grandfather called to accept the prize," Arnold admitted, pushing his round wire-rimmed glasses up his short nose. "But she claimed she was eighteen on the application."

Dillon's tanned, large-featured face grew baleful. "She lied, Arnie."

"In writing!" Arnold round face was aghast. "Disgusting, the youth of today."

"Not everyone is quite as conventional as you are, Arnie," Dillon pointed out philosophically, lacing his large fingers together. "Julianne of Coronado may consider her age a minor detail in the larger scheme of things."

"Yes, yes," Arnold conceded, shaking his head. "Women! When they really do get older, they go the other direction and pretend they're younger. Can't they ever be happy about their ages?"

"I really don't know, Arnie." Dillon had the feeling Kristina Jordan was quite content with who she was. A strong woman probably born on Independence Day.

"I suppose it could've been worse," Arnold grumbled with a huge sigh. "If the mother hadn't called you about the kid this morning, we wouldn't have found out until you arrived at the restaurant."

"A call? It was a volcano eruption!" Dillon stroked his square stubbled chin in contemplation, wincing as he relived the point of impact. Finding out the mother was young and a doctor to boot was a bit hard to stomach. Dillon normally had his dealings with the public sewn up quite tightly. Because of his careful maneuvering few surprises bounced in his direction. He'd been embarrassed by her revelations, irritated by his embarrassment. "She chewed me up one side, then down the other protecting her young one," he reported.

"Sounds like a real tigress," Arnold cracked with contempt.

"Sounds like a good mother," Dillon shot back in an uncharacteristic flash of sensitivity. His temper had simmered down drastically since his telephone encounter with the witty Dr. Jordan. Once the smoke had cleared, he'd come to respect her position. A parent who cared was a person to admire. Sure, she was snippy, sneaky, and no easy mark as most women seemed to be. But her intentions were good. Sure, she'd treated him like dirt, stringing him along before laying out the facts. But her intentions were the best. She loved her kid.

Dillon had no firsthand knowledge on the subject of caring parents. And he habitually ran like hell from emotional females. Being raised in a succession of foster homes had kept him on the move—physically and emotionally. Whenever he'd dared care for any adult, they'd ended up separated by the vagaries of bureaucracy. There was always some reason why things didn't work out. A foster couple divorced, or they couldn't afford to adopt him. Eventually he simply grew too old to be considered cute. The idea of bonding became too painful, the concept of building lasting relationships too difficult. By the time Dillon was eighteen, he knew better than to open up to anyone.

Fortunately the intimacy of Dillon's talk show fulfilled his desire to be needed and appreciated, and at the same time gave him the distance he was so accustomed to. Dillon truly loved women. But he always made love to them in hotel rooms or at out-of-the-way inns. There was always a detached feel to Dillon's relationships. An inner shield to protect him from the disappointments of his youth.

"Well, bravo for motherhood," Arnold grumbled under his breath as he reached into his desk drawer for a gumdrop. "Just explain to me what a kid her age is doing up so late on school nights."

"Didn't you ever do anything risky at fourteen?" Dillon inquired, wry amusement curling his full mouth. "Perhaps smaller than the huge crime of lying about your age or staying up past your bedtime."

"No! I did what I was told." He popped the piece of candy into his mouth with an obstinate look.

"Yes, how shortsighted of me."

"Have your fun taunting me if you wish, Dillon. But this development is, as you say, catastrophic. A program director's nightmare." Arnold jumped up from his chair and began pacing the floor. "I expected a huge return from this date. The *San Diego Sun* is set to cover it for next Wednesday's entertainment section. The publicity was meant to be a real boost for the station."

Dillon was familiar with the plan—intimate snapshots of the couple at the restaurant, quotes from the starstruck lady. A ratings dream. "I hated this entire thing right from the start."

"But you agreed to it," Arnold reminded him. "You promised to make the best of it."

"Yeah, yeah," Dillon said, waving a dismissive hand. He

did everything he could to make his show a success. He thrived on the air. His professional persona was wide open. But his private life was another matter entirely. His residence was a well-kept secret, his phone number unlisted. He realized that the paradox never ceased to amaze Arnold Rodale, along with the entire WXNT staff. But he handled them quite nicely with his vaguely intimidating off-air demeanor.

"So, what did you tell the mother?" Arnold stood over his chair now, wringing his smooth hands nervously.

"I stalled her, told her I couldn't make a final decision without first consulting you."

Arnold beamed over Dillon's reply. "So, shall we ditch— uh, disqualify the girl?"

"Lawsuit, Arnie." Dillon clucked with disapproval. "Just the sort of thing those national gossip papers love. I can see the headlines now, Station WXNT Takes Candy From Baby." Dillon's gut lurched at the thought of being featured on the cover of a scandal sheet.

"But it's all so disappointing," Arnold groaned. "I envisioned a different image altogether for our winner. Some gorgeous babe who preferred listening to you rather than watching the *Tonight Show*."

"The girl can't be swept under the rug," Dillon insisted. "You'll only be asking for trouble."

"Too bad the mother didn't forbid the girl to accept the prize," Arnold grumbled. "That's the way my mother would've handled it."

Dillon muffled a chuckle with a cough as he envisioned a young Arnold tangling with his mother over a poetry contest.

"I agree it would've been the easy way out for us. But," he pointed out realistically, "things rarely turn out as we wish. Let's include the mother, then put the whole episode behind us."

"Everybody wants to get in on the act." Arnold rolled his eyes. "Show biz..."

"Call her back and set things up," Dillon directed, rising from the chair.

"I wonder if the mother is a fan, too," Arnold mused. "Imagine trying to horn in on the kid's good fortune."

Dillon grimaced. Kristina Jordan a fan? Not on a cold day in Hades. "It really doesn't matter, does it?" Dillon was determined not to allow any of it to matter. He'd turn on his on-air personality for dinner, smile for the camera. If the mother was nice-looking... Perhaps a nightcap. No emotional involvement.

Arnold, who had an uncanny way of reading Dillon's thoughts sometimes, cast him a worried frown. "Remember to ooze with 'after dark' charm Saturday night, won't you? You can go back to your cave Sunday morning."

Dillon stood over Arnold, his six-foot-three frame dwarfing him. "I'll try not to beat my chest during the entrée."

"Oh, yes," Arnold continued, his eyes leveled on Dillon's breastbone. "I've made arrangements for a tuxedo."

"One of yours?" Dillon queried mockingly.

"Hardly!" Arnold retorted, then looked up to discover Dillon was jesting. "Very amusing. I'll be chuckling over your humor all day long."

"Enjoy yourself."

"Uncle Roger says you may keep the suit. Compliments of the station."

Dillon's suntanned face crinkled with delight. "Gee, just what I've always wanted."

"Oh, and Dillon...Please don't try anything sneaky like wearing one of your fluorescent T-shirts under the jacket. No one thought that stunt was amusing at the Jukebox Awards banquet last year—except for perhaps a few of your more exotic fans."

"I promise," Dillon pledged solemnly, "to wear the traditional pleated dress shirt. Now I want you to promise me something, Arnie."

Rodale sniffed, pushing his wire-rimmed glasses up his nose again. "Certainly, if I can."

"Never, ever give my private telephone number out to a stranger again," Dillon said in a lethal tone.

Arnold cleared his throat, eyeing the toes of his Italian

loafers. "Sorry. As you've discovered yourself, Mrs. Jordan is quite a persuasive woman. I'll never do it again."

Dillon stabbed a long tanned finger at Arnold's chest. "See that you don't."

"I'm sure she won't let it leak out, Dillon."

"She's going to rip it to shreds and burn it," Dillon informed him matter-of-factly. "Stomp on the ashes for added security."

"Ah, a thorough woman then," Rodale said with elation, moving toward the door. "You've nothing to fear, man."

Nothing to fear? Dillon gazed after Arnold with silent grimness. The woman had just turned him inside out in a verbal duel. Had totally taken him in, then strung him up in his own trap! Verbal seduction was *his* specialty.

He'd have his way before this contest was over, if he wanted it. It just so happened that Dillon had just the cure for stiff-backed doctors. Lots of bed rest. Flat-on-the-back bed rest.

3

"PLEEEZE—DON'T SLOUCH," Julianne implored with desperate violet eyes.

"I don't mean to—"

"You don't want to look like a crotchety old lady, do you, Mom?"

Kristina straightened up under Julianne's encouraging gaze and smiled politely at the middle-aged man in a gray suit sharing the glass elevator with them at the Crestview Towers. He appeared puzzled over the exchange, but politely turned to the glass wall to studiously scan the hotel's lavish tropical courtyard floors below. Kristina took the opportunity to tug at the white knit minidress which Julianne had lent her for the occasion.

What an uncomfortable way to spend a Saturday night, Kristina silently complained. Dressed in her daughter's outfit, meeting a man who worked the night shift with the seductive style of Dracula.

She smoothed the front of the dress with a sweeping hand, as if willing it to somehow magically lengthen over her thighs. The polka dots were the worst part. The small dress was covered with stark black, nickel-sized polka dots. Kristina wasn't in the habit of calling attention to herself through her clothing. But this little knit number was screaming a huge hello, in design and fit, Admittedly, the flared skirt did cover her hips, and the strapless knit bodice did conceal the swell of her breasts; but it was a close call on both ends, especially when she straightened her spine.

An evening with Dillon Danvers. Julianne's first date. Kristina eyed her daughter standing a couple feet away, shifting from one yellow spiked heel to the other. She'd en-

visioned this momentous occasion a hundred times over
since her daughter's infancy, wondering what it would be
like. Sometimes it was the prom. Sometimes it was the movies. It was always with a pimple-faced boy driving his father's station wagon. Julianne was always a well-scrubbed
cherub in frills.

It was hard to erase her illusions, but Kristina was forced
to as she gazed again at her daughter. Julianne's dress was a
tight bright orange spandex. Her face was layered with
makeup. And her hair... Kristina grimaced. She'd somehow
pulled it together on one side of her head with a pink binder,
causing it to stand on end like a black feather duster. It was
all for Dillon, she'd been told.

Kristina's appearance had been scrutinized, criticized, and
supervised as well. Julianne had boldly come to Kristina's
room that afternoon and rejected her best gold shirtwaist
dress as boring with a capital *B*. She'd tugged Kristina back
to her messy den of dust and fixed her up with the polka dot
frock, complete with dark panty hose. After some consideration Kristina had gone along with it all with a sporting
spirit. It wouldn't hurt to be daring this once.

"You look radical, Mom, honest." Julianne interrupted her
mother's thoughts with a bolstering grin.

"Thanks, honey."

"Just hope you don't stretch that top..."

The danger of stretching fabric drew the male passenger's
attention away from the glass. Kristina could feel his eyes focusing on her breasts as he fumbled with his tie. To her further chagrin he emitted a low whistle of approval before ex-
iting on his floor. Kristina blushed as the elevator doors
closed.

"Don't crumble over one whistle," Julianne anxiously
pleaded. "It must've happened to you before. Think back..."

"I was whistled at last week, young lady," Kristina informed her with staunch pride. "And I was wearing a real
dress at the time!"

"You're in a real dress now! It's so real that it cost me four baby-sitting jobs," she added grumpily. "Be sure not to spill anything on it."

"I won't." Kristina assured her.

"And please don't talk about those loony patients of yours," she begged, clasping her hands in prayer.

Kristina gasped in amazement. "I would never betray a patient's—"

"And don't drink too much wine," Julianne cut in. "You get all giggly."

"I do not!" she objected, aghast.

"Not so fast." Julianne shook a chiding finger at her. "Remember Uncle Phil's wedding last year? One bottle of champagne and you were up on stage with the band doing some dance called the mashed potato."

"It was the twist," Kristina corrected, then added with a reflective grin, "I thought I was pretty good at it."

"You got so dizzy jumping around that the drummer had to hoist you up on his shoulder and take you outside."

"Seems to me I returned in short order and did do the mashed potato."

"They'll be taking pictures this time," Julianne pointed out significantly. "Pictures for the *newspaper*."

"I'll remember to say cheese."

"I just want this night to be perfect," Julianne confided, grasping her mother's hand in her clammy one. "Dillon means everything to me. He's dreamy. Ever so dreamy."

"Remember what the station manager told your grandpop. Dillon is thirty-five years old—over twice your age."

The reminder only caused the girl to close her eyes and moan with ecstasy. "Oh, yeah, but he's so well-preserved!"

"He's a year older than I am!" Kristina exclaimed with affront.

Julianne shook her head in disbelief. "The man is a walking talking miracle. He's got to be at his age."

"Oh, sure," Kristina mumbled.

A troubled frown crossed Julianne's young, slim face. "If he wants to call you Mom, you won't make a fuss, will you?"

Kristina's painted lips thinned. If that man called her

Mom, she'd—she'd sink her spiked heel into his micro-phone!

"What I mean is... He sort of may have the idea that you're an older woman..." Julianne trailed off bleakly, staring off into the distance.

Ah-ha. So Julianne's talk-show charade was finally catch-ing up with her. She was having second thoughts about hav-ing portrayed Kristina as a dowdy old biddy.

"This funky dress was your idea," Kristina reminded her. "Perhaps I should've gone for the frumpy look."

"No," Julianne replied seriously. "I thought about letting you dress on your own. But our family pride comes before anything else. We all should look fun. Even Grandpop, when the time comes."

Kristina was sorely tempted to confess that she knew all about her late-night talks on the radio, but kept quiet. It would make the date far more uncomfortable if Julianne knew her mother had already bickered with Mr. Dreamy. When Arnold Rodale had called to confirm the arrange-ments, Kristina had requested that Dillon not mention to Ju-lianne that he'd spoken with her mother ahead of time. She figured she had a fifty-fifty chance with the D.J. The smooth-talking Dillon on the radio would keep the secret. The gruff, sleepy hermit on the phone most likely wouldn't.

Once at the restaurant's entrance, Julianne informed the hostess they were here to dine with Dillon Danvers. Kristina was impressed. Dignity couldn't be very easy to maintain when one had a clump of hair springing from the side of one's head like a fresh oil gusher.

The pair followed the hostess through a maze of tables in the elegant dining room of ornate mahogany woodwork, glittering crystal chandeliers, and rich burgundy carpeting.

"It's him, over by the windows," Julianne paused to whis-per in a squeal, jabbing a finger at him behind her clutch bag.

"Oh, Lord." Kristina's heart stopped as they edged closer. He stood on their approach, pulling his chair aside with a flourish.

"I warned you he's a gorgeous hunk," Julianne murmured. "Keep your cool. Just let me do all the talking."

The man was a Greek god, Kristina decided in wide-eyed wonder as he rose to full height. A tall, tanned dream in a black tuxedo and crisp white shirt. Just the sort of man she used to fantasize about—back in the days when she indulged in that sort of thing. She didn't know they made 'em like him anymore. Julianne was right. He was dreamy. Awesomely dreamy.

"Good evening, ladies," he greeted huskily. "I'm Dillon Danvers." His voice was even richer in person, a fluid caress, a mental embrace.

Kristina turned to Julianne, anticipating a giggled rush of superlatives from her. Surprisingly, her heavily glossed mouth was open, but nothing was coming out.

"I'm Dr. Kristina Jordan, and this is my daughter, Julianne," she finally announced in the dead air.

"It's so nice to meet you, Julianne," Dillon intoned, capturing Julianne's small ringed fingers in his hand and bending over to kiss her heavily blushed cheek.

"Oh... Gee..." Julianne responded in a small, hushed voice. So much for guiding the conversation.

"So nice to meet you as well, Doctor Jordan," he added with a solemn expression.

Kristina drew a breath of relief as Dillon clasped her hand with a brief squeeze. He was willing to play the stranger after all. Thank goodness!

Dillon smoothly did the honor of seating them at the round linen-covered, candlelit table—Julianne at his right, Kristina beside Julianne. Kristina slipped her napkin onto her lap and stole a glance at Dillon to find his eyes were twinkling like two bright blue Christmas tree lights. What was his game? She'd clipped him to a quick over the phone. Was it possible Dillon Danvers had a playful side between night and day? It seemed more conceivable that he'd added a dollop of hemlock to her water glass!

A sudden jolt of electricity passed over the flickering candles as Kristina met his consuming look head-on. Think cool, Kristina cautioned herself. Babbling brooks. Icy breezes.

It was no use! Every time she matched eyes with the velvety-voiced talk-show host, she felt nothing but a prickly heat of passion licking at her insides. She shifted in her chair, finding no position comfortable.

Dillon wasn't especially handsome really, she judged with discrimination. At least not in a clean-cut, even-featured way. His looks were distinctive, probably appealing only to a select group. Not everyone would go for his wide, square chin, slightly crooked nose, and prominent cheekbones. His mouth was especially generous, too large for the silver screen, but quite right for kissing the hell out of somebody. His rich blue eyes were universally appealing, she conceded. But his hair was on the shaggy side—wispy around his collar, sunbleached almost white-blond, and combed straight back off his forehead, leaving his features open in glaring forthrightness.

Dillon was definitely for the discriminating taste.

Until he spoke.

When Dillon's rich, melodic voice flowed from his lips he was elegant, eloquent, and quite irresistible in every way.

Kristina began to study the menu with forced intensity as memories of his show invaded her mind. She had initially pictured him in a tux or a dinner jacket as he sat behind the microphone, perhaps puffing on a pipe as he sorted out a caller's dilemma, or sipping a snifter of brandy while relating some amusing anecdote from his endless stockpile of experiences. All these romantic images had continued to float in her mind all week long despite their little tiff over Julianne. She just couldn't bear to close the curtain on her fantasies of the late-night seducer. She was a regular listener now.

A "Dillon After Dark" addict.

So what if he'd barked at her on the phone? So what if his advice was totally unprofessional in her professional opinion? The excuses for him poured freely through her mind as she eyed him with yearning. Perhaps she had caught him at a bad moment the other morning. Most people weren't at their best when awakened by the telephone. She'd certainly been at her worst, yelling at him the way she had. And he did sincerely seem to have believed that Julianne was at least eighteen. Falling for him would be notoriously easy, she realized with a mixture of anticipation and alarm.

More to his favor, Dillon was now making an effort to draw Julianne out of her shell with a genuine expression of interest. Her daughter's severe attack of timidness was beginning to subside as he questioned her about her schoolwork and hobbies, complimenting her on her winning poem.

Maybe Dillon was a chivalrous knight after all, she mused with uncertainty. Could a knight work under the cover of darkness, wooing damsels with certain tricks of the trade? Kristina sensed a sincerity in him, did she not? And she should know. She evaluated people every day.

Dillon shifted in his chair as he listened to Julianne rattle on about herself. Now that she was geared up, there was no stopping her. He liked the girl. She was honest and open like a kid should be. But the mother...

Kristina Jordan was trouble with a capital *T*. Wild and lethal-looking. He caught her watching him over her menu. Those arresting violet eyes... They were shifting in shade and light over the candle's flame in the oddest way. It was kind of spooky. The daughter's eyes didn't do the same thing, he noted, making a comparison. Hers merely sparkled with innocence. But the mother's were stripping him, studying him.

What the hell was the matter with him? he questioned himself severely. The answer was most unwelcome. This woman had edged him further into a corner with her beauty. She was pulling the rug clear out from under him with one steady look. It wasn't fair. He liked to jerk the reins of control. He needed those reins back. But how to get them?

This psychologist was a siren plain and simple. She shackled men with her eyes and turned them to Jell-O. Brought them to her knees in her tight white dress and then, and then—healed them! Suddenly all he could see were spots. Black, nickel-sized, polka dots!

Dillon raised his finger to loosen the knot of his bow tie; it was tightening at his throat, choking him. His dress clothes seemed too tight as well. Even his shoes felt crowded. His heart was pounding, his head hammering. He wished he was alone at his beach house. He wished he was battling the waves on his battered old surfboard. Oh damnation, what he really wished was to glide a hand down her black-stockinged leg and press his mouth on her creamy exposed shoulder...

"Your wish, sir?" a waiter asked with polished politeness, appearing at his side.

"Excuse me?" he blurted out, wondering if he'd spoken his thoughts aloud.

"On my recommendation, the ladies have ordered the Crestview's special lobster dinner," the waiter calmly explained. "I am wondering if you would like the same?"

"Yes, please," Dillon said, clearing his throat. "I made some prior arrangements concerning the wine."

"Yes, certainly. Shall I bring it now?"

Dillon nodded and the waiter quietly disappeared with the menus under his arm.

"I ordered champagne," Dillon explained, regaining his sanity as he spoke of concrete things. "Ginger ale will be served in Julianne's glass of course."

"Maybe you should have ginger ale too, Mom," Julianne suggested anxiously.

"I prefer champagne," Kristina told her with a no-nonsense smile.

"Your mother must know her own mind," Dillon told a disgruntled Julianne in a soft, soothing tone. "Just as you so charmingly do."

"I suppose it's all right," Julianne conceded, aglow over his compliment.

Kristina was beginning to wonder if there was no end to Dillon's power. He's set Julianne straight with simple diplomacy. "I could use your kind of service every day," she murmured without much forethought.

Had she really said it? Kristina wondered with instant panic. The statement sounded so provocative. She peeked at Dillon over her water glass. The burning gleam in his crystal-blue eyes told her that the double-edged meaning of her words had seared him.

Kristina Jordan sear Dillon Danvers? It hardly seemed possible. She couldn't remember the last time a man had gazed at her so amorously. Maybe he was thinking how nice it would be to stroll with her in the moonlight. Maybe he wanted to hold her, kiss her, whisper sweet nothings only to her.

Dillon wanted to devour the delectable woman across the table in one bite. Take her to his bed and explore every inch of her ripened body. Just one night in this wild woman's arms... No strings. No pain. No talk. Nothing but pure pleasure. Kristina certainly appeared to be up to the challenge. She seemed to be returning his signals with great acceptance. And if her spirited attitude during their phone battle had been any indication of her steely will, she'd be quite a challenge indeed. An all-night-long challenge. She'd stop talking soon enough. She'd barely draw a breath!

But dammit, the timing was all wrong! There was the daughter to consider. Dillon lowered his lids to slits, anxious to break eye contact with Kristina before his desires manifested themselves for the world to see. Think lobster. Think anything! Then there was certainly Arnold to think about. He was due to arrive with the photographer from the *San Diego Sun* any minute. The obstacles seemed insurmountable and his passions insatiable. It would be a lesson in abstinence to remember.

The seafood proved to be excellent. Kristina attacked hers with a healthy appetite while Julianne picked away at her shell with a doe-eyed expression. It was a shame to see her daughter's meal go to waste, for Kristina knew the first thing the girl would do when she got home was raid the refrigerator.

"Eat, Julianne," Kristina urged, dipping a forkful of tender lobster into her twin bowl of warm melted butter.

"I'm not hungry, Mom," she protested, casting Dillon a loving glance. "Would it be okay if I combed my hair, before they take the pictures?"

"Of course." Kristina set down her fork. "I'll come along if you like."

"No! I can manage," Julianne's face clouded with exasperation. "You know I like to be on my own."

"Yes, certainly, dear. I'll wait here."

Dillon rose briefly as Julianne hopped up with her satin purse.

"Nice kid," he remarked as she nearly skipped off toward the ladies' room, her ponytail bouncing against her ear.

"Nice energetic kid," Kristina agreed.

"More champagne?" he asked settling back in his chair.

"Yes, please."

Dillon reached for the bottle nestled in the ice bucket at his elbow and reached over to fill Kristina's fluted glass, then his own.

"Thank you for not mentioning our previous conversation to Julianne," Kristina ventured, surprised by the shy lilt to her own voice.

Her daughter certainly was her weakness, Dillon observed, openly studying Kristina's dainty features. "You aren't as I pictured you," he remarked carefully.

Kristina's small smile was rueful. "If you pictured me as Julianne described me, I believe they would've had to wheel me in on a hospital bed equipped with a respirator."

"No, I drew my own portrait."

Kristina easily read his brooding look. "Oh, I see, the man scorned."

"Do you always toy with men over the telephone?" he asked silkily, his eyes betraying a smoldering fire within.

Kristina gasped in surprise. "No, I certainly do not. You were an exception." Kristina sipped her champagne. "Actually, I want to apologize for flying off the handle. I'm not certain exactly what got into me. I'm usually far more patient."

Dillon quirked a blond eyebrow. "Ah, progress."

"Progress?" Kristina set her glass down on the table with a thump.

"I got to you. You to me." He leaned over the table, resting his large brown hand over her slender creamy one. "Progress, my love."

Kristina inhaled rather shakily as Dillon's fingertips pressed into the smoothness of her hand. Julianne needn't have worried about her mother jumping up to do the twist or the mashed potato. All Kristina wanted to do was cup her hands on Dillon's unique, angular face and kiss his full sensuous mouth. She'd kiss his temples, his throat, nibble his earlobes and listen... Listen to his magical hypnotic voice as it wound silken strings around her, trapping her in his web.

This woman could indeed use the "Dillon After Dark" cure of bed rest. "What do you say we rendezvous later," he rasped, his blue eyes shimmering slits under sweeping blond lashes. "I reserved a room here at the Crestview Towers, just in case..."

Bedroom eyes... Kristina lightheadedly pondered his proposal. She felt as if she were floating on a champagne bubble through the romantic fog of his provocative tone, his massaging fingertips and finally his penetrating gaze until the blatant invitation hit her consciousness with the force of a backhanded slap.

Dillon Danvers wanted to bed her! Tonight!

She began to fume as the reality of his proposition hit home. Kristina Jordan, pick of the night. He probably moved with agility from the studio to the bedroom. As night turned to day, day to night. Studio to bedroom and back again. This man didn't have a life. He spun round and round in a revolving door from microphone to mattress!

Dillon drained his final dribble of champagne, watching Kristina's expression move through an unreadable exercise. "Well?"

"I don't wish to be your Saturday-night conquest," she replied stiffly.

"You aren't actually insulted, are you?" he demanded

with sincere perplexity. "We're two adults. Two adults attracted to each other."

She gaped at his lack of understanding.

"You must get proposals like mine all the time," he asserted, his eyes roving over her with appreciation.

Kristina snatched her hand from his, rubbing her temples dizzily. He was insulting her with his invitation, yet complimenting her beauty. What was she to say? 'Sorry, Dillon, I don't appreciate getting asked to bed on impulse. Physical attraction isn't enough with which to hit the sheets. But thanks for letting me know I'm a turn-on." Sputter that mumbo-jumbo and she'd be inclined to have herself committed!

"Can't I persuade you?" Dillon asked quietly, lifting a bleached eyebrow in hope.

Kristina's eyes widened in panic. "No! A hundred times no. A thousand times no!"

"A hundred nos would've kept me at bay," he returned with cool eloquence.

Cool, lying eloquence.

Kristina had already worked her way under his skin like a rash. A quick spreading, itchy, uncomfortable rash that left him squirming. Left him dying for just one scratch!

Thank God he's spotted Arnold and a newspaper reporter near the entrance. Another minute alone with Kristina Jordan and he'd surely have pulled her into his arms to sample her small rosebud mouth, read her shifting violet eyes like the most intriguing story ever told. Well, the night would soon be over, he rationalized. He would never have to see Kristina again. He'd survive her rebuff.

All he had to do was convince himself that Kristina wasn't the perfect blend of wit and beauty. That she didn't somehow manage to play doting mother and tender temptress at the same blasted time! He would eventually forget her as he had all the others that had passed through his life. The sparkle of her exotic eyes would fade in time. If only he could manage to live that long!

4

DILLON DANVERS was simply impossible to forget.

Kristina stared down at the entertainment section of the *San Diego Sun* on Wednesday morning pondering the impossibility. She'd hoped it would be over once the newspaper article was out. But obviously no one brushed off the great Dillon Danvers without a battle scar or two. The man couldn't resist the temptation to extract his pound of flesh from her in the end. Hostility, disappointment, and a sense of betrayal simmered within her as she gazed down at his black-and-white revenge.

Just because she hadn't slept with him, Julianne was cheated out of her moment of publicity. Her daughter was to suffer for her mother's decision. The black-souled buzzard! She took an angry slurp of coffee, drawing her father's attention across the kitchen.

"Something the matter, Krissy?" Howard moved through the spacious country-styled room, the coffeepot in his hand. With a long-armed reach across the large round table, he refilled her cup with steaming brew.

"Look at this, Pop!" she sputtered, spreading the paper flat on the calico print tablecloth. "Look at the stunt Julianne's idol has pulled."

Howard stood over Kristina's shoulder, his bushy gray eyebrows lifted in confusion. "Nice picture of you, honey."

"That's not the point, Pop," Kristina huffed in frustration. "The picture should be of Julianne."

"She's there," he said, stabbing a finger at the grainy figure of his granddaughter, standing at Kristina's right.

"They cut half her arm off!" she exclaimed. "Read the caption." She jabbed a finger at paper. "Kristina Jordan and Daughter. It doesn't even say she won."

"Doesn't say she didn't," Howard rumbled thoughtfully. "Pretty sneaky, I'd say."

"I should've followed my original instincts about this whole date business," Kristina muttered with self-recrimination.

"But Julianne came home so upbeat about Dillon on Saturday night." With a heavy sigh, Howard moved to replace the coffeepot on its hot plate. "As I recall, you never did say anything."

Kristina shrugged evasively. Sharing with her father Dillon's invitation to join him in the sack hadn't at all appealed to her at the time. "I wasn't certain what to make of him on Saturday night," she replied carefully, "but I never thought he'd pull a stunt like this. He seemed genuinely fond of Julianne. Oooh, he makes me so damn mad," she fumed. "Turns his charm on and off like a faucet."

"I think you're mad at yourself because you can't figure him out," Howard surmised.

"Of course I am!" Kristina exploded. "I'm trained to figure people out. It's a low blow to fail when the well-being of Julianne is at stake. I—"

"Good morning, wonderful family units!" Julianne floated into the kitchen in a bright green blouse and shorts with rose-colored piping. She bent to kiss Kristina's cheek. "You already have the paper, Mom?" She dropped into a bow-backed chair and rested her upper torso on the table to scan the article.

"Julianne—"

Julianne twisted her body to confront Kristina, her young face full of hurt and betrayal. "What have you done to me?" she cried. "You spoiled the whole deal!"

"This isn't my fault, kiddo."

"Yes, it is!" she cried with certainty. "The paper makes it look as if you won the contest and dragged me along."

"Now, Muffin," Howard interceded, setting a glass of juice beside Julianne.

"You dazzled him in my dress," Julianne accused, glaring down at the newspaper. "He thinks you're hot because you wore it. He likes you more than me."

"You asked me to wear the dress," Kristina reminded her. "You insisted."

"I just wanted you to fit in," she said in a choke, her eyes misting. "Not steal the show!"

"I'm so sorry, Julianne." Kristina's heart lurched as her daughter fell back in her chair, limp as a rag doll. "I truly think Dillon was impressed by you," she said slowly, her sense of fair play at war with her resentment of the man. "Maybe he isn't responsible for the mistake."

"I hope not! I told all my friends I was dating him," she confessed, rubbing her eyes. "They ask me every day if he's called me back yet."

Kristina's slender delicate face clouded with disapproval. "You went too far, Julianne," she asserted firmly. "He's not going to call you."

"Haven't I proven to you that I can handle him?" she demanded. "I cleaned my room, didn't I? Even under my bed! I brought all those dessert plates back to the kitchen and washed them one by one."

Kristina was amazed at her simplistic overall view of maturity. "He's of an entirely different generation! He's thirty-five years old."

"He's more your mother's age," Howard put in, popping two slices of bread into the toaster.

"They're not the same!" Julianne cut in with swift fervor. "Dillon's not old like Mom. He lives free—on some romantic beach somewhere. He doesn't dress up in old-man clothes and mess with papers and meetings all day the way most older people do. He doesn't live by other people's rules!" Julianne clenched her fists, tears welling in her eyes.

"We all live by some rules," Kristina asserted gently, rising to get Julianne a tissue from the box on the counter. "I'm sure even Dillon has his own code. A schedule he follows. For instance, he knows he has to be behind the microphone six times a week, three hours a night. Sounds pretty routine to me."

"He's different!" Julianne dabbed her eyes with the tissue, and traced a long pink fingernail over Dillon's face in the newspaper photo.

How could Kristina honestly argue the point? Dillon was one of a kind. She stood behind her daughter, and focused on the picture over the girl's shoulder. She pulled the lapels of her white terry robe over her collarbone, tensely wondering if Julianne was shrewd enough to pick up on the sensuous nuance so clear to her own eyes. Dillon's attentive gaze as he stood over Kristina. The way his arm curved tightly around her bare shoulders. She could still feel the pressure of his fingers on the tender skin of her upper arm. She shuddered slightly at the memory of the odd sensations that had traveled up and down her spine. While the picture was being taken she'd suppressed her anger over his outrageous proposal still fresh to her ears.

But the mutual attraction between them was impossible to deny. It had been a long while since Kristina had been turned on so instantly, so electrically. And the man in question was nothing more than a hustler!

"Maybe we're judging him out of turn," Howard proposed. "Maybe this mix-up wasn't his doing."

"No matter whose fault it was, I'll be the biggest fool in school today," Julianne cried. "Nobody will believe I really won the contest."

"I could call the station's program director, Arnold Rodale," Howard proposed. "He seemed cordial enough when I spoke to him last week."

"Maybe if I explained it to your friends," Kristina suggested. "I could tell them about the mix-up. They'd believe me."

"You'd wreck my social life for good! Everybody would think we were both a couple of geeks." Julianne sniffed, and hopped off her chair to pace anxiously around the room. "There must be something we can do. I can't face the guys without proof that I actually won the contest."

"You have to go to school today, Julianne," Kristina insisted.

Julianne turned on her heel, a mortified look on her tear-stained face. "You'd really make me go?"

"Julianne, this isn't a life-and-death matter. I can't call your principal and tell him you're indisposed over 'Dillon After Dark.'"

"I really do feel sick," Julianne complained, clutching her middle. "Sick all over."

Kristina knew the feeling. Her own stomach was curled in knots over the guy. "I still feel I could convince your friends that you won the contest, without looking too geeky."

"No!" Julianne shot back. "You can't do it."

"I could tell them," Howard offered. "I could put on my uniform and go down to the school."

Kristina bit back a grin as she watched Julianne wrestle with some polite dissuasion. To her grandpop, she was always polite.

"No thanks, Grandpop," she eventually replied staunchly. "I'm old enough to handle this myself. I'm going to talk to Dillon. Find out what happened."

Kristina shot her father a warning glance as his head began to nod in approval. "Julianne, I'm afraid you might be in for a disappointment. You're not sure who to blame at this point..."

"I think she was originally blaming you for dazzling him," Howard interceded helpfully.

"Thank you, Pop," Kristina replied with sarcasm.

"Just trying to sort it out," Howard claimed defensively.

Kristina shot him in exasperated look. Whenever her father tried to sort something out, she ended up on the short end of the deal. "Julianne," she ventured, turning back to her daughter, "Dillon may not expect to hear from you again."

"Get real!" Julianne cried with emotion. "You just said he liked me."

"Yes. But he's a busy man. And... I just don't want you hurt any deeper than you are now."

"I have to find out, Mom. Maybe he just doesn't know I'm

in a tight spot with my friends. Maybe he doesn't know I love him."

"Maybe we should just put this behind us," Kristina advised.

"I have to talk to him. I'll call the show if I have to," she threatened.

"We made a bargain, young lady," Kristina reminded her. "You got your dinner with Dillon on the condition that you stop calling his show in the middle of the night."

"Your mother's right," Howard inserted to their mutual surprise.

"Why, thanks, Pop." Kristina brimmed with relief.

Howard nodded. "Krissy, you make the call."

Kristina was aghast. "What?"

"Find out if he can fix things with Muffin's friends," Howard suggested.

"Gee, I guess it would be better than nothing," Julianne conceded with a heavy sigh.

"Thanks for the vote of confidence," she retorted dryly. "But I think we should just drop Dillon from our lives."

"I don't understand why, Krissy," Howard said in puzzlement. "Just call the man and ask if he can stop by the school or something. No big deal."

No big deal? Kristina tensed as she thought back on his brooding sensuality. Dillon Danvers was one damn big deal.

"I'll die if you don't help me," Julianne whined. "Please, Mom."

"Get this over with one way or the other, Krissy," Howard prodded.

Kristina looked from one stubborn face to the other, caving in. "I'll call him from the office."

KRISTINA PICKED HER WAY across the white beaches of Oceanside two hours later, her best suede pumps sinking deeper and deeper into the damp sand with every step. When Dillon's phone had buzzed with a busy signal for over an hour, Kristina had decided to physically track him down. It paid to have a friend who worked for the telephone company. It had taken the promise of a free lunch, but Kristina had succeeded in obtaining the address of Dillon's beachfront home.

During his program Dillon had talked of living near the ocean, but she hadn't expected to have to literally chase him down to the sandy shores of the Pacific in her navy blue suit and bow blouse. As the wind whipped under her skirt, she began to wonder if she'd plunged in over her head. When she realized exactly what he was all about, it took all her willpower not to jump back into her Camaro and spin off down his long gravel driveway.

Though his skin was tanned a rich golden color, and he spoke of the water during his show, she'd hoped he wasn't a surfing fanatic. But all the signs were there—the modest redwood and glass house perched on a bluff just above a beautiful private cove, the surfboard wax and rag on the front doorstep. Dillon had sunk the bulk of his money into his land rather than on his house, just for the privilege of living on a plot of secluded beach property.

She realized Dillon didn't merely talk about the beach on the program. He *lived* the beach. Dillon Danvers was probably the worst possible thing a man could be.

He was a beach bum.

Kristina paused near the rippling foam of the backwash, taking in the splendor of nature's liquid blue fury, scanning the horizon for a sign of him. The ocean was especially turbulent today, roaring and hissing with untamed energy under the blazing sunny sky. The high blue crests moved forward, gaining height and power, curling with feathering foam before slamming to the rock-riddled shoreline with a hissing sound.

It had been a long time since Kristina had stood on the fringes of the Pacific on a weekday morning, feeling the seductive embrace of sea and salt air. Surfing conditions were ideal today. The sun was brilliant and warm in the cloudless sky. The waves were strong, rolling in with high, smooth faces. Oh, yes, she knew what she was missing. Fifteen years ago she and her ex-husband Wade would've been paddling into the horizon on their boards, anxious to sail on a surging mountain of water only a few feet below heaven.

Kristina shook her head to clear such sentimental reminiscences from her mind. That kind of life was a million years ago! Raising a hand to shield her eyes from the glaring sun, she watched the horizon for a glimpse of Dillon. She eventually spotted him lying on his surfboard, piloting it toward open water. Kristina shifted uneasily on her feet. It wouldn't be long and he'd be back.

Dillon noticed the woman on shore the moment he turned his board around at the surfline. He sat upright, his muscular legs dangling over either side of the board, watching and wondering. His head spun back at the rising peaks of water, then at her, and back again. She was spoiling his timing. She was trespassing. Dammit, he hated intruders. If only the ocean surrounded his home like a vast, bottomless moat. That would make the world go away!

And he would make her go away, he declared inwardly, timing a swell forming behind him, intent on catching it.

Kristina watched Dillon spring to his feet on the surfboard, gliding atop a gradually rising swell of water. Against her will, she found herself immersed in his ride as if it were her own. He'd chosen a wave that Kristina judged as challenging for even the most experienced carver. He'd taken it early in its formation, gaining momentum along with the rising swell. Up, up he climbed, cutting a graceful, powerful figure on the horizon, maneuvering the board beneath his feet with razorlike precision. Kristina's heart pumped rapidly as he rode higher and higher over the wave's frothy lip, then down the smooth watery face. With arms extended he balanced and twisted on the board, ultimately cutting across the wave as it curled over his head, following it down the line in it's hollowest sections.

Kristina puffed a breath of release as he shimmied toward the shallow shoreline, hopping off his board with practiced ease. He sloshed a short distance through the foamy soup, leaning over to scoop up his red and white Fiberglas board, deftly tucking it under his sinewy brown arm.

It was over. He'd met and conquered. Kristina was amazed at how involved she'd become in the ride. It was ridiculous to feel so exhilarated. After all, she hadn't even gotten her feet wet!

The itch to ride the tubes was long gone. It had to be! But Kristina had to admit that the lure of the sea had always been dangerously inviting. And in the end it had brought her nothing but heartache. It was the greatest seducer of them all, with its siren whine and turbulent, ever-changing face.

Though she was describing the sea, she suddenly realized that the same words could define Dillon as he stalked toward her with power and purpose in his stride. His bronzed body was corded perfection, on display in black nylon trunks that revealed more than they hid. He looked so raw. So basic.

Dillon's bleached eyebrows drew together as he squinted at the woman several yards ahead of him. She looked like a banker in her dark blue suit and harnessed hairdo. A dumb banker. Whoever heard of wearing stockings to the beach, anyhow? What had drawn him to the stockings in the first place? he wondered with a jolt, stalking his prey warily.

It was that pair of legs, naturally! They were long and lean and decidedly mean. There was enough leg there to start a whole new girl. He shook his wet head in confusion. How could he be so certain about the thighs concealed above that knee-length hem? How could he be instinctively positive that they'd be luscious to the touch? He delved deeply into his memory. When was the last time he'd felt compelled to reach out and touch someone? He shrugged his broad shoulders. Naw! It couldn't be her! Could it?

"Kristina Jordan." Dillon tossed aside his board, running a hand over his water-slicked hair as he approached. Within seconds he was standing over her, his massive figure easily shading her space.

"Hello." Kristina's voice was an embarrassed squeak. Somehow he'd been easier to rebuff while he was elegantly clad in a tuxedo. What was it about a tux that gave men an air of propriety?

She stood her ground, quickly discovering she was at eye

level with his chest. His shoulders hadn't seemed quite this wide in the restaurant, she recalled thoughtfully, her eyes lingering on the smooth muscled flesh. His taut, tanned chest was the color of honey gold, with a layer of matted bleached hair. Kristina stood silently, intrigued by the rivulets of water running along his sternum, down to his narrow waistline. She lowered her gaze, tracking the droplets as they welled in his navel, disappearing beneath the low-riding elastic band of his swimming trunks.

"What do you want?" Dillon abruptly demanded, his mouth curling wickedly as she raised her eyes from the area of his hips. He couldn't help giving her a hard time. Seeing her in street clothes was enough to destroy a man's faith in dreams-come-true.

Dillon's erotic fantasies of the past several nights had centered on the Kristina Jordan of Saturday's dinner. The skintight white minidress. The black stockings. The free-flowing tide of raven hair gleaming blue-black in the candlelight. He had loved her a thousand times in his dreams. Every way. Over and over again. The conservatively dressed woman standing before him in gaping confusion was a distinct disappointment. Maybe getting her out of his system was going to be far easier than he'd imagined. Maybe he'd get some sleep for a change. The past four nights had been yearning, restless ones.

Kristina's pulse hammered in her ears as she confronted him. His anger hadn't stopped him from moving in at very close range. He was so close now that some of the water rolling from his shoulders dripped to her face. She winced as a single drop suddenly landed on the tip of her nose, and she couldn't lift her hand to rub it away without brushing against his torso.

The drop stayed where it was.

"Doctor, I really hate intrusions on my privacy. And quite frankly, I believe we once parted for ever and ever."

"Look, I had to come," she blurted out uncomfortably.

"Giving in to kismet?" he goaded unkindly.

"You arrogant ass!" she exclaimed daringly, not quite recognizing herself.

Her angry outburst shocked him, as well. "You came all the way out here to tell me that?"

"No," she replied with affront. "I've got a bone to pick with you."

"Pick away, lady," he invited in a cynical grunt, which, if uttered on the air, would have cost him every fan he had. He waited, spellbound by the drop of water hanging right to the tip of her upturned nose even as she wrinkled it in anger.

"The newspaper article was grossly unfair!"

"Really?" he bit out in surprise. "Why?"

"With the use of some clever wording and photography, it appears I am the one who wrote the poem," she reported in mortification. "Did you do it because I turned down your proposal? Are you so petty?"

"Oh, c'mon! Do I strike you as a man scorned?"

"You look like a barbarian!"

"Is that a yes or a no?" he mocked, his eyes glinting dangerously.

"I just don't know," she admitted, at a loss for words.

"Hey, a lot of women would like to be in your place," he informed her immodestly. "Relax and enjoy your moment in the limelight."

"Your method of operation is really primitive, isn't it? Love 'em, tease 'em, please 'em."

"I leave 'em the best. So if you'll excuse me." He tipped his head toward the path. "Happy trails."

"I can't leave yet."

"Why ever not?" he growled in his most intimidating tone. She had to be wearing armor underwear beneath her business suit.

"Julianne is all torn up over this article. She told all her friends she won the contest and now she has no proof."

"There is nothing I can do," he claimed distantly. "As I explained the other day, it was a promotional gimmick sponsored by the station."

"How can you open your heart on the air, then snap it shut in my face?" she asked, genuinely perplexed.

"You've already had my best offer, Kristina Jordan," he told her forthrightly. "My very best."

"Regardless of what you may think, I'm not accustomed to indulging in one-nighters." Kristina shot back, watching as the crystal-blue eyes hovering over her lost their glint of smugness.

"You aren't, are you?" he relented quietly, seeing the whole woman quite clearly all of a sudden. The Kristina standing before him was not a panting fan, no matter how he wished it so.

"Finally convinced?"

"Yes. I made certain assumptions out of habit, I guess. But you really can't blame me for dreamin'. You were one tempting babe in all those polka dots."

His compliment hit home, despite Kristina's attempt to dismiss it. She couldn't remember the last time she'd turned into an emotional mess over a man. But she knew her feelings were beside the point. Julianne was her main concern.

"Look, Dillon, I'm here because I desperately need your help. My daughter thinks she loves you!"

"You have a funny charm about you, Doctor. You just called me an arrogant ass!" he said incredulously.

Kristina raised a palm. "I can't explain why I said it. You seem to bring out the worst in me."

"I apologize."

"I want to handle this crush thing very carefully. Teenage girls are fragile, you know..."

"Whoa! I don't know anything about teenage girls. Let me off the hook. I can't help you."

"I could go see your station manager," she threatened.

Dillon's angular face grew oddly hesitant. "To tell you the truth, Doctor, the only reason WXNT gave Julianne the prize was to avoid a lawsuit. The management doesn't care about your feelings. As far as they're concerned, the contest is over."

"It would serve them right if I sued their pants off!" she huffed.

Dillon rubbed his whiskered chin to camouflage a lustful leer. She could have his pants if she wanted them, just as long as she didn't try to wear them, or iron them. "Would a lawsuit really benefit your kid? I don't know much about family life, but I'm sure it would cause a lot of grief around the house before it was over."

Kristina nodded in defeat. "You're really the only one who can help. Couldn't you go to her school, give a little talk or something?"

Dillon lowered his lids in mental retreat. "I—I can't."

Kristina balked at his refusal. "You must do promotional appearances all the time!"

"I don't," he said flatly. "I prefer to stay out of the lime-light."

"How can you separate yourself from your listeners?"

"Quite conveniently until now!" he said in a dry tone.

"You purposely get females all worked up!" she accused shrilly, uncomfortably aware that she was speaking of her own plight rather than Julianne's. "And over what? A few phony coos on the airwaves."

"I do my job six nights a week," he stated plainly. "I pay my dues. They call me 'Dillon After Dark.' Not Dillon in the morning. Not Dillon at school. Not Dillon the baby-sitter! So back off, lady."

Kristina balked at his audacity. "I never—"

"Not lately I'd wager," he snapped. "And you had your chance." He reached out and rubbed the drop of water from her nose.

Kristina gasped in shock as the roughened tip of his thumb grazed her skin.

Dillon almost laughed out loud. After all he'd done to her in his dreams, touching her nose seemed pretty tame. With a fluid motion he picked up his surfboard and started crossing the sand toward the bluff.

"Hold on there! You hold on!" Kristina scampered through the sand in his wake. He was moving along at a

good clip, taking long pantherlike strides. Kristina's pace
was more like that of a jumpy chicken as she picked her way
along, fighting the wind billowing her skirt. She pursued
him relentlessly, slipping off her shoes along the way to gain
speed. He had no right to speak to her that way. To touch her
nose!

"Damn you to the fires of hell, Dillon Danvers!" Kristina
screamed at the top of her lungs, her self-control lost somewhere on the ocean breezes.

Dumbfounded by her burst of rage, Dillon stopped short.
He whirled around to find Kristina right on his heels.

"I don't dig you, woman! You're fire, then ice. You're sane,
then crazy. What's a man to do!" he roared in outrage.

Through his tide of anger he suddenly saw it—that exotic
violet flash in her eyes. Sparkling streaks of light and dark,
identical to the sensuous shades of purple passion which
made him squirm in the restaurant.

He couldn't leave it like this! Not knowing just what Kristina Jordan was really made of would eventually drive him
mad. He had to act swiftly before his appetite for solitude
outweighed his craving for the doctor. He tossed his board
aside in the weeds and with a huge wet hand grabbed the
silky bow of her cream-colored blouse, drawing her face up
toward his.

"Wh—Dillon!" The breath was knocked out of Kristina's
chest as Dillon's looming figure leaned forward. With agile
swiftness, he wound an arm around her waist, thrusting her
up against his hard, wet body. The small of her back rested in
the curve of his arm as he urged her higher into the solid
length of him.

Kristina started a small noisy protest, her eyes widening in
shock as Dillon's mouth covered her lips. He groaned audi-
bly, savoring their sweetness with open pleasure. She was
just as he'd imagined, sizzling on the inside. She was kissing
him back now, tentatively, probably instinctively. Her shoes
fell from her hand, plopping into a chaparral shrub beside
the path. Her fingers rose to his chest, reaching and explor-
ing the solid span of his shoulders.

Kristina went under for the last time as she tasted Dillon. He was a tantalizing blend of the salty sea and his own unique flavor. His full lips were just as inviting as they'd appeared—smooth, hard, consuming. He nearly smothered her with his mouth, the stubble on his face rubbing against her tender skin. Kristina wanted to stop him, stop herself. But not now, not while she was swept up in the tidal pool of his urgency, nearly drowning in his needs and demands.

Now confident that she welcomed him, Dillon released his hold on her blouse and moved his hand to the back of her neck, pushing at the pins securing her hair. Glossy black tresses tumbled to her shoulders, blowing softly in the wind like a billowing banner. He buried his face in the soft strands, inhaling the scent he remembered so well. If he closed his eyes she was the polka-dot she-devil, the temptress of his fantasies. But how long could a man keep his eyes closed?

"Enough!" Breathlessly Kristina eventually broke from Dillon's hold. Excitement drummed through her body, making her visibly shudder.

"You enjoyed it," Dillon uttered with gruff pride.

"Are you for real?" she asked sincerely, rubbing her whisker-burned chin.

"If you fell for me in that monkey suit Saturday night, you're way off the track."

"Fell for you?" she gasped, embarrassed by her transparency. "I turned down your abrupt, rude invitation if I recall."

"Yeah, but you felt the sparks between us." He paused, daring her to deny it. She couldn't. "But I can tell you it's been a bitter disappointment today to find out you wear funeral clothes in the daytime. Probing people's minds was bad enough news."

"You're a bit of a letdown yourself you...you...beach bum!" Before he could respond, she rattled on. "Psychology is a very respectable profession. A benefit to humanity. Which is more than I can say for a D.J. who leads women on with his husky murmurs of seduction."

"I have some pretty satisfied listeners, if the poems from

the contest are any indication." His mouth widened in a mirthless smile. "There are a lot of ways to give humanity a boost."

"I'll take your word for it," she said coolly, though her puffy lips and inflamed chin acutely reminded her of his red-hot talents.

Flames licked through Dillon's body like a raging forest fire, but he fought it. "You're a snob! You think your therapy is more useful just because it's more conventional!"

"I certainly do," she returned. "Your 'after dark' schlock has caused a lot of trouble for me. And hurt my daughter deeply." With a heavy sigh she started to move past him. "If you will excuse me, I have real patients to see. Not that I wouldn't mind getting you on the couch for an hour!"

"If you ever got me on the couch for an hour, I guarantee not a word would pass between us!" With a waist-deep bow, Dillon moved aside.

As Kristina moved past him, she made the mistake of looking back. Dillon's eyes instantly locked with hers for one brief electric moment, before his lids lowered to hooded, cool slits of azure.

Kristina's heart pounded in her throat as she scampered up the trail, the sound of his lush mocking chuckle on the wind with the roar of the surf. What the hell was he laughing about? she wondered, rattled to the core.

It wasn't until she got back to her Camaro that she realized she'd left her shoes behind in the sagebrush. How entertaining for him! With a string of muttered curses she fired up the engine, slammed a stockinged foot on the accelerator, and sped down his long gravel driveway, the wheels of her car kicking up a dustbowl.

Caught between the devil and the deep blue sea. Reduced to quivering jelly over a sweet talkin' snake who could coax the angels to peel off their halos! All because of a radio, a poem, and a grandpop who could never say no!

5

"WHY, DOCTOR!" Ethel Burns, Kristina's secretary, bustled into the office that afternoon just as she was slipping in through the back entrance.

"Hello, Ethel," Kristina greeted the petite, gray-haired woman breathlessly. "Is my one o'clock here yet?"

"Just arrived," Ethel confirmed, shutting the door between the connecting rooms, as she stared at Kristina's disheveled appearance in curious wonder.

"I know I look a bit out of sorts," Kristina said with a self-conscious smile, tucking her blouse farther into the waistband of her wrinkled blue skirt.

"You found Dillon Danvers?" Ethel asked dubiously, planting her hands on her small hips.

"Yes!" Kristina declared with forced brightness. "I suppose you're wondering about my shoes," she added as Ethel's gaze dropped to the doctor's feet.

"As long as you've mentioned it yourself, Doctor," Ethel coaxed. "I can't say I've ever seen you in sneakers before."

Kristina grinned sheepishly. "They belong to Julianne. You see, I got my suede pumps wet on the beach, and as luck would have it, I found these in the back seat of my car."

"Lucky break, all right," Ethel agreed with hesitation, frowning at the stained, tattered canvas shoes.

"Ethel, I'm going to need your assistance," Kristina told her in a harried tone.

"Yes, Doctor," Ethel chimed in, perking up with her usual efficiency. "Anything I can do to help."

Kristina dug into her purse, extracting her wallet and handed the older woman some bills. "I want you to run across the street to Carlisle Clothier and buy me a pair of shoes. Navy blue. Size seven. Some hose, too, please."

"All right. Shall I send Mrs. Mathews in right away?"

"Get her file for me, then give me a few minutes," Kristina instructed, settling in behind her desk.

"Shall I dispose of the sneakers now that you're seated?" Ethel asked, moving toward the file cabinet.

Kristina's eyes grew merry. "We don't dare! According to Julianne, they're finally broken in just right!"

"I see. I think." Ethel gave her the file with a dubious look on her face, then headed for the door. "Well, I hope your trip to Oceanside was fruitful, Doctor," she said, disappearing into the reception room.

"Fruitful, my foot," Kristina grumbled to her empty office as she opened her bottom desk drawer, reaching for her emergency makeup kit. If ever she had an emergency, this was it. She opened the case, raising the mirror to her face to survey the damages.

No wonder Ethel looked so disconcerted! Kristina's reflection frowned ruefully back at her, her complexion a bright pink, her makeup smeared, her hair a windblown tangle. She swiftly worked with her comb and blusher, trying to recapture some of her former dignity.

Put Dillon Danvers out of your mind, she chided herself. Cover his amorous effects with a quick touch-up. She worked carefully, applying eyeliner, shadow, highlighter. She thought she had control until she ran her lipstick along her lips. Her tender swollen mouth brought him rushing back into focus. Dillon flooded her senses. He was miles away, but his touch was as fresh as the initial encounter.

There was not an ounce of justice in the situation. He'd taken unfair advantage, smothering her with a burning kiss, squeezing her in a wet embrace, leaving both her face and suit a blotchy mess. Kristina could barely express the horrible word which bluntly described the feeling between them. The very mutual pull which drew them together as they hurled harsh words at each other. There was only one explanation.

It was chemistry. Pure, passionate chemistry.

Kristina shook her head in disbelief, but her dark purple eyes mirrored the truth. Kristina was utterly intrigued by Dillon Danvers. He turned her on. Turned her inside out! And it was all wrong.

Dillon was absolutely nothing like the men she usually dated. She was accustomed to choosing her male companions very carefully. She'd comfortably fallen for career-oriented businessman who drove four-door cars, who dabbled in the stock market. They wore suits like second skins, ties with smooth neat knots, and liked to stay downtown after work for cocktails and chitchat. Sex was selective, without pressure. Usually without much passion, either, she admitted to herself ruefully.

Dillon was passion itself. He'd swiftly taken her emotions in hand from the first time she'd listened to him on the radio. But how much of it was genuine? He certainly seemed genuinely angry today. Genuinely aroused. But it was quite clear he didn't shoot for enduring relationships. His method of operation seemed to be a verbal lure, followed by a quick physical merger.

She just couldn't be falling for him. She'd always played it safe.

There were so many reasons why Dillon was all wrong for her. He was unpredictable, audacious, a loner, a surfer. He was quite simply too hot to handle. Too dangerous.

A knock on her office door brought Kristina back to the moment. But the lingering doubts would rest firmly in the back of her mind throughout the afternoon. How could a mother explain away a man like Dillon Danvers to her fourteen-year-old daughter? How could a woman explain him away to herself?

KRISTINA SET HER briefcase on the kitchen table after work, following the sharp tomato aroma to a pot gently bubbling on the stove.

"Krissy?" Howard's voice rumbled from the direction of the living room.

"Sure is, Pop," Kristina called out. "I'm here to pay homage to Coronado's chili king!"

"Krissy..."

Kristina took a slice of cheese from a plate on the counter and headed for the front hallway. "I had no time for lunch and I'm starved!" Kristina entered the living room in full steam, only to stop short on the living-room carpet. Seated between her father and daughter on her floral chintz sofa was Dillon.

"No wonder no one's watching the pot boil," she erupted with the first lucid phrase that entered her mind. She bit back a nervous laugh as she gazed down at the huge man dressed in a bright Hawaiian print shirt, snug-fitting jeans and brown leather sandals, sitting on one of her pristine cushions. He'd dried out completely, his blond hair now fluffy and dry, curving in wisps at the nape of his neck. The picture would've been forever etched in her mind in hilarious infamy if her old photograph album hadn't been open on his lap; for a man who cherished his privacy, he certainly invaded hers without compunction.

"Dillon was kind enough to pay Julianne a visit," Howard explained, beaming from ear to ear.

"Brought me WXNT bumper stickers, and some 'Dillon After Dark' posters," Julianne reported excitedly, her head and hands in motion.

Dillon lifted his chin to meet her gaze squarely with a guileless smile. How dare he play the innocent after manhandling her on the beach? Kristina folded her arms across her chest, determined not to break eye contact first. Dillon held her eyes for several seconds, then lowered his gaze down her body to her legs, then to her feet.

Damn him! He was smugly taking in her new shoes! With a swift movement, she yanked her photograph album off his lap.

"Hope you don't care about the beach-bunny book, Krissy," Howard inserted without a care in the world. "Julianne told Dillon you once were a surfer yourself, and he just couldn't imagine it."

Dillon shrugged his broad shoulders with a mocking look of apology. "Guess I'm the skeptical type."

"So we showed him the proof," Julianne piped up proudly.

"Julianne tells me you drop her off at the beach, but never stay yourself," he said with disapproval.

"I swim at a health club," Kristina returned stiffly. "A swim is a swim."

Julianne balked. "Unreal! Like, surfing is a whole different high."

"Unreal is right," Dillon agreed, sending Julianne into a swoon on the sofa.

"I believe my chili is almost ready," Howard announced with a quick glance at his watch.

"Then you better take your test spin," Dillon told him.

"Test spin?" Kristina repeated in confusion.

"Dillon says we can take his car out for a drive," Julianne informed her, popping up off the sofa. "We're going to roll by Cindy's and Amy's and Angie's. C'mon, Grandpop," she prodded. "Let's go."

Kristina shook her head as her daughter whirled across the living room as if on air. She could read Julianne like a book. Dancing on the clouds. In love with love. She couldn't help wondering about Julianne's trip back to earth. Would it be a long hard drop?

Dillon lifted his hip off the cushion and reached into his pocket for his car keys. "Keep it under a hundred, Admiral."

"Aye, aye, sir," Howard promised with a happy salute. Like a couple of children, the pair disappeared out the front door.

"What are you doing here?" Kristina demanded, hovering over Dillon like a thundercloud.

"You sure are a puzzle," Dillon griped. "You begged me to come over just this afternoon."

"I didn't think you'd show up here! Now. Like this."

"Like what?" Dillon rose to his feet, looming over her.

Kristina inhaled sharply as he invaded her space, the loud print of his shirt blurring her vision. He was so large that the fabric stretched across his chest seemed to span miles, cornering her like a bright brick wall. She held the photo album in the crook of her arm as a buffer. "You know what I mean. You give me the big hermit speech—"

"And the big hermit bear hug," he finished for her, an infuriating grin splitting his face.

"Yes, yes, yes!"

"Stop complaining for a minute and appreciate the happy ending," he suggested. "Julianne thinks you're a heroine because you convinced me to come a callin'."

Kristina took pleasure in delivering him an elbow jab in the ribs as he tried to close in. Instead of tangling with her as she expected, Dillon snatched the album from her arm.

"Give it back," she ordered sharply, making an attempt to recover the book.

Dillon easily held it out of her reach, opening it to some colorful beach shots. "You still have this purple bikini?"

"Of course not! It went out the door about the time my ex-husband did."

"This him?" Dillon asked, pointing to a wiry young man with a surfboard in his hands.

"Yes!"

"Is he the reason you hate the beach?"

"I don't hate the beach," Kristina snapped. "Julianne is quite a little surfer, and I admire her skill. I—I just don't care for fanatical sun worshipers."

"Oh, so your 'beach bum' gibe was straight from the heart then," he said with new understanding.

"In short, yes." Kristina grabbed the book, snapping it shut. "I'm going to ask you again, what are you doing here? And don't give me one of your lines, because I'm fresh out of patience." She backed off a couple of steps, tossing the album on a nearby chair.

"I... I got to thinking about everything," he confessed, his angled face fleetingly boyish, vulnerable. "It's true I don't know much about kids, but I do remember being let down once or twice in my youth. I decided I didn't want Julianne to look back on me with resentment."

"Very thoughtful," Kristina conceded. "Now that you've done your good deed, don't let me keep you."

"Your father has my car," Dillon reminded her, his eyes twinkling with mischief.

"Right you are!" Kristina said, squirming under his lazy scrutiny.

"Baby has a new pair of shoes." Dillon's observation was a low mellow crow, his expression honed once again to sensuous perfection. "Stockings, too."

Kristina backed up again, this time hitting an end table. "So, where are my pumps?" she asked awkwardly.

"In my Porsche. The minute your father drives up, I'll go out and get them."

"No!"

"Why not?" With a look of feigned innocence, he took a step forward.

"Just because," Kristina hedged, avoiding his face.

A dry chuckle filled the air. "A professional knows better than to reply with such an evasive answer."

"You already know the answer!" she replied, annoyance in her tone.

Dillon nodded with an infuriating grin. "It could be a difficult moment. Explaining to the admiral how I kissed the very shoes off her feet."

"You didn't!"

"I could have." A complacent smile slanted his mouth. He could have kissed the clothes right off her back. Every single stitch.

Kristina pinched her lips shut, wishing she could pinch *his* smirk away.

"Just forget about the shoes," she told him in a nervous rush.

"Just put them right out of my mind?" he asked incredulously. "As if they never existed?"

"Yes!" she hissed, clenching her fists at her sides.

"Okay," he agreed, studying his long flexing fingers. "Actually, they're ruined anyhow. I just brought them along in case you didn't trust my word. Do you trust me, Kris?" he asked softly.

Kristina quivered under her wrinkled suit as she warily monitored his face, the way his lids lowered, the way his jaw worked. She'd seen those signals before. It was prelude to trouble.

Within seconds his mouth was melting over hers, his tongue urging her lips open. His hands were pressed against her back, holding her fast against his solid chest. She gave in with a soft moan of surrender. Why did his touch toss her common sense out the window, his tender smoky murmurings strip her of all rational thought? She clung to him like a swimmer going under. She urged him closer, rubbing her legs against his, savoring the tingling sensations.

Dillon whispered softly in her ear, moving his mouth along the silken column of her throat. A tiny alarm pulsed at the back of his mind, reminding him that this intelligent, vibrant, complicated doctor was different from any woman he'd ever known.

A man didn't love and leave Kristina Jordan. Not a man with a lick of sense anyway. Suddenly it was as if a red exit sign flashed in front of his eyes. Leave. Leave before you can't leave. But the pumping surge of his mounting desire soon quelled the warning signals. The "Dillon After Dark" persona may belong to thousands of females, but Dillon himself belonged only to this woman. She only had to say the word. He'd lay it all out for her without another thought.

"Incredible," he groaned, moving over her lips once more.

"Impossible, Dillon." Kristina broke free of his grasp, raising a hand to her mouth.

"I'm sinking in quicksand!" Dillon thundered in desperation and frustration. "You toss me a lifeline, then you yank it away!"

Though Dillon confronted her with eyes glazed to a hard, icy blue, Kristina could read the fear in his face, the sense of betrayal. It sliced cleanly through her heart, softening the rebuttal on her lips. "What shall I do?" she asked tenderly. "Indulge in a fling with no thought, no real foundation for the future? Everything I do affects my life, my daughter's life. You can take such risks and land squarely back on your feet. I have...obligations."

Dillon ran a hand through his bleached hair with a rueful chuckle. "I very much doubt I'll be landing on my feet anytime soon."

"Oh, c'mon," Kristina protested. "I've made a lasting mark on you?"

Dillon reached for her upper arms, drawing her close against his solid body. "Just the fact that I'm here at all should prove something. It's my first house call, Doc," he admitted softly. "And you know it." He shook her gently, as if to awaken her desires. "You've gotten to me in a strange way I can't understand. It's new. It's disturbing. I want to explore it. And I think you do, too."

Kristina's heart hammered in her chest as she confronted his wild-eyed look, as she registered his desperate pleas. She could barely believe that this was the same person who guarded his privacy like a mad caveman. "I'm confused. Of course I want you. But Julianne believes she loves you. It makes this situation so much harder."

"She is a child, Kris. Next week she'll love somebody else."

Kristina shook her head with uncertainty. "I need time to think."

"You think all the damn time! Close down your brain and open up your heart for a change. Start feeling."

"What an unfair thing to say!"

"Prove me wrong," Dillon challenged, giving her a shake. "Can't you see this is one of the hardest moments of my life? I want you so much."

"I...I can't just let go without a clear head," Kristina explained.

"Nobody let's go with a clear head," he muttered sadly. "Maybe you're just too wound up to spring into passion." Dillon released his grip on her arms, his huge shoulders sagging under the weight of her rejection. "I won't bother you again," he assured her tersely.

"Please don't be this way," Kristina called after him as he headed for the front door.

"I'll wait for my car outside. Good day, Doctor. Thanks for the heart transplant. You've convinced me that I do indeed have one. Although right now, I wish I didn't."

Kristina bit her lip as he stalked out to the street with his hands jammed in his pockets. How could she wound a man so big, so physically powerful? He'd seemed invincible on the beach. But he'd totally let his guard down under her roof. She hadn't meant to flatten him. She was confused, stunned. She just couldn't switch gears fast enough to accept his mood swing. She wasn't the loose, impulsive type.

"YOU LOOK FARAWAY, Krissy." Howard leaned against the front porch railing later on that evening, watching his daughter gently rock on the wooden glider butted up against the house.

"I'm closer than you know, Pop." With a deep wistful sigh, she tucked her bare legs beneath her on the chipped wooden bench, rubbing her arms with her hands. The beach was less than half a mile from the house and the ocean breeze was chilling. It felt good to feel something. Even if it was cold, damp air on her exposed skin. It somehow made Dillon's assertions concerning her insensitivity seem all the more wrong.

She did feel, dammit!

But she was also backing away. She was backing away in the same manner he most likely did whenever his emotions became erratic. They were actually quite alike in some ways. Neither of them had been searching for commitment. Both were snug in a comfortable rut. Both of them cherished their privacy. But his visit was such a shock to her system. It would've taken so much for her to give in to him on the spur of the moment.

It must have been quite a stretch for him to reveal his innermost feelings, she realized. Kristina's realized that he'd freed his emotions this afternoon, and she'd shoved him aside because his intensity had frightened the hell out of her.

"You shouldn't be out here in shorts and a T-shirt," Howard chastised.

"I know, Pop," she agreed.

Of course Dillon hadn't exactly made her any promises, she rationalized. He'd come forward to admit there was a spark of something between them, but he was making no promises.

"How was my chili tonight?" Howard inquired, gazing up at the stars.

Kristina shot him a small smile. "Fine, Pop. Very tasty."

How could Dillon make promises when he was trying to be honest? Had he started professing all sorts of romantic notions, she'd have swiftly labeled him a charlatan. Could he have won this afternoon's round with just the right phrasing? Probably not, she silently, reluctantly admitted.

"Julianne had some tricky algebra problems," Howard informed her, drumming his fingers on the wooden railing, "but I believe we figured them out okay."

"Thanks, Pop. I don't have much of a head for figures."

"Love to help out, honey," he assured her, lifting his bushy gray eyebrows with delight. "You know I do."

"Mmm...yes."

"I was thinking of testing a new recipe for barbecued ribs tomorrow night," he confided. "I'll leave it up to you. I know we usually have meat loaf on Thursdays... Krissy, are you listening?"

Kristina perked up. "What was the last thing you said?"

"Meat loaf on Thursdays."

"Before the meat loaf."

Howard shrugged, stroking his jawline. "Only that it's really up to you."

Kristina uncurled her legs, hopping to her feet. "You're a genius, Pop," she proclaimed, planting a kiss on his cheek. "Thanks for the discussion. Good dialogue is the best way to work things out."

Howard shot her a puzzled, but pleased look. "My pleasure, honey. Call on me anytime."

6

"MORNIN', SUGAR."

"Good morning, Ariel." Dillon entered the lobby of WXNT, saluting the sassy young receptionist seated behind the front desk. As always, Ariel exuded the trendy image of the station. Today she was dressed in an orange jumpsuit, her short rusty colored hair spiked to attention with a glossy sheen of hair spray.

"Ooh, don't you look fresh outta my dreams," Ariel purred, running an appreciative eye over Dillon. From the sunglasses resting atop his thick mass of bleached hair down to his seam-busting running shorts, he looked downright hunky.

"So, is my mail ready?"

"It's Friday, isn't it?" Ariel reached under her desk and set a grocery sack full of papers and gifts on top.

"Through rain, sleet, or hail, Ariel." Dillon smiled gratefully, reaching into the bag. "I can always count on you."

"Oh, yeah, this mum came for you yesterday," Ariel informed him, gesturing to a yellow plant set precariously atop her In basket.

"Oh?" Dillon stopped sifting for a moment to cast a sideways glance at the droopy flowers.

"It's from the lady."

Dillon lifted a dubious eyebrow. "What lady?"

Ariel waved a heavily ringed hand. "You know, the mother. Kristina Jordan."

"What!" Dillon nearly lunged over the desk like a hungry tiger.

"Hey, loosen up, lover," she squealed in astonishment.

"When did it come?" he demanded gruffly.

"First thing yesterday morning."

"Why didn't you inform me yesterday morning?"

"Don't blame me," Ariel shot back defensively. "You never deal with the mail before Friday. If you've said it once, you've said it a thousand times, 'Ariel, I don't want to deal with the fan mail more than once a week.'"

Dillon slapped his forehead, quickly calculating just how deep a hole he was in. He'd seen Kristina on Wednesday, she's sent the flowers first thing Thursday. It was now late morning on Friday. Dammit, she must think he'd brushed her off. She'd come around full circle to meet him and he'd missed her.

"Gushy card came with it," Ariel volunteered.

"You actually read it?" Dillon was aghast. "A personal note from *her?*"

Ariel gasped in disbelief at the distraught man she thought she at least half understood. "Her? Her? All the notes are from a her, you big dumb oaf! I read all your mail! It's part of my job, remember?"

Dillon grabbed the sack and dumped its contents over the desktop. "Help me find it."

Ariel frowned at the litter of envelopes, jewelry, and lingerie scattered over her fashion magazine. "Women send you everything from garter belts to motel-room keys and you flip out over a dried-up mum plant."

"Sure it's dried-up. You didn't even water it." He glowered accusingly.

Ariel drew back several inches as his breath singed her face. "Everyone knows I'm not a nature person. I'm a material girl who walks on concrete and thrives under fluorescent lighting."

"Water it." Dillon handed her an empty glass from the corner of her desk. "Please."

"Now?"

"Yesterday!" His impatient snap crackled through the air. "And set it on the windowsill behind you. We'll have to revive it somehow," he mused half-aloud. "She can't see it like this."

"Gosh, no," Ariel oozed with a sarcastic squeak. She jumped out of her chair and yanked the glass from his hand.

"Now, what did the envelope look like?"

Ariel paused in thought. "It was lavender, I think. Had a florist's name on it." With her spiked head held high, she marched across the tile floor to the water fountain.

Dillon pawed through the pile ferociously.

Ariel returned and unceremoniously dumped the water into the pot. "There! I believe the operation's a success. Now to post-op." She picked up the pot and set it on the windowsill, then returned to her desk, pausing to pat her intense co-worker on the back. "I could just tell you what it said—"

"Don't you dare!" he roared with a murderous gleam. "It's private—it's personal!"

Ariel reached down into the clutter, hooking a black lace panty in her forefinger. "Women throw underwear like this at you day after day and you fall apart over a plant?" Her eyes flashed teasingly. "Boy oh boy, but knowledge is power. One word to the press and this room would be full of mums."

"The mum is a symbol, you little dope," Dillon explained, as he tore into a third lavender envelope. "She could've sent me a frog and I would've had the same reaction."

"Bite your silver tongue!" Ariel openly shuddered. "I don't dig slippery creatures. Be forewarned, Dillon Danvers."

Dillon was no longer listening. He'd found Kristina's card.

Let's explore the possibilities.

                                                        KRIS

"I could've told you it wasn't much." Ariel grinned, her almond-shaped eyes sparkling.

He snapped his fingers in her face. "Look her up in the phone book."

"Didn't you exchange addresses during your tête-à-tête?"

"Look up her office address," he ordered in curt, distinct syllables.

"Okay, okay, don't get snippy." Ariel reached into the bottom desk drawer for the San Diego phone directory. "She work here downtown?"

"Yes!"

"I still can't believe it took a doctor in her thirties to snap your strap," she grumbled, thumbing through the book. "Go figure." She pinpointed Kristina's address, jotted it down on a slip of paper, and handed it to Dillon.

"I'm off." Dillon jammed the card and paper into his shirt pocket, turning on his heel to flee.

"Hey, just a minute, sugar. You forgot your mail." Ariel swiftly started to toss everything back into the paper sack.

Dillon reluctantly halted in his tracks. "Give me a break. I'm in a hurry."

"You know the rules. Mr. Rodale insists that all the D.J.s accept their mail, so if a disappointed fan calls about an unanswered letter, the station can honestly say it was forwarded."

"Yeah, yeah." Dillon gracefully accepted the sack and took off toward the entrance in a sprint. *Don't let it be too late*, he silently prayed. *Don't let Kristina slip away, not when she is so close.*

"EXCUSE ME, I'm here to see Dr. Jordan." Dillon stood in Kristina's outer office fifteen minutes later, talking to a middle-aged woman bent over some magazines on a coffee table.

The sound of Dillon's rich melodious voice tinged with urgency caused the woman to drop the stack of magazines and bob up to full height. "The doctor isn't in at the moment," she announced, pushing her bifocals up her nose to scrutinize him. "Have you been here before? I don't seem to recall..."

"No, I've never been here before." Dillon stepped closer. "Is she at lunch?" Her eyes flicked from his icy stare to his bare muscular legs and she visibly flinched. Realizing that she mistook his impatience for hostility, he stopped advancing. It was understandable, he decided. He wasn't wearing much clothing for an office visit of any kind and because of his imposing physique he did seem to loom over people—especially in close quarters. "I merely wanted to speak to her on a private matter," he explained in softer tones.

"Do you have an appointment?" she asked briskly.

She thought he was a patient! Dillon didn't mind being mistaken for King Kong, but a patient... He struggled to keep his temper under control. It was so much easier to simply stay on the beach until dark. "My name is Dillon Danvers. I'm a friend of Kristina's."

"From the radio?" The small woman's face warmed with pleasure. "I'm Ethel, Dr. Jordan's secretary. You must excuse me for not recognizing your voice. I listen every night."

"Ethel," he began, aware that she was advancing on him, her bifocals peeled from her face and dangling from a string around her neck. Why did women always take off their glasses? "I must speak to Kristina as soon as possible."

"Oh, my." The older woman's round face beamed conspiratorially. "Well, she leaves the office early on Fridays. As a matter of fact, you just missed her by thirty minutes."

"Is she playing golf or something?"

"Heavens, no. She sets aside the afternoon for Beacon House. You see, she donates her counseling services to the poor souls residing there. I'm sure she wouldn't mind your stopping by. It's a pretty informal place."

"Where is Beacon House, Ethel?"

"Not far away, on the outskirts of the city. I can give you the address," she offered coyly, as if in possession of the biblical tempting apple.

"I would be most grateful, Ethel."

Ethel glided to the desk and reached for a tablet of paper. "I would so like to hear a Johnny Mathis song tonight on your show."

"No problem, Ethel."

Ethel picked a pen. "Dedicated to me, of course."

"Naturally!" Dillon promised. He'd have promised her anything.

ETHEL'S PRECISE directions led Dillon to an old white stucco two-level home in a low income area of town. Beacon House was dated, but in decent repair with a couple of eucalyptus trees in the small square front yard. Dillon eased his Porsche up along the curb behind Kristina's Camaro and swiftly moved up the cracked concrete walk. He had her now. He'd have her in his arms before long.

Dillon rang the doorbell, absently wondering what sort of "poor souls" resided here. He thought back to his conversation with Ethel and realized he and Kristina had never touched on the subject. It was just another example of Kristina giving to those who needed her. The list was growing—Julianne, Howard, her patients, and now the residents of Beacon House.

To help people on such an intimate level took courage, the ability to lower one's defenses, to get emotionally involved. The guts to open up was an awesome, dangerous prospect to Dillon. But for the first time in years he felt ready to do it. It was totally because of Kristina. She was a siren lure, her violet eyes seducing him spiritually and physically. The plant had him believing that she could be there for him, too. She'd come halfway. After all the years he'd fought the temptation to make a commitment, he'd been with a fifteen-dollar mum. No wonder Ariel was mystified. His lusty fans would be, as well. But none of them understood his needs. If there truly was a way to combine romance with sex, Kristina would be the one to show him how.

The door of Beacon House flew open suddenly, drawing him from his reverie.

"Hello. Sorry we didn't hear the bell. The TV is kind of loud."

Dillon gaped at the girl in the doorway. She was only a few years older than Julianne, but the swelled belly under her yellow smocked top put her a lifetime ahead of Kristina's daughter. "I'm looking for Dr. Jordan. I understand she's here."

"Oh, sure. Please come in." The girl moved through the small entry hall, beckoning Dillon into the living room. The television was indeed blaring, a heated game show in progress on the screen. Several young ladies, all in different phases of pregnancy, sat on worn furniture surrounding the set, second-guessing the show's contestants. They all turned their attention to the ruggedly handsome man who could've stepped out of a come-to-California commercial.

"He's here to see the Doc," the girl beside Dillon informed them. A round of chirps, which sounded very juvenile to Dillon's ears, mingled with the game-show noise. He suddenly wondered what would happen to all those babies. Would they find happy homes? He pushed aside the momentous question with forced effort.

"I'll tell her you're here," the yellow-smocked girl offered.

"If she's talking with someone, I can wait."

"No, she's not counseling right now. Dr. Jordan does all sorts of jobs around the house. Be right back." With a hand pressed against the small of her back, she started up the scarred white staircase.

Dillon nodded at the girls and wandered toward the stairs. Their light, merry chatter lingered in the background, as if they were planning a school pep rally. He wondered if they'd be all right. If each one had a survival plan.

"She says to come up," the girl called over the railing. "It's the last room on the right."

She didn't have to tell him twice. Dillon took the stairs two at a time.

"It's you!" Kristina exclaimed moments later at the sight of Dillon in the bedroom doorway.

Dillon took in the scene: Kristina perched on the third rung of a stepladder, a paint roller in her gloved hand. Her shiny black hair was pulled back in a high ponytail, leaving her delicate face wide open and unassuming. A huge paint-speckled flannel shirt cloaked her pink blouse and frosted jeans. "You're expecting another man?" he demanded shortly.

Kristina erupted in nervous laughter at the sight of his distressed expression. First he strings her along for two days, then he bursts into Beacon House like a harried lover. His unpredictability would take getting used to. "Pop has been threatening to show up here, one day. I thought perhaps he was my male visitor."

Dillon turned and shut the door with deliberate force, pushing it solidly into place, locking it with a distinctive click.

Kristina focused on the large palm pressing against the wood. She felt suddenly tense with desire. People shut doors every day, locked them, too. Yet there was something so intimate about Dillon's simple gesture. Something so intense about the blue flame lighting his eyes. She gripped the roller in her hand, her nerve endings raw with anticipation.

He narrowed the space between them, his eyes pinning her in place, his voice husky and hypnotic.

"Thank you for the plant."

Kristina cleared her throat. His shorts were *so* short. Nearly riding on his rear end. His shirt was open at the neck, exposing a wide triangle of his hairy chest. "You're welcome," she managed evenly.

"Solid sturdy plants, mums. A plant a man can appreciate."

"You must get flowers all the time, don't you, Dillon?"

"I get a lot of stuff. But your gift was nice. Real nice."

"I was beginning to wonder if you'd received it. I sent it to the station figuring it wouldn't be left on the doorstep."

"It arrived and it's as healthy as can be," Dillon said reassuringly. "Ariel, our receptionist has been baby-sitting it for me. Insists on keeping permanent watch over it, as a matter of fact."

"Why the hell didn't you come to me yesterday?" she finally blurted out, her coolness shattering with wounded force.

"My darling..." Dillon murmured, closing in her.

Kristina raised the roller like a weapon, looming over him like a thundercloud. "Answer me!"

"I shall," he promised, extending his hands up toward her.

"Without touching me," she added with a frown.

She was a tough one. Dillon paused a step away, his expression apologetic. "Look, I didn't receive the mum until today. I pick up my mail at the station once a week and Friday happens to be the day."

"Oh, I see," she murmured, her guard falling away.

"It was a misunderstanding. Nothing more." Dillon shrugged uncomfortably, rubbing the back of his neck. "I've been thinking about you a lot. I tried to forget you, but it was a useless exercise."

"My thinking has slowed down a bit," Kristina admitted softly. "I've decided to ease up."

"Ease up and let nature take its course." Dillon reached up and grazed the hollow of her cheek with his finger. "It's been a long journey here," he confided. "First I found your gift, then I had to search for the card. Then I rushed to your office and Ethel was certain I was a deranged patient. I headed over here, all the while knowing you must be furious with me."

"Poor baby." Kristina gingerly set the roller on the paint tray attached to the ladder and grinned down at him. "Maybe I can make it up to you."

"No doubt about it." He tugged at the large tan cotton gloves on her hands, tossing them over his shoulder. He lifted his gaze to the violet eyes that were lingering over him with a burning that made him ache. He pushed aside the flannel shirt covering her front and nuzzled her stomach through her gauze blouse, inhaling her wildflower scent beneath the thin layer of fabric. His hands clasped her waist, then glided along the slope of her hips, pressing her to him.

Kristina's hands dropped to his chest, her fingernails nesting in his blond chest hair.

"Kris..." Dillon raised his face, his eyes aglow with a sensuous sheen. Clamping his arms snugly around her, he lifted her from the third-step perch, setting her down before him on the worn blue rug.

No sooner had Dillon covered Kristina's mouth with his own than a sharp knock on the door interrupted them.

"Hello in there!"

"It's the director of the house," Kristina whispered.

Dillon looked down at the arousal straining his shorts. "Women are coming out of the woodwork here!" he muttered.

"Too close for comfort, huh," she tossed back with a playful wink.

"I'm in no condition to meet another female," he snapped under his breath. "Get rid of her."

"I can't!" she mouthed, turning sharply at the jiggling doorknob. Kristina frantically scanned the room, eyeing the four-drawer maple dresser she'd pulled away from the wall. "Stand over there," she ordered with a jabbing finger.

"Kristina, are you in there?"

"Yes, Mrs. Chambers," she called out. "I'm coming."

"Oh, all right!" Dillon marched behind the dresser as if he were entering the gas chamber.

Kristina unlocked the door, and the live-in director of Beacon House barged in. Despite Mrs. Chamber's bad timing, Kristina smiled at her. The woman quite simply brought out the best in people. Her red hair was dyed a bit too bright, her solid figure was a trifle too heavy, and her voice was like an earthquake rumble, but she was a hard worker and loved the girls who lived under her roof.

"Land sakes, there is a man in here!" Her beady brown eyes twinkled at the sight of Dillon, his muscular forearms propped on the top of the dresser.

"Mrs. Chambers, this is my friend, Dillon Danvers," Kristina announced.

"Pleased to know you, Mr. Danvers."

Dillon extended his hand over the dresser as Mrs. Chambers strode forward.

"Firm grip," Mrs. Chambers declared, pumping Dillon like a slot machine. "I like strong men."

"Me too," Kristina said lightly.

"I can't tell you how indispensable our Dr. Jordan is around here," Mrs. Chambers said proudly. "She advises, she paints, she decorates, and most importantly she listens." Her expression grew serious as she leaned over the dresser, her face inches from Dillon's. "A lot of the girls residing here are really down for the count. Either no one cares, or those who do can't stop shouting long enough to listen."

Dillon swallowed in the face of those shrewd beady eyes. His shorts were feeling roomier by the minute, but he prayed this earthy, direct woman wouldn't round the dresser to punctuate her point. These things took time.

"Do you realize how tough it is to find nonjudgmental people these days?" Mrs. Chambers continued. "Kristina is a rare one, a real giver. Donates herself without reservation."

"I couldn't agree more," Dillon assured her honestly. If only people would back off, he'd have the chance to take one of her donations!

The redheaded woman studied Dillon for several seconds, her faintly freckled face narrowing in thought. "You could be just what we need around here yourself."

Kristina watched Dillon pale under his tan. Those had to be the last words he wanted to hear from this woman. He looked totally freaked.

"Actually it may appear that we've had too much contact with the opposite sex under this roof," Mrs. Chambers hooted bluntly. "It was just a joke, Mr. Danvers."

"Yes, of course." Dillon mouth curved without real amusement.

"Real muscles are a rare commodity at Beacon House, even during visiting hours. Got plenty of sweet talkin' hustlers," she confided, giving his forearm a pat. "But it doesn't get the job done, if you know what I mean."

Did he ever! Kristina bit her lip, shifting from one foot to the other. Dillon was the master of sweet talkin' hustlers. But there was far more to him. She was betting everything on it.

"Mrs. Chambers, did you want something in particular?"

"Why, of course! Don't I always?" The woman's bosom jiggled beneath her large royal blue shirt. "I rushed in here because I heard your boyfriend was a strong one." She turned back to Dillon. "We could use some help rearranging our recreation room. Naturally the girls shouldn't be lifting

anything heavy... You and I would make a great team. I just
know it."

"You wouldn't mind, would you, Dillon?" Kristina said,
the question a rhetorical one.

This was so much more than he'd bargained for! Every
time he tried to get close to Kristina there was someone else
blocking his path. Could he learn to share her with so many
people? Dillon cleared his throat uncomfortably as Mrs.
Chambers circled the dresser to give him a slap on the back.
Luckily he was in a condition to receive visitors once again.
"I'll help out while Kris is painting," he relented impetu-
ously.

"That's the spirit!" Mrs. Chambers linked arms with him,
pulling him toward the door. "Say, do you know anything
about plumbing? The kitchen sink is down to a trickle."

"I can probably fix it," he admitted like a harried defen-
dant under cross-examination.

"And why on earth would a lawn mower cough like a kid
with the croup?"

"Might be the choke."

"Nearly threw my back out trying to start the thing. It
made a *ger-ger* sound when I pulled the cord."

"*Ger-ger?*"

"I'll tell you all about it in the rec room."

"Indeed."

"Is it ever nice to have a capable man around the house!"
Mrs. Chambers declared airily. "One with some practical
things on his mind."

Kristina shook her head in wry amusement, picking up
her roller. Dillon practical? Dillon the fix-it man? It stood to
reason that if a man wished to live like a hermit, he'd have to
be fairly handy around the house. Kristina couldn't imagine
him welcoming the electrician and the plumber into his sanc-
tuary. This would be good for him, she decided. He needed
to make contact with people one-on-one. He'd isolated himself to ridiculous extremes.

Dillon glanced over his shoulder at Kristina as Mrs. Chambers hauled him out the door. She was actually grinning

from ear to ear, her ponytail bouncing with a gleeful nod. Well, she'd have her way for the moment, but she'd pay at day's end.

She'd pay the "after dark" way.

7

"GREETINGS, my fellow American. The admiral, the doctor, and the prizewinning poet are presently unavailable to take your call. All hands will be on deck shortly, so I urge you to leave your message after the beep. Anchors away."

Kristina listened to the "new" message on her answering machine with a mixture of amazement and annoyance as she stood before Dillon's floor-to-ceiling living room window overlooking the sea later on that afternoon.

"This is Kristina, Pop. It's exactly seventeen hundred hours. I'm going to be late tonight, so you and Julianne can have dinner without me. Anchors away," she couldn't resist adding with a sarcastic edge before hanging up.

"Here, sailor." Dillon crossed his small cozy living room with two glasses of wine. "I'd offer you some ale, but Captain Hook drained me dry of the stuff."

Kristina accepted the long-stemmed glass and set the phone on a nearby end table with a huff of frustration. "My father is incorrigible. Sometime during the past week, he changed the message on my answering machine. Little by little he's taking over, pushing me back farther and farther into the background."

"Sounds as if there are one too many leaders around your place," Dillon surmised with a humorous twinkle in his eye.

"Yes." Kristina sipped some wine, watching him curiously. "What are you grinning about?"

Dillon looked around the room, his eyebrow quirking in triumph. "I finally have you all to myself."

Kristina's face softened. "I guess it is the first time, isn't it."

"Trust me, it is. I've been keeping close tabs on this almost-affair of ours. I've had to battle droves of females to get to you. Your daughter, your secretary, and the houseful of 'em this afternoon. Mrs. Chambers worked me like a dray horse all afternoon." His mouth twisted ruefully as he added, "Beacon House can't be repaired by one man in a single afternoon."

"Involvement can get sort of habit-forming," she said coyly. She sauntered forward, grazing his forearm with hers. "One person brushes against another person, then he finds himself in contact with another, and another."

"Exactly!" he exclaimed awestruck. "It's like a tidal wave. A tidal wave of women." He rolled his eyes, gulping his wine. "I'm not accustomed to face-to-face encounters."

"It's far better than airwave fantasy," Kristina assured him. "It's real. Something you can hold on to." Kristina watched Dillon, his eyes anxious as he entered his small open kitchen area to refill his glass. She so desperately wanted to reach him, to draw him out of his self-imposed isolation.

"Something to hold on to," he repeated grimly, leaning against the counter separating the two rooms. "Look at those youngsters of Beacon House. They got involved, didn't they? They ended up with the short end of it. The support of strangers. No partner. No family."

Kristina was startled by his sudden turn of emotion. The lighthearted banter between them was replaced with heavy issues. Social issues fueled with some very subjective undertones. Kristina wondered just where Dillon was coming from. He'd certainly hit a particularly sour note on the word *family*. Impulsively she scanned the sparsely furnished room for a sign of his family. There was nothing. His house reflected no warmth, no personal history. There was not a single photograph hanging on the cedar walls, not one high school trophy on his bookcase. Only a few papers were stacked on his small writing desk.

It was as if Dillon had dropped out of the sky in the form of a fantasy man. No past. No foundation to build on. Kristina put so much faith in the tangible.

"If you're looking for a college diploma or a congressional

medal of honor, you're wasting your time," Dillon surmised shrewdly over the rim of his glass. "I'm self-taught and self-centered."

Kristina spun on her heel, regarding him with a straightforward gaze. "Stop toying with me! We want to be together, so...here we are!"

Dillon studied her with intent consideration. "Sorry. I'm defensive by nature. You of all people didn't deserve that speech."

"We have a beginning," she told him gently. "Naturally we'll learn more about each other as we go on." Kristina broke eye contact with him and busily gazed down at his desktop.

Dillon could sense a lingering wariness in her words and gestures. She didn't trust him yet. Perhaps he shouldn't expect her to. But he so yearned for her confidence. "Julianne's poem is there among those papers," he volunteered. "You can tell her I plan to hang on to it."

"All right." Kristina picked up the sheet of paper, eager to read Julianne's masterpiece. "Why, this is downright sappy," she declared with a mother's tenderness, then read aloud:

"Dillon rides waves of air at night, as he does the ocean
when sun shines bright.
Soaring higher and higher toward the velvet black skies,
his voice touches all our lives."

She shook her head in disbelief. "This was the best of the bunch?"

"Many of them were too scandalous to read on the air," he confided. "That tipped the odds in her favor a bit."

Kristina's face still betrayed her disbelief. "It sounds so juvenile. It was your favorite?"

Dillon frowned, rubbing his square, stubbled chin. "You've got me cornered. Ariel, the station's receptionist, chose the winner," he admitted. "She's on the immature side herself. Barely twenty."

Kristina groaned in disappointment. "What a fraud you are, Dillon Danvers! Julianne—all your listeners thought you sifted through the entries one by one yourself."

"I said I glanced at some of them," he shot back defensively.

Doubt pinched her features. Had she merely imagined Dillon's inner qualities? Could she be so easily fooled? Was her heart twice the size of her head where he was concerned? He was watching her now, obviously aware of the suspicion sifting through her eyes. Perhaps Dillon was too good to be true. When she finally spoke, Kristina's voice was puzzled, pleading. "You are for real, aren't you?"

Dillon gulped his wine, setting the glass on the countertop with a clatter. "My feelings for you are the real thing, Kris."

"I want to think so, Dillon," she said on a sigh.

"Stop thinking and let it happen," he coaxed huskily.

Dillon rested his elbows on the counter, rubbing his face with his hands. Reasonable doubt was a human trait; he had to accept it, deal with it. There was nothing more he could say at this point to convince her of his sincerity. He understood her reluctance considering his stock and trade. He was in a trap of his own making. He seduced women for a living—for a harmless airwave thrill. Now, when his caressing words had real meaning, he had no way of proving their sincerity. There was not one thing he could say to change that. Dillon's biggest asset—his voice—was suddenly his biggest liability.

"Kristina, do you want to know me, to love me?"

Dillon's sharp direct question made her flinch. She watched him as he rounded the counter, his eyes pinning her in place. She stood frozen to the floor, waiting for him.

"Very much so," she told him with quiet certainty.

"You understand that I'm not a blue suit you can analyze after ten minutes of casual questioning?" He hovered a short distance away, his large body tensed for the truth.

She nodded numbly. Dillon was the first man in years who

could turn her legs to rubber with just a murmur. Blow her circuits with a kiss. True, he was reclusive, arrogant, and stubborn as a mule. But she was hopelessly dazzled by him. "I guess you could say I'm just plain stuck on you," she admitted softly.

"Me too." He moved toward her with new confidence, unbuttoning his colorful shirt along the way. He could satisfy her sexually. He knew it just as sure as he knew the sun rose every morning. The mattress was Dillon's favorite playground, second only to the sea. Dillon acknowledged without modesty that he knew all the right physical moves. Finally, after all these years, he had the sense to make them with the right woman.

Dillon's heart hammered in his chest as he stripped off his shirt. There was so much he wished to tell her! And he would do so...eventually. But first he would show her. Once he'd shown her, she'd believe the silken words. But not before, that much was clear. He threw his shirt on the sofa as he approached, his gaze never leaving her wide-set violet eyes. It was all there to read in those incredible eyes. Lust and tenderness. She felt as he did, her feelings reflected in those purple shimmering pools. He'd counted on it as he'd worked the afternoon away under Mrs. Chambers's bellowing direction. Hell, he'd counted on it since the moment he'd grabbed Kristina on the beach. It was time to move ahead.

It was time for show-and-tell.

"I'm like no one you've ever had before, Kris."

His words were liquid passion, a velvet-gloved threat. Kristina watched the shifting blue of his eyes, seeing the smoldering promises, the gleaming animal-keen instinct. Desire had set over them like a hot humid August afternoon. Kristina's pulse quickened as he drew her into his arms. She already knew enough of him to ache with need. His touch was as resonant as his voice. And he was going to really touch this time. Touch her secret places.

Kristina trembled as he pressed her closer, his lips grazing her temples, her nose, her jawline. He sought her lips, overpowering them with his full mouth. His hands moved to her back, arching her against him with a thrust. He held her fast, deepening his kiss, feasting on her mouth as if he were a starving man.

Kristina wound her arms around his neck with a luxurious moan, returning his kiss with feverishly. She was losing herself to Dillon, bonding against the length of his muscled body. He slipped his tongue between her lips, delving into the sensitive recesses of her mouth. Tasting, heating, satisfying an impatient thirst.

Her senses were raw with sensitivity as she followed his every move. His fingers were running a course over her back, tugging at her pink gauze blouse until it got out of the denim waistband of her jeans. He eyed the buttons with ardent frustration, then peeled the blouse up over her head, tossing it behind him.

"You popped one of my buttons," she accused with passion-heavy breath.

"I'm about to pop one of my own, as well," he muttered intensely.

Kristina only had to press her stomach against him to feel the power of his arousal. "Are you, ah, going to stand behind a dresser again?" she teased softly, gazing down at his strained shorts.

He cocked an eyebrow in surprise, then smiled wickedly. "You little witch," he uttered, unsnapping her bra and disposing of it nonchalantly. With an admiring look he clasped her small rounded breasts and kneaded them in his huge hands. He massaged them with a circular movement until her nipples hardened against his palms. Kristina moaned in response, flattening herself against him. Holding her fast he dipped his head, nipping at her earlobe, placing a ribbon of kisses along her creamy shoulder. Then his hands glided down her spine to her waist, tugging at her jeans and panties until they fell to her ankles.

Dillon's breath caught in his throat as he watched her step out of the clothing. She was a pale, delicate flower. The most feminine of creatures. "Ready for bed?" he asked huskily, stroking the length of her satin-smooth back.

Languor seeped into her bones as Kristina faced the smoldering desire in Dillon's hooded gaze. "Yes," she whispered, her hands pressed against his chest. "I...I'm a little frightened."

Dillon understood her trepidation quite well. The unconsummated passions between them had escalated into an intoxicating force. "Everything will be all right, sweetheart." With ease he lifted her into the cradle of his arms and strode into the bedroom.

Dillon deposited Kristina on his single bed, stripping away his shorts. He dropped a knee onto the mattress, the length of his corded tanned body stretching over her creamy white limbs. Skin against skin. Dark against light.

Kristina smiled up at him, her voice shaky. "Do your fans know you have a single bed?"

"All hideouts have single beds." He paused over her for a brief moment, his expression sober. "Is this a vulnerable time of the month for you?"

"I'm safe," she assured him. As safe as a woman could be in Dillon's bed! she dizzily decided.

Dillon moved over her, propping his weight on an elbow. Dillon's hair-roughened skin against Kristina's creamy soft flesh caused a sweet, agonizing friction. Kristina savored the sensation, quivering as his lips covered hers with a ravenous hunger. She hungrily kissed him back, skimming his body with her fingertips. He growled in exquisite agony as she caressed him, explored him.

Blood pounded in Dillon's ears as he counted all ten fingertips working their magic on him. Shifting position, he parted her thighs with his knee, gently stroking her tender flesh, kissing her inner softness.

Kristina clung to him, her reins of control loosening until she gave in to him completely. Her cries of abandonment played musically in his ears. She'd surrendered to him. Trusted him all the way.

With restless urgency Kristina drew him over her. Ever so slowly Dillon entered her, watching the interplay of emotions on her face. He began to move within her, tension swiftly accelerating as she followed his tempo. His eyes never left her face. She was responding so wildly, so freely, as openly as she lived from day to day.

With one last intense thrust, he climaxed. Her finger stroked his cheek as he clung to her, spiraling back down to earth. He knew he could count on that face forever. When he told her he loved her, she was going to believe it.

"GUESS I FELL asleep." Dillon stepped out through the sliding glass door to join Kristina on the redwood deck later on. He'd watched her from the darkness of the living room for several moments, standing in the glow of the moon, staring out to sea in contemplation. He hadn't meant to spy, but it was the most beautiful sight he'd ever seen, a sight to savor.

Dillon's insides were a mess at the moment from the seesaw of emotions he'd endured. He'd panicked when he'd awoken to find her missing from his bed. Had she escaped like everyone else he'd ever loved? Could she slip off after what they'd just experienced together? Jubilation superseded despair when he spotted her outside. It was almost more than his battered heart could take.

He could feel the trauma begin to subside as he padded barefoot across the redwood planks, the mild ocean breeze washing over his body like an old reliable friend. Although his breathing eased to a near-normal pace, his heart was still racing just a bit. She looked so delicately dressed only in his lime green shirt. It flapped like a banner in the air, revealing the curve of her creamy white bottom over and over again. Everything was all right. Kristina hadn't left him. She wasn't going anywhere.

"You were dead to the world," she informed his over the roar of the sea, still focusing on the churning black waters.

Dillon weaved a hand through her loose black tresses and emitted a low deep-chested growl. "You exhausted me with your demanding ways."

"Still, it's only nine o'clock. It seems an odd phenomenon for San Diego's night ow—" Kristina's mouth froze in an O as she leaned back against Dillon to discover that he was completely naked.

"I often come out here in the nude." He raised his arms in the air. "Total freedom. You should try it."

"We'll see," she said, under his devouring gaze.

"You look perfect against the Pacific. Wild, uncontrolled. And thoroughly sated." He smiled with male pride, pulling her to him. "Kiss me back to paradise," he urged, tasting the sweetness of her mouth all over again. When the breeze lifted Kristina's shirttail, Dillon's hand was there to cup the smooth tender flesh of her bottom.

"Save it for now," Kristina whispered, pressing her fingers against his lips.

Dillon's eyebrows narrowed in confusion. "I'll never run dry, honey."

Kristina lowered her eyes. Dillon pinched her chin and lifted her face back up to his.

"Kris, what's the matter?"

"What's going to become of us?" she asked quietly.

"I just showed you how I feel!"

"I need more."

An odd glimmer of humor touched his shadowed features. "Are you ready to believe me now, Kristina? Listen to the words I say?"

"Yes," she responded eagerly. She understood his position. He couldn't tell her what she wouldn't accept.

"I know my on-air reputation isn't the best calling card, but I want your trust—more than I've ever wanted anything in this world."

"You have it, my darling. My complete trust."

"Yes, I believe I do." He pulled her close once more, resting his forehead against hers. "I love you, Kris. For the first time in my life, I know what it feels like."

"Feels pretty good." Kristina rested her head against his chest, her voice thoughtful. "I can't help but wonder how we'll ever mesh our lives, though."

"I believe we both are counting on managing somehow," Dillon said with a wry chuckle.

"Yes. For instance, you can see how much I count on structure. I like to plot goals, follow them through."

"Once you send a man a mum... Look out!"

"Very funny," she said, gently jabbing him in the rib cage. "Don't misunderstand me, Kris. I admire how you've made a home for your daughter. I'm... Let's just say I'm new to this guarantee business," he confessed.

"How is it possible? Have you no family at all?"

Dillon looked off into the horizon with a heavy sigh. "My mother was very much like the girls at Beacon House. She was young, pregnant, and single. She gave me up for adoption—for whatever reason—fear, humiliation."

"It wasn't commonplace to have a child out of wedlock thirty-five years ago," Kristina whispered sympathetically.

"Even today she wants nothing to do with me," he said remotely. "I went through the whole search bit about ten years ago. She has a family. A family who doesn't know about her 'mistake.'"

Kristina's heart twisted in sympathy. To be thought of as a mistake was pretty rough.

"I was almost loved a few times," Dillon continued. "But mainly I was shuffled through a series of foster homes."

Tears stung the back of Kristina's eyes as she watched the pain sheath his face. It explained so much. No wonder he kept his fans at a distance. "Oh, Dillon. I'm so sorry." Kristina hugged him close, stroking his head as he buried his face in her hair. "Are you sure you can handle the Jordan package? Julianne, the house in Coronado, the admiral?"

"I want to make it work." He raised his head, pressing his lips against her cheek. "But I can't help wondering if Julianne will ever accept it."

"It won't be a snap," Kristina conceded. "She'll reel in her Reeboks when she learns we're a couple."

"But you think it's possible, don't you, Kristina?" he questioned urgently. "Don't gloss over the truth."

"Of course it's possible! But it'll take patience and communication to bring Julianne around."

"I tell my listeners to take one day at a time."

Oh, the things Dillon told his listeners! His damn after-dark show was the biggest obstacle they faced. Kristina now understood why Dillon used his show to gain the approval he yearned for. Women loved him, counted on him, dreamed of him, and fulfilled his need to be needed. But he'd never been called upon to put himself on the line, never dared to risk the rejection he'd faced as a youth.

Intimacy without risk. The entire concept scared Kristina out of her wits! Dillon definitely had the best of intentions with his show, but he didn't quite understand that everything had its risks—even airwave seduction. Dillon had just beaten the odds so far.

If Kristina could fulfill his needs, he wouldn't need his sensuous, adoring audience any longer. He could toss his crutch aside and be the man of her house.

"Chilly?" Dillon asked solicitously as she shivered in his arms.

"A little. Are you?"

"I am a bit undressed. C'mon," he invited, his voice growing husky with passion once again. "I know a warm place."

Dillon paused to close the sliding glass door behind them, his arm still snug around Kristina's shoulders. With a fluid motion he began a second journey of seduction, pushing the baggy shirt up her spine with an anxious shove, nuzzling his face against her breasts.

Kristina shuddered as his magic touch ignited her with renewed passion, far richer this time around with the promises made. Tomorrow would be soon enough to worry about the trouble spots ahead. But not tonight. Kristina didn't wish to look any farther than the bedpost tonight.

8

"IN THE STUDY, Krissy."

Kristina had hoped to get to her bedroom without running into her father, but found herself trapped in the front hallway outside the study. She peered into the lamplit room to find Pop sitting in her favorite easy chair, watching an old black-and-white Western on television.

"It's after ten o'clock, Krissy."

"I know the time, Pop," Kristina responded, struggling with her patience. After her passion-filled hours with Dillon, she didn't feel like playing the contrite daughter. She reluctantly stepped into the room, recalling when it was her space, her nest away from it all. Now it was the admiral's, too. He'd invaded her sacred territory soon after his arrival, hanging his framed certificates and plaques on her paneled walls, filling her oak shelving with his precious books on military warfare, and the biographies of respected leaders. His carved burl pen-and-pencil holder now held the prominent place on her rolltop desk once reserved for her ceramic mug full of stubby pencils and stray ballpoints.

It struck a nerve as it always did. Kristina felt as if she was a visitor in her own study.

The feeling would often slowly seep into her conscious mind as she sat behind her desk, absorbed in her casework. There was no gradual realization tonight however. Facing Pop's stern parental glare against the backdrop of a huge photograph of his ship, the USS *Phoenix*, drove the feeling home. She was on his turf. Or so he believed.

"We were expecting you hours ago," he chided, turning down the volume of the television with the remote control. "Where in the blazes have you been all this time?"

Kristina shook her head in disbelief. She felt as if she'd stepped into a time warp, a scene that should have occurred twenty years ago. "Pop, I left a message on my machine."

"You know Friday is poker night over at the officers club."

Kristina sank down on the arm of the chair beside him, her face blank with amazement. Since Howard's return in October, he'd joined his fellow retirees over at the Naval Air Station for cards exactly three times! "Pop, if you wanted to play poker, you should've gone."

"But what about our Muffin?"

"Julianne could've managed a few hours here by herself."

Howard's bushy gray eyebrows and blazing pale eyes fell into moping self-pity.

"I have a life of my own, you know," Kristina retorted impatiently.

Howard expression grew serious. "You and that Dillon fella. You were with him."

"Yes," she admittedly calmly, suppressing her surprise. He knew already! Record timing. "He dropped by Beacon House and stayed to help out," she ventured in explanation.

"Break a few hearts over there?" he grumbled sarcastically. "Seems like those girls have received enough false promises out of life."

"He didn't seduce the household. He moved some furniture, fixed the plumbing."

"Ah..." He trailed off skeptically.

"I don't understand you, Pop. I thought you liked Dillon."

"I liked him as a temporary visitor. Now he's tangled up with both you and our Muffin. I never thought he'd..." He trailed off in frustration. "I just never thought this far ahead."

"I suppose you told Julianne."

"Julianne told me."

Kristina's heart jammed her throat. "Told you what?"

"Julianne called your office this afternoon and Ethel told her Dillon had dropped by looking for you."

"I see." Kristina's heart weighed heavy in her chest. "What does she know, Pop?"

"She doesn't know where you've been all evening. She still has stars in her eyes. But she's not a cynical old man," he pointed out crustily. "She doesn't know about the stars in *your* eyes yet."

Kristina moved across the room and shut the six-paneled door. "I care about Dillon. And he cares for me."

Howard twisted around in his chair, glaring at her incredulously. "How can you be sure about him, Krissy?"

"He says he cares and I believe him."

"He says whatever it takes." With an incensed oath Howard leaped out of his easy chair, nearly tipping the cumbersome thing over.

"I'm not a lovesick child." Kristina folded her arms across her chest, a defiant lift to her chin. "I know what I'm doing."

"What about our Muffin? Couldn't you choose another man to satisfy you? A man your daughter doesn't worship?"

"Pop, I'm not indulging in a fling. If I was that sort of woman, men would be hanging from the light fixtures."

"You're talking commitment?" The word was spat out with horror and disbelief. A raw recruit most likely would've melted under the lethal look he leveled at his daughter.

"Naturally!" she cried. "I wouldn't ask Julianne to make this adjustment if I wasn't certain this was real."

"You hardly know the man!"

"I know all I need to know."

"Can't you see he could woo the birds from the trees? Talk the stars from the heavens? As a psychologist you should be able to see through him."

"I see *him*, Pop. I see him as a complicated man."

"Chemistry is for hot-to-trot kids," he scoffed darkly.

"Not so!" she objected, her body still tingling proof. "There's no age limit on spontaneous combustion. Thank goodness!"

"Let's leave the lab tests out of it then," he said with a dismissive hand. "Can you stand there and tell me you respect his job?"

"I respect the man. The job choice..." she reluctantly conceded, "is not the best for him."

Howard's face grew mirthlessly smug as he raised a warning finger. "He'll never change enough, I guarantee it."

"You're accustomed to dealing in absolutes," she asserted coolly, leaning her arms on the back of a chair. "Perhaps it works in the military. But civilian life is different."

"Too blasted bad!" he ranted. "Always know where you stand aboard ship."

Her father always did have trouble shifting from military absolutes to civilian abstracts. She clearly remembered the hours he spent home on leave, staring blankly at the walls, at the television set, trying to adjust to everyday pandemonium. He was trying to change, to loosen up. But why did he have to bulldoze her to do it?

"As a matter of fact," he continued, "I—"

The door flew open suddenly, and Julianne came flying into the room in her Garfield nightshirt, a pink beauty mask on her face, a towel turban covering her hair. "It's about time, Mom! I've been waiting for hours and hours."

"It's after ten, kiddo. Time to hit the sack." Kristina flashed her father a warning look. She and Dillon had agreed to speak to Julianne together. Break the news of their relationship as a team.

"Are you kidding?" Julianne squawked, her violet eyes wide. "Sleep on a night like this?"

"Your grandpop says you know Dillon came to see me—"

"I called you this afternoon and Ethel was a gooey mess over him. What did he want? Did you ever find out?"

Kristina grimaced as she watched Howard walk toward Julianne and his arm tightened around her daughter's shoulders, as if to shield her from an impending blow. But she forced a smile and kept her voice bright. "Dillon wanted to invite us to visit Sea World tomorrow."

Julianne covered her masked face with her hands and squealed in ecstasy. "You're joking! How radical. A real date!"

"A family outing," Kristina corrected.

"Sure, Mom, whatever you say," Julianne shook her turbaned head with a humoring look. She walked away from Howard and blew him a kiss, pecked Kristina on the cheek, and dashed for the door. "I gotta go. My facial mask is cracking."

Howard listened for Julianne's gallop to die away before he spoke. "I hope he is the one, Krissy. I hope the chemicals are mixed just right. Because if something goes wrong, it'll be a waste. Julianne will have had to deal with your relationship with Dillon for absolutely nothing."

Kristina wanted to reel on him in fury. Tell him just how far and often he'd outstepped his place. But she couldn't. There was such a forlorn tinge to his lecture that she knew she must resist. With all the willpower she could muster, she turned on her heel and followed her daughter upstairs.

Kristina turned on her radio as she prepared for bed. Leaving Dillon's warm embrace for the cool evening air had been difficult. Hearing his mellow voice soothing the women of San Diego would be rough, as well. He had assured her that his listeners meant nothing to him now that he had her. She wasn't certain his assurances would be enough to soothe her feelings as she eavesdropped on his showmanship. She promised to try to handle it. At least for the time being.

Mellow music filled the bedroom as she unbuttoned her blouse, mentally noting the missing button. Maybe he could hunt for it tomorrow. She braced herself for his next caller, reminding herself that it was all artificial.

"Hello? Dillon? It's me, Julianne."

Kristina froze in the center of the room, clutching her blouse as though it were a dishrag. It couldn't be! Julianne had strict orders not to call the station! She had strict orders not to listen anymore!

"I have to talk to you," Julianne was saying in breathless urgency.

A silence fell over the airwaves.

Kristina squeezed her eyes shut. "Cut to a commercial, Dillon," she commanded the clock radio.

"WXNT's poetry contest winner," he finally managed in a

low controlled voice that might pass for sexy with his listeners. But Kristina knew better. He was walking a tightrope, not sure what to do with her daughter.

"Look, I talked to you-know-who," Julianne confided conspiratorially. "About you-know-what."

"Hmm... Very interesting. Hang on a minute, Julianne. I see it's time for a station break. A word from Malibu Musk Suntan Oil. The oil that lubricates and stimulates. Don't leave your mate alone on the beach wearing Malibu Musk."

Dillon was like a caged animal in the studio as he pushed a button on his control panel, and a sultry voice coaxed a beach god to share his bottle of Malibu. He tore off his headphones and picked up the telephone.

"Hello, Julianne? Are you still there?" His heart was exploding in his chest. Kristina had decided to tell her alone. In a way he felt let down, but on the other hand it was over and the girl was still speaking to him, even anxious to speak to him.

"I know I'm not supposed to call you during the show, but I couldn't wait to talk to you."

Dillon hesitated with uncertainty. "You talked to your mother then?"

"Oh, yes, she couldn't wait to tell me everything. I'm so happy, I could bust. You're the most wonderful man in the world."

"I am?" he repeated hollowly.

"Absolutely," she pledged.

"You aren't too disappointed, are you?"

"Well... A teensy-weensy bit. Like, I thought we'd be alone at first, but I'm sure it'll be cool."

"Oh, Julianne, I can't tell you how relieved I am. I care for you of course. But in the way an adult is fond of a youngster."

"Say, what?"

"I may be wording this awkwardly..." He sighed with a chuckle. "I definitely am. Quite ironic for a man who makes his living with words. But I love your mother more than I can say. And I want you to be a big part of it. Julianne? Are you there?"

"I—I have to go Dillon. Bye."

Dillon hung up the phone, deflated by the soft teary farewell on the line. He'd apparently blown it somehow. But how? The technician on the other side of the glass wall was wildly signaling him. The series of commercials was over. With a swift curt intro he put on some romantic mood music. He leaned back in his chair, wearily moving a hand over his face.

The most important night of his life and he'd screwed it up. But how? Hell, he didn't have a clue!

He was just plain no good at nurturing relationships, no good with children. If he had a dog, it would chew his leg off. Kristina would kill him. And he deserved it. Julianne would probably never forgive her mother and it was all his fault. Whatever had gone wrong had been his fault.

"OPEN THE DOOR, Julianne." Kristina demanded, pounding in desperation with a tight fist. She'd barely stopped to slip on her robe, once the Malibu Musk commercial cut into the program. By the time she was down the hallway, Julianne was storming around her room with thumps and bangs. "Julianne!"

"I don't have to talk to you! Go away and leave me alone."

"We have to talk," Kristina insisted. "We always talk!"

"Dillon told me everything. Just go away."

Kristina pressed her palms against the door with desperation. "I don't know what Dillon told you, but I have a right to explain, don't I?"

"No!"

"Let me in, Julianne, or—or I'll jimmy your lock with a nail."

Kristina tightened the sash on her robe, her hopes rising as she heard movement on the other side of the door. If only she could get inside without theatrics, without attracting Pop's attention. With the slightest hint of trouble, he'd be trailing behind her, spouting off with a father-knows-best litany.

The moment Kristina heard the lock click, she whisked inside, locking the door behind her. Julianne had already retreated to the far side of the room near her bed. She'd washed the beauty mask from her face and taken the towel from her head. Her small face was pale and her long black hair hung in damp clumps over her shoulders.

Kristina couldn't remember the last time her daughter had looked so vulnerable.

"Julianne, we can work this out."

Julianne glared at Kristina, then at the bright green boom box on her bed. It was still tuned to WXNT, sending strains of mellow music into the tension-filled room. In a sudden flare of anger Julianne swung her arm in a pitcher's arc, knocking the radio off the mattress. The box sailed through the air and hit the floor with a thud, leaving the room in silence.

Mother and daughter stared at each other for a moment, both shocked by Julianne's burst of rage.

"Everything all right, Muffin?"

Kristina stiffened as her father's voice drifted up the stairs. "Everything is fine, Pop," she called through the door.

"Oh...I'll get back to my show then."

"Okay, Mom." Julianne lifted her head with a defiant sniff. "You want to talk?"

"Julianne, what did Dillon say to you?"

"He told he he wants you! Is it true, Mom?" Her small face softened, her voice was a desperate squeak. "It's a mistake, right?"

"Oh, Julianne." Kristina swiftly closed the gap between them, drawing the lanky girl into her arms. She gently stroked her daughter's damp head as the girl shuddered in soft sobs. Despite the circumstances, despite the fact that Julianne was nearly Kristina's size, it felt so good to hold her. Julianne thought she'd outgrown so much—curfews, hair ribbons, and hugs from her mother. In truth, Julianne needed her mother more than she ever had. If only she'd come to realize it.

"It can't be true," Julianne cried in disbelief and accusation. "He wants me! He's mine!"

"Dillon cares about you, Julianne," Kristina quietly explained. "But not in a romantic way."

Julianne broke free of Kristina's embrace. "He does love me with all his heart! We've been talking on the phone for months and know each other really well! You don't know him the way I do."

"Be reasonable, Julianne. He had no idea you're a youngster."

"I found him first. You stole him away!" Julianne stomped her foot and turned away to wipe her eyes with the back of her hand.

Kristina shook her head in sorrow. She'd hoped to solve this dilemma without a stormy scene. Dillon had obviously handled his end of this all wrong. Contempt for him surfaced for a moment, then quickly subsided. Whatever had transpired between Dillon and Julianne on the phone had been a human blunder, nothing more. He had warned her that he'd had no experience with teenage girls. He was certainly right!

"When you calm down, kiddo, you'll see things as they really are."

"Not your way," Julianne snapped succinctly.

"Yes you will, honey."

"Why can't I have him?" Julianne whirled around to confront her mother with a pleading look. "You never date a guy very long. You'll drop him the way you did the others," she predicted, much to Kristina's dismay. "He'll start to bore you and you'll give him his pink slip. Goodbye. See ya round."

"Dillon isn't like the others," Kristina told her mildly.

"I'll say he isn't," she cried.

"I hope to build something of value with him," Kristina attempted to explain, wringing her hands as she searched for the proper words. "I—I want Dillon to become part of what we share here."

Julianne's eyes blazed with fury. "He doesn't want to settle down with a boring family. Dillon's too free. Too special. Can you just see him watching the ten o'clock news in his skivvies? Washing the car in the driveway? Dropping by the 7-Eleven for milk and bread?"

"I think he already does all those things. Alone."

Julianne shook her head vehemently. "No, he doesn't. He doesn't want to be trapped."

"Committing yourself to those you love is what makes a person special," Kristina asserted gently. "Existing without direction is the easy way out. It isn't freedom, it is a long lifetime corridor of loneliness."

"Dad lives to be free. It works for him."

"I don't consider your father a very happy man," Kristina told her honestly.

"You're still mad at him for leaving us."

Kristina shook her head. "My angry feelings toward him fizzled years ago. I only pity him now because he's missed out on the pleasure of raising you. To me, that's what life is all about—being trapped in the most wonderful way possible, in a snare with your loved ones."

"You'll never get Dillon to buy all of this," Julianne declared stubbornly, a pouty set to her mouth. "He likes his space."

"He's already begun to realize through us what he's missed. He doesn't see entrapment. He sees possibilities. Endless possibilities. He'll convince you if you give him the chance, give *us* the chance."

"Well, you won't be seeing much of me," Julianne announced righteously, folding her arms over her chest.

"You're going to be off for the next two weeks for spring break," Kristina argued.

"So?"

"So I've cleared my calendar for the first half of your vacation! We'll be together. I suggest we make it a threesome instead of a pair. Take the opportunity to see if we can make it work."

"I'm going to stay with Dad," she announced, triumph

lighting her red-rimmed eyes as Kristina's mouth dropped open. "In Hawaii."

"He isn't expecting you until July," she scrambled to protest, "as always."

"That's the trouble with you, Mom. Everything has to be planned."

"Hah! The way things are going, my girl, I don't dare plan any further ahead than sixty seconds."

"I'm going to call Dad. Right now."

Kristina closed her eyes and took a steadying breath. "Please sleep on this, kiddo. You can't run away from this problem."

"I'm so sick of your shrinky mumbo-jumbo. 'Confront your problems,'" she mimicked, "'keep your cool.' Well, I've had it! You wrecked my whole life and I want to get out of here!"

Kristina nodded, realizing Julianne couldn't be reached tonight. "We'll talk tomorrow."

9

THE KITCHEN WAS deadly quiet the following morning. Kristina sat alone at the huge oak table in the center of the room, her long fingers encircled around a warm coffee mug, her eyes staring vacantly at the wildflower pattern in the wallpaper. Saturday mornings at the Jordan house were usually noisy confusion. French toast à la Admiral bubbling on the stovetop, the titter of cartoons à la Julianne wafting in from the study, and the newspaper spread around the room in drop cloth fashion. Kristina loved every minute of it.

But this was not a regular Saturday. The stove was stone-cold and the tick of the kitchen clock was the only audible sound in the painfully silent house.

Kristina pushed her plate of cold dry toast aside along with the neatly folded newspaper. She was in no mood for food. After being spoiled rotten by rich French toast smothered in syrup, she couldn't bear to settle for her own dry replacement. Nor was she in the mood for San Diego's latest updates. The newspaper's headlines couldn't possibly top the note she'd found taped to her refrigerator in Pop's narrow scrawl.

Krissy:
   Have taken Muffin to airport. She wants to catch the first flight to Hawaii in a.m. The attendants will take good care of her in First Class. The beach bum meeting her at the airport. Know you'll understand.

Love, Pop

The ceramic mug jiggled precariously in her hand as she angrily slurped her coffee. Know you'll understand, he'd said! One word to Kristina in advance would've put that myth to rest but quick! Julianne had never before run to Wade to evade having to face her mother. Not once! Problems had always been kept under the Jordan roof.

Kristina had been quite up-front with Julianne about her natural father as soon as she was old enough to start asking direct, intelligent questions about why her daddy didn't live with them and have a regular job. Kristina thought that Julianne understood that Wade was a million miles away in his own little tropical world of sugar shacks and surfing championships. He wasn't the least bit interested in child-rearing responsibilities. Until today the realities of everyday parenting had been kept from Wade Jordan. Boy, was he in for a baptism of fire!

Kristina's heart ached for her daughter. How would Wade handle the crisis soon to be thrust upon him? Julianne was normally upbeat whenever she paid him her annual visit. Wade was her good-time dad who traveled all over the world to surf the meanest curls. Julianne accepted Wade as he was—or seemed to. How could Julianne possibly expect Wade to guide and comfort her now? The idea of Wade adding something constructive to this problem was beyond Kristina's comprehension.

Damn the busybody admiral! Kristina could've smoothed things over this morning, kept Julianne where she belonged. If only she hadn't overslept. If only she'd heard something— a slamming door or the running faucet in the bathroom. Any noise to rally her. But she'd tossed and turned most of the night and hadn't drifted off until the wee hours of the morning.

None of it mattered now, Kristina silently mourned. Julianne was out of her reach. Perhaps for the duration of her spring vacation.

The creak of the back door cut through the quiet kitchen a short time later as Kristina stood at the counter refilling her coffee cup.

"Ah, so you finally joined the ranks of the living," Pop greeted with false brightness.

"Have I?" Kristina glared at her father's bulky figure looming in the doorway. He stepped inside rather awkwardly, the kitchen door snapping closed behind him. He carefully hung his key ring on the wooden rack beside the door frame, whistling a bit under his breath as he straightened all the household keys lined up on their proper pegs. It was an openly false gesture. His neck was ramrod stiff, his jaw set rigidly. And he was watching her guardedly out of the corner of his eye, waiting to see where he stood. Kristina didn't keep him waiting long.

"How dare you, Pop?" she accused.

"How dare I make my granddaughter happy?" he blurted out. "How dare I grant her her wish to spend her vacation with her bum of a father? It's what she wanted, Kristina." He shook his gray head. "I see no harm in my actions."

Kristina's thin black eyebrows arched knowingly. "If it's all on the up-and-up, why didn't you awaken me?"

"Because..." He stumbled momentarily, looking into space. "Because it didn't seem necessary," he eventually managed, forcing a confident tone unbefitting his extremely lame excuse.

"Because you wanted to be her hero, her savior, again!" Kristina leaned back against the sink, sizing him up as he wordlessly lumbered across the room toward her in his creased cotton slacks and pinstripe shirt. He must've taken great care in preparing for the airport run. Swift, stealthy care.

Howard busily took a mug out of the cupboard and poured himself a cup of coffee, avoiding her penetrating gaze, only twelve inches away. "Too weak," he judged after twice sampling the brew with an irritated scowl. "The coffee's too weak."

"It's just right for me," Kristina responded evenly stepping out of his way as he set his cup in the sink. "As a matter of fact, Pop, I've been deciding what is right around here for a long, long time."

"She had to get away," Howard asserted in a burst to plead his case. "She needs time to lick her wounds. And you need time too, Krissy. Time to come to your senses." His bushy eyebrows narrowed in her direction.

"We don't run away from our problems under this roof, Pop," she told him with the shake of her finger.

"You think I enjoyed sending her off to the beach bum?" he demanded, genuinely shocked. "I had to make a decision on the spur of the moment, so I did what I thought fair. It's over and done with, so no use crying over it. But let me tell you," he added with a pained, pitiful look, "it's tough being a grandpa. I'm all tuckered out."

"Pop, it's tougher being a mother! As much as I like to please Julianne, I call the shots in the big matters. Little girls don't decide when to hop on airplanes."

"I only wish to be her ally," he grumbled. "Give my family something after all these years." Arms folded across his large chest, Howard began to pace between the refrigerator and the stove. "I could've gotten a place of my own, anywhere in the world. I came here to live with you because I hoped we'd capture a family feel among the three of us. I paid off this house with part of my savings so you could feel free of that burden."

"You know I protested that gesture, Pop," Kristina reminded him, a proud lift to her chin.

He raised a palm to silence her. "The pleasure was mine. A contribution to a daughter who never had a fancy wedding or a father to give her away at the altar. I've done it all out of pleasure, Krissy, the cooking, the cleaning, the shopping, the laundry. I've done everything I could think of to be useful, to be part of things."

"I love you for wanting us," Kristina blurted out passionately. "But you've taken your good intentions too far. You've teamed up with Julianne against me." There! She'd finally said it out loud. Kristina drew a breath, watching for his reaction.

Howard's weathered face clouded in amazement. "Is that how you really see it, Krissy?"

Kristina slowly nodded, continuing with rising irritation. "You've undermined my authority again and again over the past six months. The moment I deny Julianne something, she rushes to your side, wheedling your cooperation. And you gleefully step in every damn time to shut me down. It isn't fair, Pop. I've paid my dues as a mother. I deserve my daughter's respect."

"Of course you deserve it," he returned quietly. "But under the current circumstances, I felt I should make—"

"I know what you thought you should do," Kristina cut in, still finding it difficult to believe what he'd done. "You tiptoed around behind my back and put my daughter on a plane to stay with a man you dislike—just because she demanded it."

He cast her a wounded look. "Well, you've cut to the bone of the matter, haven't you?"

"Naturally a fourteen-year-old's first instinct would be to flee," Kristina conceded. "But if Julianne hadn't been given an airline ticket, the feeling would've passed."

"You mean to say she's never rushed to the bum before?" he asked, somewhat surprised.

"It was beyond her realm of thinking before! Before she had an in-house indulgent grandpa with a driver's license and Visa card in his pocket. If everybody had a grandpa like you, the planes would be full of pampered children jetting off to escape their problems," she predicted with frustration.

"I merely wanted to shield her from further hurt," he fired back defensively. "She's hurting bad, Kristina. And that, my girl, is on your head."

"Pop, Julianne cannot be wrapped up in gauze and set upon a satin pillow until her Prince Charming comes along to take her to paradise. She's in it for the distance with me, weathering the rough times as well as the good ones. She cannot learn to deal with disappointment if you smooth her every step."

"You can get her back, Krissy," Howard declared, tossing the challenge in her court with a sweeping hand. "Get rid of the Dillon fella. Say goodbye to him and our Muffin will come flying back."

Kristina reeled in shock. Wouldn't he ever learn that he couldn't pull all the strings? "I care for Dillon," she proclaimed. "Deeply care for him. I will not humor Julianne by turning him away. I need him, Pop."

"Well, we'll see what the man of darkness is made of. Just wait until he hears about today's developments. The rebel child, the meddling admiral and you, Kristina, the woman caught in the middle. We'll see how he handles real heartaches face-to-face. You aren't one of his phone-line tootsies that he can hang up on and forget. He's right smack in the middle of the action this time." Howard chuckled mirthlessly. "The fun and games are over. It's time to get down to real life."

"We'll see, Pop. We'll see you wrong!"

"Won't take long to ferret out the truth," Howard wagered. "He must already know there's trouble. Julianne must've given herself away last night on the telephone." Howard gestured toward the telephone. "Call him up. I challenge you."

"I will handle this in my own way!" Kristina cried with affront. "As far as I'm concerned, Pop, you've done quite enough meddling for one morning—for one lifetime!" With that parting shot, Kristina stormed across the kitchen, grabbed her purse from the counter, ripped her keys from the neatly arranged rack, and barreled out the back door.

Kristina sat out in the driveway behind the wheel of her car to catch her breath, the ignition key clenched in her balled fist. She needed time to think! The key dug into her palm as she replayed the morning's events, but she barely noticed the pain. Oh, how she hated bitter disputes. But it had to be done. Pop had to be called on his interfering ways. After all the good work she'd done with Julianne, she had to fight to preserve their relationship.

She had to fight for Dillon, too. He was the answer to her dreams. She'd been waiting years for just such a man, clinging to the hope that there was one—just one, who could make her shudder with anticipation. He could handle this crisis. He was strong. He was intelligent.

He was also a lifelong bachelor and a full-time hermit.

Kristina's heart grew heavy as the doubts began to surface. He was so accustomed to the status quo. Child-rearing was a roller coaster ride. Teens indulged in lots of dramatics. And Julianne was barely on the threshold of her impossible years. Dillon was bound to get so much more than he'd bargained for. Would he be willing to deal with the entire Jordan package?

Pop's dire predictions cast doubts in her mind, as hard as she tried to suppress them. Dillon could very well back off once he got the lowdown on the situation.

The fear of rejection sliced through her like a knife. She couldn't bear to watch their dreams for the future collapse before they'd barely been rooted.

She longed to call him now. Run to him. Pour out her anguish and rally his support. But it was a gamble she couldn't take at the moment. She was too fragile to test him. Perhaps later she'd muster the strength to face him. Lay out the unvarnished facts. But for now she was going to lick her wounds. For the first time in her life Kristina was going to slip away from confrontation. She was going to run off and hide just as her daughter did.

THE HAMBURGER was lukewarm and the soft drink nearly flat.

Dillon barely noticed the condition of his snack as he munched his way through a long instrumental version of an Elvis tune during his Saturday night show. He consumed the last of the hamburger, tossing the wrapper across the studio into the wastebasket. After hitting his target with the paper, he turned forty-five degrees on his wheeled chair to face the control panel, adjusting the long-armed microphone to its proper position. Joe the technician, seated on the other side of the glass, raised a finger to get his attention.

"One minute, dark man."

Dillon nodded and put his headset back on. It was nearly

midnight and Dillon's "Saturday Night Special" was bombing out in the worst way. The calls were pouring in as always. The women on the line were wired for him. Their tones were tinged with the same longing and sexual frustration that made him the master of his "after dark" universe.

They'd put their customary faith in him. They were counting on his navigational skills to guide that old familiar magic carpet ride, to soar over the clouds, skim the world of fanciful pleasure.

But Dillon found he couldn't woo them tonight. Couldn't clasp their hands across the airwaves, tickle their libidos with his trademark chuckle. He had no desire whatsoever to launch their fantasies into flight.

For the first time since the inception of his seductive Man of Night persona, Dillon didn't care enough about his listeners to even fake it.

Kristina had dropped off the face of the earth and it was driving him out of his mind.

"THIS IS 'Dillon After Dark' here on WXNT 103.9 on your FM dial. The show is moving right into the midnight hour. As I mentioned earlier, I'm expecting a certain listener to call me tonight. You know the number."

"Hello, Dillon?"

"Yes, Dillon here."

"This is Elaine. Am I the one? The special caller?"

"No, but I'm always happy to hear from you, Elaine. What's on your mind tonight?"

"What's on *your* mind, that's the real question!"

"I don't understand, Elaine."

"You're taking all the words right out of my mouth, Dillon. I'm the one who does not understand! You're just not yourself. You haven't been the same man the last few nights."

"I'm doing my level best, Elaine. If I can help you in some way—"

"Tonight's your worst ever! There's something missing,

Dillon. I can't quite put my finger on it. It's as if your spirit's drained dry. You're not touching me as you usually do."

"I'm sorry, Elaine."

"I need to be touched, Dillon. Now. Tonight. Touch me in my secret places."

"The show's winding down, Elaine. I apologize if you're not fulfilled."

"You have a wall up, Dillon. It's brick solid."

"I am only human, Elaine. Perhaps my frailties are showing tonight."

"Please don't change, Dillon. Believe me, I know you're human. As human as the male of the species gets, actually. You're a living, breathing romantic. The perfect man."

"You've been reading my press releases, Elaine."

"I've been reading you, my love. I've been all the way with you."

"Good night, Elaine."

"Sweet dreams, my prince. Don't change. I need you. We all need you."

KRISTINA NEEDED HIM. Or so he thought.

Dillon maneuvered his Porsche down the winding oceanfront highway an hour and half later, the windows wide open. It was an unusually warm spring—this night was no exception. But it wasn't hot enough to explain the perspiration veiling his face. He didn't sweat often under stress. Never for a woman.

It suddenly occurred to him that he hadn't stopped sweating since Kristina entered the restaurant in that polka dot excuse for a dress. She'd controlled his every move since the night they'd met.

The poetry contest dinner... Had it really been only one short week ago? How did men manage lifelong relationship when he was a total wreck after only a few days?

He pressed down the gas pedal harder than necessary. The open windows sucked in the warm sea air as he picked up speed, until he felt as though he were riding atop a whizzing black bullet. The wind plastered his damp skin, numb-

ing it like Novocain. Dillon welcomed the numbness. He was
a little weary of the emotional roller coaster.

Dillon eased up on the accelerator as he turned up the narrow gravel road leading to his beach house. A hot shower
was first on his agenda. Stinging hot water, followed by cool
soothing sheets pulled tight as a drum. A perfect plan—save
for the fact that his sheets held the intoxicating scents of Kristina. The intoxicating blend of lightly sweet perfume and
musky body scent.

He would change the sheets!

No, he wouldn't. He knew he couldn't. If that was all that
was left of her, he'd savor it. With a heavy sigh Dillon hit the
brake and rested his head against the steering wheel for a
moment, simply overcome by his own contradictory behavior and the seriousness of it all.

He squeezed his eyes shut, finally giving in to the flow of
emotion riding his back. The black car idled in the darkness,
its headlights piercing the desolate distance as he wallowed
in the pain, accepted its presence. He exhaled shakily, trying
to make sense of the situation. How could she simply vanish
without a word? Had he blundered so completely with Julianne that Kristina couldn't face him? He'd tracked her all
day long. Called her house, her office, dozens of times.
Never once had he gotten an answer. Eventually he'd driven
to Coronado, pounded on her back door until his knuckles
were red. He hadn't wanted to intrude on a private moment
at the Jordans, but he was a desperate man. And God help
him, the desperation had only escalated over the hours.

Dillon was as desperate as an abruptly abandoned lover
could be. He'd lived without commitment for thirty-five
years and within the course of a week he felt bonded for eternity.

All because of her.

Dillon raised his head, slid his foot back to the gas pedal to
go up the road. His headlights hit the redwood house as he
swung a hard right to shoot into the garage. With an uttered
curse he hit the brakes, stopping short in front of a car.

It was Kristina's Camaro.

KRISTINA PERKED UP her ears from her spot on the beach, certain she'd heard an engine. No, perhaps not.

She sat at the base of Dillon's bluff, digging her feet into the sand, watching the ocean rise and fall in the silver moonlight. She cocked her head to listen once more, then retreated back to her hunched position. Perhaps she'd been wrong, confused by the roar of the sea, the whiz of the wind. Whatever had attracted her attention was gone now. She was again alone with her surroundings.

It had to be getting late. The show was long over. She'd left the house in such a rush after his on-air plea, that she hadn't thought to put on a watch. Or underthings. Or socks. She'd only taken time to pull off her nightie and throw on the mint-green cotton sundress she'd worn that afternoon to the mall.

"Kris!"

She twisted around to find Dillon edging down the dirt path with practiced surefootedness, dressed in his old cutoffs and a faded red shirt.

"Where the hell have you been?" he demanded, his muscular arms and legs flexing in the moonlight.

"Dillon." Kristina's response cut to a gasp as he grabbed her arms and hauled her to her feet.

"Answer me, Kristina!"

His face was contorted in fury. Kristina would've been frightened if his voice hadn't been steeped in anguish.

She blinked nervously under his gleaming gaze. "I couldn't face you today, Dillon. I'm sorry."

"Sorry?" he roared. "You ran out on me and you're sorry?"

"It's been only a day."

"It's been an eternity for me!"

"I came as soon as I heard your broadcast."

"Why didn't you call the station?"

"Because your listeners are already doubting you," she placated. "Professionally you couldn't afford my phone call."

Dillon groaned with frustration. She had been thinking of

his career. A career she disliked. How tough it was to fault her.

"I had no way of knowing you were so upset," she continued. "I never did hear exactly what transpired between you and Julianne, and I needed time to calm down. Sort things out."

"It was an honest mistake," he insisted. "I thought she knew about us... She said you'd told her everything. I jumped the gun and assumed her everything was *our* everything."

She sighed with new understanding. "It was an honest mistake."

"You don't blame me, do you?" he asked anxiously.

"No, of course not."

"Then why didn't you come to me, Kris? Why did you need your space so badly?"

"Because there were big fireworks at our house." Kristina confessed with defeat. "Julianne and I had a blowup last night and she threatened to spend her vacation with Wade in retaliation."

"But we were all going to spend the week together."

"I had no intention of letting her run off."

"So, what happened? Is she at home?"

"She left for Hawaii this morning."

"But how could she without..."

Kristina looked at him expectantly, her tone dry and sad. "Care to guess?"

"Howard."

"He deliberately tiptoed around in the wee hours and bundled her off to the airport. Naturally, I was out of my mind when I woke up and found his note. Naturally, we—" she paused to wipe her eyes "—had a whopper of a fight."

"Oh, honey."

"Hold me, Dillon. I need you to hold me."

Dillon drew Kristina rather awkwardly into his arms. His heart was still pumping erratically with his surge of fury, his emotions a jumble of confusion, sympathy, and subsiding anger. He had no experience in comforting women. He usually held them close when they were aflame with desire. But it felt natural to press her close, to bury his face in her soft clean hair. She was curled up against him like a helpless kitten, clinging to his T-shirt with balled fists, crying into the hollow of his shoulder. He couldn't believe how much he'd been missing.

"You should've called me at the house when Howard's temper was in full bloom," he gently chastised as her sobs quieted.

"I wanted to," she assured him. "I thought about it."

Dillon lifted her chin up to study her face, his words direct. "Why didn't you?"

"Because Pop said—I thought—" she stammered helplessly, knowing he wouldn't be instantly receptive to her explanation.

"You didn't believe in me." Dillon drew back toward the sea, his voice heavy with disappointment.

Kristina followed him to the wet sand. "I was afraid our troubles would overwhelm you. Our relationship is so new, I didn't want to spoil it with a catastrophe so soon."

"Spoil it with a catastrophe?" He balked at her as if she were an alien being. "Woman, can't you see that my life has been a three-ring circus all week long, spectacular enough to put Barnum and Bailey out of business! Have any idea what I've endured these past several days?"

Kristina gazed down, watching the incoming waves roll over her feet with a foamy hiss. "It seemed as though we'd just had our fun and the problems were upon us."

Dillon hooted incredulously, kicking at the lapping water. "Fun? My whole life has been literally turned upside down by you. I was perfectly comfortable for a long, long time with being close to the women I cannot touch. Distant with the women I do touch. You stroll into the picture with the most intriguing eyes I've ever seen and dazzle me senseless. A crusty admiral's bellow and a child's tantrum aren't going to knock me flat." He cupped her face in his hands. "I love you for keeps. Nothing is going to change my mind."

"Say it again."

Dillon exhaled with exhaustion. "All of it?"

"No, the love part will do nicely."

"I love you." He closed the gap between them and kissed her tear-stained cheeks. "I love you. I will always love you."

"I love you, Dillon."

"Don't ever leave me hanging in midair again," he told her roughly. "There's not a problem we can't handle together."

"It's bound to get crazy once in a while," Kristina warned him.

"It's been nothing but crazy since the beginning," he muttered, bending over to cover her mouth with his. His need to claim her was urgent. The tensions of losing her, tracking her, hating her, then loving her had culminated over the passing hours. A tight knot of need the size of California twisted inside him, begging for release.

Kristina leaned into Dillon as his warm moist lips glided over hers, first for a taste, then with grinding pressure.

His arms soon slackened at her sides as his hands began to roam her back with a heavy touch, traveling the length of her spine over the soft fabric of her mint-green sundress.

With anxious fingers Kristina tugged at his T-shirt, pulling it up his bronzed chest and over his head. She wound her arms around his neck and standing on tiptoe, rubbed herself against him.

The pressure of Kristina's breasts against his hair-dusted chest made Dillon shudder. She wasn't wearing a bra under her dress. The tips of her breasts were dark and hard against the lightweight cotton fabric. His darling doctor was certainly out of uniform tonight.

Dillon's hand glided down the curve of her hip, then under the hem of her dress, stroking up the length of her trim leg. His fingertips climbed higher grazing greedily along smooth creamy thigh. His breath quickened as he palmed the soft curve of her bottom.

She wore nothing under the dress.

Kristina arched into him, her stomach rubbing against his swollen groin. He stiffened with desire, waves of passion jolting him. It was just like last night; she was a woman stripped of her Ph.D., stripped of her family ties, shackled only to him for the most intimate of bonds. The added bonus tonight, was that she was stripped of her panties, too....

Kristina captured his mouth once more, her toes actually leaving the ground this time as she clung to him like a necklace.

Dillon reached down and clamped his hands on the backs of her thighs. With a grunt he hoisted her up, perching her upon his waistline. She instantly locked her legs around him, balancing herself easily on his sturdy torso. She tilted her head back to look at him, marveling at his sheer physical presence. He had strength like she'd never experienced before.

Kristina was the hottest thing he'd ever seen, her black hair flying wildly in the wind, her dress bunched up over her hips as she rode him. Her most intimate place moistly fused to his abdomen.

Eyes glazed with passion, Dillon lowered his head and traced the hollow of Kristina's throat with his tongue. Clinging to his shoulders, Kristina tipped her head back to the star-studded sky, releasing a low moan as she felt his wet trail over her collarbone, down to one breast, then another, nibbling at them through the flimsy fabric, drawing each rosebud tip to a rock-hard point. All the while he balanced her on his hips.

Liquid fire coursed through her veins as she writhed against him, her limbs locked possessively around him. "Take me now," she eventually coaxed when she could take no more, her voice a siren's lure on the sea breezes.

His hands left her briefly as he undid his jeans, and she clung to his shoulders while nipping at his ear with her teeth. When his touch returned, it was without further ceremony. He lifted her hips, then entered her with a swift thrust.

Kristina shuddered with a sweet cry of delight, throwing back her head as an explosion of fireworks intermingled with the stars overhead.

Together they collapsed in the sand, the incoming waters

rushing over them with a foamy hiss. They rested together in the ocean's embrace for a long while, the backwash flowing over them again and again like a cool watery blanket.

Dillon held her fast in his arms, pressing his lips against her ear. "You are staying the night," he stated firmly.

"Just try to chase me off," she moaned with contentment. "Just try."

10

"MORNIN', SWEET CHEEKS."

Kristina started at the sound of Dillon's raspy voice greeting her the following morning. She turned away from the griddle on the stove to find him peering into the kitchen at her with curious wonder.

He moved across the tiled floor toward her, dressed only in faded cutoffs. The small kitchen seemed to shrink as he stretched his massive arms while yawning.

"Did I startle you?" he asked, enveloping her against his solid length.

Kristina tilted her head back against his bare chest. "I don't know if I'll ever grow accustomed to your voice," she admitted. "I swear, every word is a seductive purr."

"All the better to seduce you with, my darling." Dillon gazed down over Kristina's glossy black hair to the pleated dress shirt she'd snatched from his closet. She looked so at home—in his house, in his only good shirt. Leave it to her to reach into the closet and choose the highest quality garment. The woman had excellent taste. Excellent everything. He moved his hands over her stomach through the linen barrier.

"Don't get any ideas, mister. It's time for breakfast."

Dillon looked around in puzzlement. "The stove is stoked in the kitchen. I can hear the washer churning in the laundry room. You gone domestic on me?"

"We can't play all the time," Kristina pointed out, waving her spatula. "We have to eat. And I had to wash my dress. It was a soggy, sandy mess."

"Guess it did have one hell of a roll last night," he mused in recollection.

"So did I," Kristina returned with a wry grin.

Dillon frowned slightly as he looked down at the circles of bubbly batter on the griddle. "What are those?"

"They're pancakes," she replied incredulously, straightening up again. "You're going to love 'em."

"I usually eat shredded wheat in the morning."

Kristina whirled around in wonder to discover he was serious. "Pancakes are a Sunday tradition at our house. Shredded wheat is so weekday..."

"I like shredded wheat," Dillon maintained, folding his arms across his chest.

Kristina flipped the pancakes, to find all four of them black. "Oh, damn! I know there's a trick to this, but I don't know what it is."

Dillon's expression grew skeptical. "This tradition a recent thing at your place?"

"No," Kristina grumbled, "Pop's our chef. I thought maybe if I gave it try, I could master it."

"Let's go cook in the bedroom," he tempted. "You're quite masterful in there."

Kristina scowled at his boyishly hopeful expression. "No! It's Sunday and we're having breakfast. We always have a fun breakfast on the weekend."

A laughfest, Dillon thought with a grimace as Kristina flipped the pancakes onto a plate with the lighter sides up.

"Just smell," she invited, waving the plate under his nose.

"Heaven," he agreed, inhaling the smokey sweetness. How had the Jordan women survived alone all those years on their own? he wondered in awe.

"I'll make more," she decided with a firm nod, setting the plate on the counter.

"No!"

"Huh?"

Dillon smiled at her aggrieved expression, so happy that she wanted to please him. "Let's eat these first," he bargained. "If they stay put, we'll see."

Kristina's eyes widened as he slipped on his leather moccasins and headed for the back door. "Where are you going?"

"Down to the end of the driveway to get the newspapers." He paused to look at the plate of pancakes, then marched back to take the spatula from her tight fist. "Relax, honey."

"I am relaxing."

"A machine gun would probably look as natural in your hand as a spatula," he observed gently.

"Okay, so I can't cook worth a damn. Julianne grew up believing the ladies on the frozen-dinner boxes were kindly relatives." She huffed in frustration. "I just wanted to make our relationship meaningful on every level."

Dillon kissed the top of her head. "I appreciate the effort, but it's not necessary to cook to make a home cozy. You have many other admirable qualities. You obviously have survived quite nicely. Julianne's living proof of it."

"But it's Sunday... Sunday's a lazy family day."

"Tell you what, we'll do some of your Sunday things and some of mine. All right?"

"All right," she conceded with a wave. "Go get your papers."

Dillon set the spatula in the sink. "I'll only be a minute. Don't move until I get back."

"But I want to serve you a meal," she persisted.

His eyes danced merrily. "Pour coffee then. *It's* real good black."

Kristina poked her rosy tongue out at him.

"You can set out those hockey cakes, too," he instructed with a wink. "I'll eat one of 'em, I promise."

They sat together at the small square table for a long leisurely time with their coffee, pancakes, and shredded wheat squares.

"How many papers do you subscribe to?" Kristina quizzed, gazing at the stack of newsprint piled haphazardly on the third chair between them.

Dillon peeked over the top of the *New York Times.* "Several dailies. Some obscure small-town papers by mail."

"Julianne would love all the comics."

Dillon folded the section in his hands and reached for his coffee. "I'm always on the alert for odd stories for the show.

It's amazing what good copy some of those tiny hometown stories are."

"Like the woman in Ventura who sat for two days on a billboard...advertising brandy," Kristina recalled.

"Yeah. Everybody originally thought she was protesting liquor sales, but as it turned out, the scantily dressed model holding the bottle was her daughter and she was only protesting the kid. I invited her on the show, and she cleared up the misunderstanding pronto."

"Mmm... Yes." Kristina blushed slightly under his endearing gaze, then spoke thoughtfully. "I like the newsy part of your show. The oddities, the interviews. It's really enough to carry an entire night."

Dillon lifted a heavy bleached eyebrow. "It's been done before," he conceded. "Jerry Majors out of Chicago does it quite well."

"Could you do it, Dillon?" she ventured, trying to restrain her anxiety.

"Are you trying to change me, woman?" he barked gruffly.

"Dillon, I just think you could be more than just a fantasy figure to your listeners."

"Are you jealous?" he queried, the corner of his lips curving with amusement.

"Of course I am!" she blurted out candidly. "I'd be an idiot if I wasn't jealous. All of those passion-hungry women, lapping up your murmurings night after night." Her feline features narrowed ferociously. "It just burns me up to think about it."

"Talking to women has been my life-style as well as my job for a long time," he told her quietly.

"They fulfill your need to be needed," Kristina automatically surmised.

"Yes, Doctor," he placated mockingly.

"Are you denying it?" Kristina wondered in surprise.

"No!" Dillon's wooden chair tipped over and skidded into the refrigerator as he jerked to his feet in a burst of temper. "I'd be an idiot to deny it," he proclaimed, swatting angrily at the air. "But I told you Friday night that those women mean nothing to me now that I have you." He roamed around the room, plowing his hand through his hair, trying to regain his composure. "I hoped you'd be able to accept things, if you knew I loved you."

"I don't think I can." she admitted quietly. "If your sensuous come-on was considered an act by everyone, maybe it would be easier. But many women take you very seriously." Her mouth curved ruefully. "If possible, you've done your job too well."

"Actors act on stage and screen all the time."

"They sometimes have big trouble with adoring fans," Kristina asserted. "Your persona is far more real because you interact with your listeners. You give advice, comfort, an erotic charge."

"So what do you want?"

"I want you to charge only me," she told him softly, rising from her chair to embrace him. "I want to be the center of your life. I can fulfill all your needs in a one-on-one relationship, if you give me the chance. Trust me to be your confidant."

"I know it," he admitted. "I feel trapped in a snare of my own making. I've grown close to women I never touch and kept my distance from the ones I do."

"You do want to turn it around, don't you," she asked anxiously.

A hint of a smile touched his lips. "You're a pushy dame."

"Dillon...." She set her hands on his chest, rubbing her thumbs on his nipples. "I want you all to myself. Forever."

"Forever." It sounded so foreign to Dillon's ears. But he couldn't hear it enough. He closed his eyes, the pressure of her massaging thumbs soothing his taut body, her murmurings calming his churning emotions.

"Here I am, prearranging your whole life," she mused. "Perhaps I've already pushed you to your limit."

"Not in any respect." He reached over and traced the hollow of her cheek, his voice enticing. "Yet. But you have to understand, I'm new to this commitment business. Long-range plans never interested me before."

"Practice makes perfect," she whispered, her eyes shining up at his.

"Let the games begin," he rasped.

Kristina inhaled as she felt Dillon's hands creep beneath the shirttail of his best shirt, stroking her smooth thighs. "Is lovemaking all you can think about?" she asked in exasperation.

"It's a lazy Sunday morning, remember?" he reminded her on a husky moan.

"So it is." She gasped as he cradled her against the length of his body.

His mouth quirked at the corners. "I ate a pancake, didn't I?"

"Mmm-hmm." she surrendered on a soft sigh as his right hand stole to the shirt's pearl buttons, urging them out from their small holes.

The third button brought the shirt down over her shoulders and to the floor, leaving her naked before him. With a devilish grin of triumph he placed a kiss on her creamy shoulder. "We're building on forever, correct?"

"Yes," she said, releasing a breathless cry as he hoisted her up over his shoulder.

"Well then," he declared, marching toward the bedroom, "let's start a new Sunday-morning tradition."

"IT'S NOT GOING TO BE as bad as you think," Dillon announced as he swung his Porsche into the Jordan's driveway later that afternoon and cut the engine.

"Are you nuts?" Kristina gripped the leather clutch bag in her hands, staring out the windshield at Howard's gray Blazer parked in the garage.

"Howard's only a man. A flesh-and-blood human being with feelings just like the rest of us."

"He's an admiral, for Pete's sake."

"It's the father title that intimidates you," Dillon speculated aloud.

"And you think *I* overanalyze!"

Dillon pulled the keys out of the ignition and stuffed them into the pocket of his jeans. "Now, now, don't get feisty. I'm not going to delay this meeting by getting into an argument out here."

She shook her head forcefully. "I don't want to face him yet. I just can't get through to him. All my life he's dropped in and out of Coronado to straighten me out. Bellows orders at me."

"He must care. Any parent who would make such a nuisance of himself at his age must care. Let's go."

Kristina clutched the short sleeve of his madras shirt. "Don't make me do it. Let's go have lunch."

Dillon gazed at her with exasperation over the sunglasses perched on the tip of his nose. "We had lunch. Remember the shrimp place on the water? We were there fifteen minutes ago."

"Dinner must be coming up. Eventually..."

"Look, you want to fiddle with my show, change my Sundays around, and wear my only dress shirt to cook pancakes. The very least you can do is take some of my advice in return."

Kristina's nose crinkled in doubt. "Maybe he's not home."

"Don't be ridiculous." Dillon set a comforting hand over hers. "It especially concerns me that you fought with the man over me, over the possibility that I'm not serious about you and Julianne."

"If it makes you feel any better we fought about his constantly interfering with my parenting, too."

"To tell you the truth, I'd take him as a father any day, warts and all. When you've starved for something all your life, you're not quite as fussy."

"I've starved for a father, too," she griped.

"Well, here's your chance to make your relationship work. He may be guilty of a sudden dose of overkill in the parenting department, but he loves you. I'm sure of it."

"He may not want to talk to me," she warned. "He's not accustomed to being told off."

Dillon shook his head, running a hand through his bleached hair. "Being a wary soul myself, the thought had occurred to me, too. So I called him while you were in the shower and told him we were coming."

Kristina snatched her hands from his grasp. "You lousy sneak!" she hissed. "No wonder you didn't want to scrub my back!"

"See the sacrifices I'm willing to make for the common good?" he asserted, absently tucking some stray black tendrils behind her ear.

"So how did he react?" she demanded anxiously. "What did he say?"

"He said he'd stop packing and pop open a cold one."

"He was packing?" she asked, hoarse with worry.

"Don't get panicky. I suspect he would've been just about finished packing whenever you happened to walk through the door."

"All for effect, huh?"

"Yeah, maybe. Your family is a touchy bunch. Touchy but loyal," he added confidently.

"Let's get it over with, then," she relented, gripping the door handle.

They found the admiral in the study reading one of his many books.

"Hello, kids," he greeted, his gaze leaving the printed page for a brief moment.

"Hello, Pop." Kristina moved over to his chair, twisting her purse strap in her fingers.

"You left without telling me where you were going, Krissy."

"You knew where I was, Pop."

"So I did." He rose from his easy chair and snapping the book shut, he replaced it on the shelf. Kristina smiled as she noted that he'd stowed it away upside down. Maybe he wasn't as confident as he appeared.

"I'm sorry I blew up at you," she ventured.

Howard nodded his gray head. "I never wanted to hurt you. I came here to help out."

"I know it," she told him gently. "But I want you to understand that there was a lot of truth to the things I said. I feel you and Julianne work against me."

"I've been turning it over in my mind," he admitted. "Could be true. Having her hugs and special conversations has made my whole life. I may be guilty of conspiring against you in order to please her."

"And this trip—"

"Was wrong," he finished. "I went too far. I humored her beyond reasonable limits. I can't even stand Wade Jordan. That's what hit home the hardest. Sending her off to a man I despise."

"Let's just put it behind us, Pop," Kristina suggested, hugging him. "Now, about Dillon."

Howard gave Kristina's back a small pat and released her. "I'm sorry, Krissy. But I can't say I care for Dillon's lifestyle." He gazed at Dillon over his daughter's shoulder with a look of direct disapproval.

"Dillon is not Wade, Pop."

"Maybe not." Howard shoved his hands into the pockets of his trousers and shook his gray head. "And, maybe I'm guilty of being an absentee father myself. But I cannot accept you, Dillon, until I fully understand your intentions."

"I want the best of your daughter, Admiral," Dillon replied calmly. "I intend to make whatever concessions are necessary to make this relationship work."

"So am I, Pop," Kristina chimed in.

"I know I'm a crusty old seaman accustomed to having his own way," he told Dillon. "But both my girls mean the world to me and I don't want them hurt."

"I admire your concern. I love your daughter and hope to make amends with your granddaughter."

Howard muttered under his breath. "It seems like such a rush-rush thing. Your mother and I—"

"You must have had one of the shortest courtships in history, Pop!" Kristina suddenly recalled with irritation.

The admiral had the good taste to look sheepish. "It was a whirlwind thing all right. World War II was upon us. Your mother was a clerk at the Naval Air Station. Actually, I got to thinking about it last night... Guess there is such a thing as chemistry."

"You're wonderful, Pop."

"I only want what's best for you, Krissy. Do you believe me?"

"Yes, I believe you," she said with a sigh of relief.

Howard rubbed his hands together, his face bright. "So whatdasay we pop open a few cold ones in celebration, then barbecue some burgers later on for dinner."

"His apron says Burn Baby Burn," Kristina told Dillon with a wink.

Dillon rolled his eyes. "What else?"

"SURE YOU WON'T come back with me?" Dillon asked as he walked across the lawn later that night to his car, glancing at his watch. It was only ten o'clock and the idea of going home alone was gnawing at his insides. After two nights of feast, famine looked like a mightly bleak prospect.

Kristina declined with regret. "No, I better stay here."

"It's my only night off," he reminded her glumly.

"I know it. But we've been together a lot."

"And it was spectacular," he needlessly reminded her.

Kristina's hands flew to his collarbone. "Everything is happening so fast between us. I think it's best to step off the merry-go-round. Besides, I want to call Julianne tonight. I think it would be easier from here."

"I understand," he relented, tweaking her nose.

"I'll see you tomorrow, then?" she asked.

"I'll drop by and pick you up."

Her eyes twinkled in the glow of the streetlight. "Since my car is at your place, I'd really appreciate that."

"It'll be after lunch sometime. I've set up a meeting at the station."

"About the show?" she asked hopefully.

"Yup." Dillon lounged against the Porsche and pulled Kristina over him for a long luxurious kiss. "When I'm in my lonely bed tonight, I'll be thinking of you," he murmured enticingly in her ear.

"Alone after dark," she mused against his cheek. "It'll be something new for you, Dillon."

A deep rumbling sigh erupted from his chest. "Something very old, my sweet. A very, very old circumstance."

"Krissy!" Howard called anxiously from the screen door. "I've got the beach bum on the phone!"

"He didn't waste any time, did he?" Kristina noted, raising a finger in response.

"Even the old admiral must like peace all around," Dillon observed kindly.

"Seems so. Good night, darling. Sleep tight." She planted a kiss on his jaw, then darted for the house.

Dillon stiffened. Watching her walk away was one of the toughest moments he'd ever endured. He'd put a stop to it soon, he vowed, climbing into his car. Kris would soon be his for keeps.

11

"COME IN, come in, Dillon."

Roger Calhoun, owner of WXNT welcomed Dillon into the station's antiseptic conference room Monday morning with a thundering voice full of genuine respect.

"Good morning, Roger." Dillon entered the room in pleated tan pants and a neatly pressed oxford shirt, nodding at his employer. He seldom dressed up for trips to the station, but meetings with Calhoun were an exception. The man at the top deserved his best. He'd hired Dillon primarily on gut instinct, with blind faith in Dillon's sales pitch and his promise to revamp the nighttime slot. Dillon had fulfilled his promise, leaving Calhoun impressed and pleased.

"Thanks for coming on only twenty-four hour notice, Roger." Dillon took a seat near Calhoun at the long steel table.

"Door, Arnold, door." Calhoun snapped his fingers at Arnold Rodale.

The program director wasted not a second leaping up from his chair and, with a hurried yes-man step, he complied with Calhoun's order.

Roger Calhoun was a dignified man of sixty with a shock of white hair, a salt-and-pepper moustache, hawklike features, and the wiry body of a sportsman. He preferred to spend most of his time fishing in Alaska and hunting in Montana, and always dressed in western-style clothing to reflect his country-boy image. But underneath it all he was a shrewd businessman who managed to watch the station from a distance with a keen eye and with considerable success.

Dillon knew better than to change the format of his show without first consulting Roger Calhoun.

"So, Dillon, what's on your mind?" Calhoun crossed one booted foot over his knee, resting back comfortably in his chair in readiness for a chat. "I figure it's important. I'm rarely interrupted on a Sunday morning by a station employee trying to set up a Monday appointment." He cast a jaundiced eye at Rodale. "Not too often, anyway."

"I've been reevaluating the 'Dillon After Dark' format." Dillon leaned forward, putting his arms on the table, his eyes never straying from Calhoun's.

Calhoun did a double take. "I'm shocked, Dillon. Why tamper with perfection?"

"We've always been up-front with each other, haven't we, Roger?"

"Absolutely! I admire your style," he assured him with a solid nod, "never been any question of it. I hired you on a gamble. Never once been disappointed. You've delivered what you promised."

"I've always been quite comfortable with the show, Roger—"

"You *are* the damn show, Danvers. You are Dillon After Dark," he proclaimed, driving his fist into his palm with every word. "Knight of the darkness. Hero of the damsel in distress. Why, my own wife is as smooth as melted butter after your show. And that's not all bad!" He shook his head with a chuckle. "Not bad at all."

Dillon sighed, rubbing his forehead. "I've found I can't go on with the format."

The pulse point at Calhoun's skinny neck throbbed. "Why not? You're better than ever. More popular than ever!"

"I noticed that Saturday's show was a bit stilted," Rodale broke in nervously. "Callers were complaining right on the air."

"Dillon will explain, Arnold," Calhoun snapped. "He isn't hiding anything."

Dillon's expression was forthright. "No, I want to be candid. My personal situation has changed," Dillon confided quietly. "There's a special woman..."

Calhoun's gray eyes sharpened and a smile creased his face. "So you've finally found a lady of your own. Wonderful news. But how does that affect the show, Dillon?"

"Quite frankly, I don't care to seduce women on the air anymore."

"But it's just show business! It's not real!"

"It's difficult to define the line between fantasy and reality when you're on the air night after night."

"Hell, no," Calhoun differed. "It's entertainment. Titillating entertainment, grant you. But phoney as a three-dollar bill. The women know it."

"Roger," Dillon said, expelling a thoughtful sigh as he searched for the words to explain. "My show isn't like a television program, with a hero slaying imaginary dragons week after week. The ground rules are clearly defined in drama. When viewers tune in, they know it's a hundred percent fiction. My show is different. I interact with my audience. They lay their real problems on me. It's a blend of fantasy and reality."

"A blend that has carried you to the top, Dillon." Roger Calhoun's hawklike features narrowed.

"I can't play the romantic knight any longer. It doesn't satisfy me as it used to."

"It's the psychologist-mother from the contest!" Arnold Rodale broke in triumphantly. "She's the one who's turned his head, Uncle Roger!"

"What's he babbling about?" Calhoun snapped.

"Leave Kristina out of this, Arnie," Dillon warned.

"She's put all these crazy notions into your head," Rodale maintained, his round face fairly glowing with insight. "She sent him a plant the other day, and Dillon went tearing out of here as though the place were on fire."

"Has all this stemmed from that stupid contest you concocted, Arnold?" Calhoun demanded, turning the tables on his program-director nephew.

"Yes, Uncle Roger," he conceded, reddening as he realized he'd shot himself in the foot.

"The poetry contest," Calhoun muttered. "Your chance to prove you had the stuff of an operator, Arnold. And you allow a child to win."

"Yes, but..."

"Never mind." Calhoun rubbed his hands together and turned his attention back to Dillon. "It isn't the money?"

Dillon shook his head, and responded simply. "No."

Calhoun shook his head. "It usually is. When all's said and done, it's cold hard cash."

Dillon lifted his broad shoulders. "I have money."

"Nobody has enough," Calhoun argued starkly.

"I do."

Calhoun glared in frustration.

"Money isn't the issue," Dillon insisted. "Peace of mind is the issue. For the first time I see a chance at having a real home life. I can't turn away from it."

Calhoun knew when his opponent was equal in strength. Dillon knew he knew and patiently waited.

"So, what do you want, Dillon?"

"I want the chance to change the format of the show. Bring in controversial guests. Expand my unusual news item spot. Drop the seduction bit completely."

"Oh, Lord! We're doomed!" Rodale buried his face in his hands.

Dillon gazed at the program director with concern. Arnold wasn't Hercules, but he knew the broadcasting business—contrary to what his domineering uncle believed about him. He hoped to garner Rodale's support, the wealth of his experience.

"Arnie, it might work," Dillon told him.

"I need an aspirin," Rodale moaned.

"Go ahead and give it your best shot, Dillon," Calhoun invited, rising from his chair. "I'm smart enough to know when I've hit a brick wall." He strode toward the door, pausing with the doorknob in his hand. "You've got the rest of the week. We'll take a look at the mail on Friday."

"Today's Monday... It isn't much time in which to test my idea," Dillon protested.

"The response will be quick and to the point. Passionate women have a way of making their desires known, don't they?"

Dillon nodded. How could we argue after his whirlwind affair with Kris? She'd made her desires known in short order!

"Please don't do this to me, Dillon," Arnold begged the moment Calhoun departed.

Dillon stood and stretched with release. "C'mon, Arnie, be reasonable."

Rodale rounded the table and clutched his arm. "I need you. My program schedule will be nothing without your hot-to-trot format."

"Can't you stand up to the old man just once?" he asked gently.

Rodale's pudgy body shuddered. "No. Uncle Roger sees me as a weakling. Has done ever since I fainted on a hunting trip at the age of fifteen. Have you ever seen a dead deer? Passed clean out at the sight of it."

"Not everybody's into hunting," Dillon consoled. "It doesn't diminish you as a man."

"It's rough when someone puts you in a certain category and is bound and determined to keep you there, Dillon. Changing a man's attitude is nearly impossible once he's labeled you. Or a woman's attitude," he added significantly.

"Tell me about it," Dillon agreed grimly.

"So what will you do if your listeners won't change along with you?"

"I really don't know, Arnie."

Rodale nodded. "I'm glad I'm not the only uncertain man left around here."

"There's a few of us still floating around, Arnie. But I'd work on Calhoun if I were you. Force some respect from him."

"Who knows, maybe I'll be pounding the pavement with you by the end of the week," Rodale predicted.

Wouldn't that be the perfect wedding present to offer Kris?

"JUST LIE THERE on your stomach, Kris. Let the passion build."

"Dillon, please..."

"Are you going to tell me you feel absolutely nothing?"

"I feel! I feel fear, Dillon. I am chicken. Okay, so you've heard my confession. Can I get up now?"

"No!"

"Your hands are digging into my arms."

"Sorry, honey."

"You don't sound sorry, Dillon Danvers! And you haven't moved your hands."

"This means so much to me, Kris."

"If you bring love into this, I'll scream."

"Forever means giving in, does it not, sweet cheeks?"

"Don't use that husky tone with me. Not now. Not here."

"Whatever do you mean?"

"Don't play innocent, you sneaky devil. Using that radio croon to make me swoon."

"Oh, c'mon, woman! It's like riding a bicycle. Once you know how..."

"I've never once gone under riding a bike."

"No puddles in Coronado?"

Kristina shifted on the hot-pink surfboard beneath her, glaring up at the chuckling man standing beside her in the waist-deep water. The Monday afternoon sun blazed above them in a cobalt sky, reflecting off the ocean, warming their scantily clad bodies.

"You loved surfing once. Those photographs in your album are proof positive."

"Those pictures are fifteen years old!"

"You're still in great shape," he determined, his hand gliding from her oiled upper arm to her back with a gentle massaging motion. Kristina's bright yellow bikini didn't leave much to the imagination. Her body was streamlined heaven.

"I don't call you sweet cheeks just because of your pretty face."

Kristina raised her upper body off the board and rested her chin in her hand. "Give me a break."

"You swim laps indoors every week," Dillon pointed out. "You're just a stroke away from some real fun."

"I feel like I'm going through my second childhood—borrowing Julianne's dress, her sneakers, and now this surfboard."

"I don't like the prejudices you've come to attach to surfing," Dillon griped. "It's good clean fun. A healthy sport."

"I admit I've probably overreacted to Wade's defection from the mainstream of society. Giving up surfing was like closing a painful chapter in my life."

"Now you're talkin', sweet cheeks. Analyze *yourself* for a change."

"No need to be so smug. It...just seemed easier to blame the sport along with the man. I'm certain if he'd chosen golf, he would've run just as long and far. But it seems too late to take surfing up again, Dillon."

"Any mother who can wear her daughter's skimpy dress can do anything!"

Kristina rested her cheek on the Fiberglas board, the salty water lapping against her head, the incoming waves rocking her with cradlelike gentleness.

"Feel's great, doesn't it?" Dillon's voice vibrated with excitement as he watched her expression mellow. "At one with the sea."

"Mmm..."

"I ate your pancake yesterday."

She hooted incredulously. "How much mileage do you expect to gain from it?"

"As long as it sits in the pit of my stomach, I figure it's fair game."

"Ha-ha."

"Kris," he said, planting a kiss between her shoulder blades. "I can't imagine our living together the rest of our lives and not sharing surfing. It would be different if you had no background, no interest."

"No, it wouldn't, Dillon," she denied flatly. "Even if I'd never surfed before, you'd needle me. You'd pester me. Even if I'd never swum a stroke, you'd have me flat on my stomach and basted with oil, just like a freshly caught sunny in a sizzling frying pan."

"So, what are you going to do about it?"

Without another word, Kristina dug her strong arms into the water, sending the board shooting ahead toward the open sea.

"Hey, wait! I have to go get my board! I have to help!" Dillon sloshed back to shore to collect his red-and-white surfboard, water dripping onto his muscular frame and the skimpy black nylon suit riding low on his hips. Grabbing his board he did a sharp turnabout, tossing it out into the rushing waters ahead of him. Then, diving after it, he climbed onto it stomach first. He paddled furiously to catch up to her, his huge arms rotating like spinning windmills.

They reached the surf line around the same time, the takeoff area just beyond the breakers. In unison they turned their boards toward the shoreline and sat side by side on the rolling waters.

"You didn't cup your hands enough while you were paddling," Dillon chided.

In irritated wonder Kristina turned to stare at his water-slicked face. "I got here, didn't I?"

"Yeah, honey," he said with pride. "Still frightened?"

Kristina's hand stole over her vibrating chest. "Scared to death! But it's exhilarating."

"Keep some of that fear," Dillon advised soberly. "It'll make you more cautious."

"Yes, sir," she teased with a drippy salute.

Dillon glanced over his shoulder to gauge the pattern of the waves swelling in the horizon. "They've been coming in sets of five or so. From a long distance too, judging by their size and shape."

"Shall we go together?" Kristina suggested.

Dillon shook his matted blond head in slow disapproval. "That stunt is a little tricky for a rookie. I'll go first. That way I'll have a front-row seat for your performance." He grinned roguishly at her to disguise his trepidation. Though he was sure of her agility, the turbulent sea was unpredictable. He wanted to be prepared to rescue her from the swallowing waves if necessary.

"So, go if you're goin'," she prodded impatiently.

He drew a hesitant breath as he gazed into her sparkling eyes. "Remember everything I told you?"

"Yes, oh smooth talkin' one."

With a reluctant grunt, Dillon took the next incoming swell upward, then he eventually glided down with swift, angled body movements. He'd never enjoyed a ride less. For the first time in his life it was just a means of getting from one point to another. He wanted to be in the shallow section facing the horizon when Kristina started her ride.

Dillon had just retrieved his board when Kristina began her ascent, rising atop the hot-pink board with the gradually cresting water, awkwardly tucking her knees under chin. His breathing became shallow as he watched her hop into position, landing on the balls of her feet in the center of the board as it soared up, up with the gradually rising swell. The powerful green wave rolled forward with increasing speed, feathering with foam, carrying its rider into the air.

Dillon's heart nearly stopped beating as he watched Kristina's bikini-clad body angle and turn on the board in an effort to maintain her balance, play the wave to sense its course. She was doing it for him. For them. He was so proud of her, so grateful she'd overcome her fears and prejudice. He silently vowed to eat her crummy breakfasts for a month of Sundays if she hung tough.

He continued to urge her on, even when he was a hundred percent certain she was going to take the fall. She'd begun to sway precariously as she shot up to the foamy lip. Her knees were visibly locked stiff, robbing her of balance. She was at the crucial high point of the ride and she didn't have the moves to cut downward with grace. Within seconds, she'd lost control and toppled into the sea, her board somersaulting into the sky like a huge pink fish. Dillon tossed his board inland and dived into the breakers in the direction of her wipeout.

Dillon emerged from beneath the surface of the water moments later, nicking his head on the edge of her board, which was bobbing along without its rider a hundred feet from shore. Where was she? He treaded water with his massive arms, scanning the waters with desperation. Where the hell was she?

"Yo! Dillon!"

Dillon turned to shore to find Kristina waving from the sand, hopping up and down in her little yellow suit. She was okay! With a firm grasp on her board, Dillon headed back in.

"Pretty damn good for a first try," he congratulated with heaving breaths minutes later, stomping across the sand to join her. He picked up a towel to dry his face, concealing his relief behind the terry cloth.

"Real damn good," she returned with a proud lift to her chin. "Guess you were right. Once surfing's in the blood, it stays."

"It's kind of addictive...like you," he intoned huskily.

Kristina tossed her head back and laughed, water specks sprinkling the air.

"Come here and get your congratulatory kiss," he invited with an extended hand.

"No way, mister!" she balked, stepping away into the backwash. "Your seaside kisses lead to the works."

His large sensuous mouth gaped open. "You complaining about the works?"

"No, but we're out here to surf, aren't we?" She scampered to the shore and picked up her board.

"We've got the rest of the afternoon—the rest of our lives."

"You're all talk, just like I've said all along," she taunted, dashing back into the ocean.

"I'll show you!" Dillon followed, board and body crashing into the waters behind her.

Kristina released a scream as Dillon's board glided up beside her own, and his arm snaked out to tip her over.

"There!" he shouted with satisfaction. "An official sea christening!"

DILLON STRETCHED OUT on the beach blanket an hour later with a deep-chested groan of contentment. "This is perfect, cheeks."

Kristina, resting within inches of him, rolled to her side and began to trace a finger along his sternum. "It's nice."

"You still down because Julianne wouldn't come to the phone last night?"

"I wasn't really that surprised. I half expected the cold shoulder," she admitted. "I'm going to call again tonight."

"It's all you can do." Dillon folded his arm behind his head, closed his eyes, and followed her featherlight touch on his soaked skin with full attention. Her manicured nail glided up and down his torso, forging through his wet springy hair, circling round and round, tracing matted ringlets around his navel, slipping lower to the elastic band of his nylon swim trunks.

"We really should go back to the house," Kristina said lazily.

"Why? No one's in sight."

"I'm thinking about your career, not sex."

"Can't you relax and accept the fact that you're on vacation?"

"But you aren't Dillon After Dark anymore," Kristina pointed out practically. "You have to prepare for tonight's show. Changing your format is going to be a challenge."

"I'm prepared," he assured her with a bored mumble, shutting his eyes. "If you clip one more fascinating fact out of the newspaper on my behalf, I'll throw the scissors into the wastebasket with the spatula."

"You want to have enough material," she returned crossly. "What if you run out of things to talk about?"

Dillon cracked open a lid to regard her with a pleased grin.

"Don't worry. I won't go into my seduction production. I promise!"

"If you do, I'll kill you."

"Ouch! Pull at those hairs again and I'll surely be halfway to the grave!" Dillon's hand moved to his abdomen to rub away her handiwork.

"Sorry." Kristina leaned over to place a kiss on his cheek. "I didn't mean to. It's just that I worry. And when I worry I get crabby."

"Nothing to worry about, Kris." Dillon sat up, pulling her onto his lap.

Kristina gazed at his twitching mouth, her voice moving from desperate to suspicious. "What have you got up your sleeve?"

"I don't have any sleeves," he teased. "I'm a ragged beach bum."

"Dillon Danvers, you're hiding something," she insisted, poking his chest.

Dillon growled in frustration. "In less than two short weeks, you've completely battered down the walls of my carefully constructed privacy. Damn near invaded nearly every part of me. Well," he declared cockily, "this is one little secret I plan to savor until tonight."

"You are so bad," she accused, winding her arms around his neck.

"Which is why I'm so good at reforming uptight surfer girls," he returned silkily, his hand unclasping the bra of her bikini.

KRISTINA WAS RECLINING on the sofa around eleven o'clock that night when she heard her father's lumbering footsteps in the kitchen. "In here, Pop!"

Howard popped into the living room with a jaunty step, sitting down in a chair near his daughter.

"How was the movie?" she asked.

"All right."

"How was your old navy buddy?"

"Very talkative," Howard reported with a frown. "We

stopped for a beer after the show and all he did was brag about his grandchildren.''

"Insensitive bore," Kristina teased.

"Don't you worry, Krissy. I showed him some snapshots of Muffin to keep things even.''

"Of course, Pop.''

"So, you talk to Julianne?" Howard asked, his worry ill-concealed.

"Yes," she replied brightly. "We smoothed things over some.''

"Good, good. She coming home?''

Kristina's eyebrows arched in hope. "She plans to sleep on it. Said she'll call us collect tomorrow.''

"Fine." Howard stroked his jaw, suddenly noting the muted music emanating from the entertainment center in the corner of the room. "Dillon?''

"Yeah.''

"How's he doin'?''

"All right. He's playing some Phil Collins right now. Trying to mix some of the old with the new. He hasn't taken any callers yet.''

"You've got this 'Dillon After Dark' show all wrong, you know," Howard objected, sinking down on the sofa.

Kristina stiffened, waiting for the blast. "How so, Pop?''

He pointed a finger to the floor above. "You should be upstairs in your room with a boom box, a dessert plate in your lap.''

Kristina laughed with relief. "Julianne can be a real sneak sometimes.''

"Things keep going the way they are now, she won't have to sit alone in her room to listen to him, will she?''

Pleasure flooded Kristina's face as she shifted in her chair. "Probably not.''

"He'll marry ya all legal like, won't he?''

Kristina gaped at his bluntness, then realized it was the justified worry of a concerned father. "I wouldn't have it any other way, Pop," she assured him with a gentle smile. "Dillon knows we're a family. He knows Julianne needs a steady home life. Because he yearned for a secure place as a child, he recognizes its value. He wouldn't want to pull half of me away from here."

"Good, good," he uttered dismissively. "Me, I could start over someplace. But Julianne's just a kid."

"I love this house, Pop. I love my life here."

"Just checkin'," Howard said defensively, jumping up to turn up the volume on the stereo as Dillon's voice murmured.

"THIS IS DILLON DANVERS, back from a rhythmic rendezvous with the popular Phil Collins. As you know this is WXNT, 103.9 on your FM dial.

"Live radio.

"As you listeners know, live broadcasting always has its own obvious risks. The frailty of the human being put on the spot, with no chance for rectifying his mistakes. I've certainly made my share of mistakes over the years, personal and professional, as we all have.

"Compassion is so necessary to keep the world turning. Digging deep within to understand those who make a mistake in judgment. We're often faced with decisions while performing 'live' in our daily routines. Mending broken hearts is often discussed on this program. Mellow moods, soothing talk, glib advice all have their place in the healing process. But there are times when hands-on participation is needed. I'm talking about action, listeners. Taking action to help those who need us.

"I have a special guest with me tonight, a woman of action. She's not an author, sports figure, or actress, but she is a celebrity to all those young ladies who at some point in their lives were living under her roof. Welcome with me Mrs. Bernice Chambers of San Diego's Beacon House, a privately funded home for unwed mothers.

"Good evening, Mrs. Chambers."

"So nice of you to invite me on the show."

"It's my pleasure."

"Why, when I think back on you unplugging my drain... I quite simply had no idea you were a radio personality."

"As the audience probably has already ascertained, I've been to Beacon House."

"Made quite a stir, too. Pitched right in to help. Strong as an ox."

"Thank you. Now—"

"Don't be so modest. Never seen such a worker. Except of course for Doctor Jordan. Dr. Kristina Jordan, the psychologist. Located downtown in the Winston Towers. Wonderful person. Good listener. In the Yellow Pages."

"Yes, she's all of those things, Mrs. Chambers."

"I know why you're smilin', Dillon. My Dr. Jordan is yours, too. Brought you to us, Dillon."

"Yes. Mrs. Chambers, I would like you to lead us in a discussion tonight concerning the needs of a house such as yours. Perhaps if our listeners knew just how they could help you out, they would step forward."

"Oh, sure. I'm here to lay out the facts. To let the good folks know how things are at the House. Well, Beacon House was founded in 1960, back when there was quite a scandal attached to unwed motherhood. Not that our girls don't have a tough time today. Not by any means. We live in a complicated world, Dillon."

"Tell us about your world, Mrs. Chambers..."

"I'LL BE!" Howard sprung out of his chair an hour later. "He really did turn the gushy stuff around, didn't he?"

Kristina shook her head in wonder. "I can't believe it. Snagging Mrs. Chambers right under my nose! I've barely left his side."

"Not too many callers, were there?"

"No," Kristina agreed soberly. "But he didn't take callers at first during his monologue on hometown absurdities."

"It was different, just like he promised you." Howard shook his bushy gray head. "Can I shut this radio down now?"

Kristina cast him an absentminded look. "Uh-huh."

"Don't worry about Dillon," Howard consoled. "I enjoyed the show. May even drop by Beacon House with you someday soon."

"You're sweet." Kristina rose out of her easy chair and switched off the desk lamp.

"Let's hit the hay, Krissy." Howard linked arms with his daughter. "You know," he began thoughtfully, "I spin a mighty mean yarn myself. Especially from my WWII days. Since Dillon's almost family, maybe we could slip me in on a slow night. Like tomorrow, for instance."

Kristina stood on tiptoe to kiss her father's lined cheek. "We'll see, Pop. We'll see."

12

DILLON APPEARED at Kristina's back door the following morning to find her leaning against the kitchen counter talking on the telephone. To his surprise she was not sportily dressed as he'd expected, but quite put together in pleated white slacks and a silky red blouse, her rich black hair curled neatly at her shoulders.

He cast her a "what's up" look through the screen.

"How lovely to hear from you," she was saying as he opened the door. "Yes, Mrs. Chambers," she continued, waving at him with a significant smirk, "it was a fun surprise. I had no idea you were to be his guest. Uh-huh, ten years younger at least. You have a youthful ring to your voice... Of course I appreciated the plug. I'm sure it'll bring new patients in by the droves."

Dillon ruffled her neatly styled hair and took an apple from the fruit bowl on the counter.

"I'm certain Beacon House will have some new backers by the end of the day. Even my father volunteered to help with some odd jobs."

Dillon dropped into a chair at the table, stretched his long tanned legs across the linoleum, and crossed his ankles with a relaxed sigh.

"As a matter of fact, my father's coming in my place on Friday," she said, studying the unruly wisps of blond hair nesting at the nape of Dillon's neck. "I've taken the entire week off. As it happens, my daughter's returning home today from a trip to Hawaii, so I hope to spend the final days of my vacation with her."

Dillon turned sharply to regard Kristina with surprise.

"Yes, sometimes one has to take care of one's own family

business first. If any of the girls urgently need counseling, let me know... Right. Pop will be there most of the day. Yes, he's quite handy... As handy as Dillon?"

Dillon's gaze centered on her mouth, his large white teeth sinking into the crisp apple with a crack.

"I don't know that they're much alike, but I assure you Pop will be an asset... No, I haven't spoken to Dillon today. But I liked the interview just fine, so I'm sure he's pleased... Fussy?"

Dillon shrugged as he munched.

"He can be a bit demanding. But I'm sure he liked your style."

He nodded in agreement.

"He hasn't called you today?" she repeated, her black eyebrows lifting in mock disapproval.

He rolled his bright blue eyes toward the ceiling.

"He's usually quite reliable. Did he say he'd get back to you?"

Dillon vehemently shook his head, mouthing an emphatic no.

"I'd certainly like to help you out..." She gasped as his hand closed with warning around her thigh. "But he's difficult to reach on occasion," she relented. "All right. Goodbye."

"Thanks for the white lie," Dillon said with relief as she replaced the receiver on its hook. "I know the truth is your torch."

"You are hard to reach at times," she asserted, slipping onto his lap. "So actually I was speaking the truth."

"Ooo, but aren't we getting technical..."

"I saved you, didn't I?" Kristina moved her fingers through his thick head of hair, resting her cheek against its fluffy softness, inhaling the herbal shampoo scent. "Just showered, huh?"

"It was hell without ya, sweet cheeks." With a mild groan he drew her closer.

"You could have said hello to her," she scolded close to his ear.

"Saying hello to Bernice Chambers is an hour-long commitment. At least!"

"Yes, I guess it is," Kristina conceded, twirling a lock of his hair around her finger.

Dillon rubbed her back. "She did a fine job last night on the show and I told her so. Last night."

"I think she's just looking for an excuse to see you again."

Dillon pinched her bottom.

"Ouch!"

"Watch your language, then."

"I think Pop will be a good match for her. They're both widowed, both love to spin yarns. They can chat each other up hour after hour."

"You're a clever shrink."

"Yeah. And you're a pretty smart guy yourself. The show was great."

Dillon frowned in uncertainty. "I hope it works out. There weren't many callers. I suppose the women listeners were in shock."

"You have to give it time," Kristina encouraged.

"I have all the time in the world. But the companies that sponsor my show may not share my forbearance," he added ruefully.

"I believe in you," Kristina said, cupping his face in her hands.

Dillon kissed her palm against his face. "Knowing you're behind me makes all the difference in the world."

"I'm sure everything will fall into place. Julianne's coming home as you heard."

"I was wondering why you were so dressed up." Dillon fingered the silky red collar of her blouse. Red was certainly her color, he mused as he watched her black curls slide over the shiny fabric in a rich colorful interplay.

"I have to leave for the airport in a few minutes," Kristina announced, glancing at the clock over the stove.

"No, I don't think you should."

Kristina's head snapped back to him in amazement.

"I'd like to pick her up, Kris," Dillon announced suddenly. "Alone."

"Absolutely not, Dillon." Kristina shook her head vehemently. "She's too angry, too confused."

"I have to start laying foundation with her sometime," Dillon argued, a bit put out that she didn't leap at his brilliant idea.

"I just don't want to rush things or see either of you hurt unnecessarily," she explained, stroking his cheek. "You barely know her really."

"Julianne and I are actually old pals in a way," he contended. "It's not as though a complete stranger were coming to pick her up. We go way back."

"Airport reunions are emotional. And this one could be a whopper."

"It would be my way of showing her that I care."

"I admit it would," Kristina said. "But I can't quite picture it."

"Julianne and I would have a chance to talk things over alone. It would prove to her that I see her as a separate person."

"I don't know, Dillon..."

Dillon grinned at her wavering mouth. She'd come from "absolutely not" to "I don't know" with promising speed. "Please let me do this, Kris," he pleaded earnestly.

Though his voice was steady, Kristina could read the need in his eyes. He so wanted to be accepted. To be a part of their inner circle. He'd certainly come a long way since their first encounter on the beach. He'd traveled the distance of a lifetime.

"Okay," she consented with a bolstering smile. "Go for it."

He sighed with pleasure. "Thanks, sweet cheeks. I'll take her to Sea World, as I'd originally promised to do."

"No lady on earth could ever turn down an offer from you," she said with encouragement.

"I DON'T WANT TO GO to Sea World with you ever!" Julianne snapped two hours later at the San Diego Airport, her young violet eyes bright with defiance.

Dillon stood helplessly beside her in the crowded terminal, already regretting his decision to come alone. The girl had paused dead in her tracks at the sight of him, instantly blocking the path of other disembarking passengers. She squared her shoulders and stood her ground as people hurriedly streamed past her with looks of anticipation, running into the arms of their loved ones. Julianne had most likely been counting on such a reunion with her mother, Dillon realized.

He'd blown it with her again.

"Come over here," he urged, gently pulling at her arm. She looked cute with her sunburned nose, pink-and-white striped shorts and top, clutching her carry-on bag to her chest like a wayward urchin. But he knew better than to tell her so. She didn't want to be cute. She wanted to be foxy. She was some distance away from foxy.

"Didn't Mom want to come for me?" Julianne asked abruptly.

Dillon tugged at the bill of her bright pink cap. "Of course she wanted to come. This was my idea."

"I bet she didn't," Julianne argued. "I bet you didn't want to, either."

Dillon would've been fooled by her hardball stance and glowering violet eyes if her chin hadn't wobbled suddenly under his stricken gaze. She'd hastily lowered her face to her shoes, but it was too late. He'd read the longing there. Maybe it would be all right. Maybe he could win this round.

"You wanted to go to Sea World a few short days ago," he ventured.

Julianne shook her head, her long black hair swinging across her back. "I did before. I don't now."

"Why not?"

"Because I'm tired, okay? I've had a few hard days and I'm burned out."

"Oh, c'mon, young people have lots of energy on tap."

Julianne wrinkled her red nose. "Where did you get that corny line?"

Dillon cast her a wry look. "A book. A movie. Maybe I just remember being your age. Look, you used to think I knew a lot of things."

Julianne lifted her chin haughtily. "Maybe I've changed my mind."

Dillon shrugged his broad shoulders, waving a hand through the air with a magician's sweep. "Maybe we can change it back."

"When you've seen one killer whale, you've seen 'em all."

"That's just the point, Julianne. I've never been to Sea World."

Julianne regarded him with genuine surprise. "You've really missed out, haven't you?"

"Guess so. Maybe we can learn from each other." Dillon reached out and took the nylon carry-on bag clutched to her chest. "I'll carry this." He slung the strap over his shoulder and lurched in mock pain. "What's in here—lava rock?"

"Souvenirs."

"Oh."

Julianne cried defensively, "I couldn't take a chance on checking them through in my big suitcase."

"Your big suitcase?" he repeated in shock. "There's more?"

"Sure! You didn't think all my stuff was in one little bag, did you?"

Dillon stroked his square chin with a rueful smile. "See, I'm learning already."

"DID IT HELP? Going away, I mean?" Dillon leaned against the tiled edge of the petting pool at Sea World an hour later, watching Julianne's slender hand gently stroke a black-and-white dolphin.

Julianne gazed up at Dillon intently from beneath the bill of her cap. "Are you for real?"

Dillon nodded solemnly. "I really want to know. I've done

a lot of running myself... So I just wondered what you thought."

"You want my opinion, so you can tell me I'm wrong?"

"No, no. I'm not in the habit of chewing you out, am I?"

Julianne jumped back a step as the dolphin dived into the water, splashing up water with its fin. "No, but everything was different before the contest."

"I thought you were a woman," Dillon whispered desperately in her ear.

"I am!" she groaned through clenched teeth.

"Okay, I thought you were old enough to vote," he amended in a calmer tone.

"A lot of people don't even bother to vote." Julianne began to walk down the circular stone path around the pool.

Dillon followed her lead, noting that the tropical landscape was breathtakingly beautiful with its lush green plants, colorful gardens, and large bright parrots. It was truly amazing how all the animals went about their business, oblivious to human intrusion. Perhaps it wasn't so amazing, he amended. He'd done it for years himself.

"So, did going away solve anything?" Dillon asked, falling into step beside Julianne.

Julianne shrugged, focusing on a pond of swans. "Wade's still the same old Wade. He thinks he's a rebel, but he's in a rut just like Mom. I mean like Mom used to be," she amended, rolling her large eyes.

"Maybe your Mom's the real rebel," Dillon suggested.

"Maybe. She was always so easy to handle. I never felt like running off before."

"Running has never helped me much," Dillon mused, rubbing his palms together. "I thought I was satisfied. Sometimes you don't know what you're missing until you're shaken up somehow."

"Mom shake you up?"

Dillon's mouth curved, his voice pensive. "Yeah."

"I didn't think she had it in her."

"She's pretty surprising." Dillon chuckled deeply with pleasure.

"She's changed," Julianne confided accusingly, her hands planted on her slim hips.

Dillon shrugged. "Change can be good."

Her black eyebrows narrowed. "I don't feel so good about it."

"Did you talk things over with your dad?"

Julianne's face drooped even lower. "Sure! I went there for help, didn't I?"

Dillon shoved his hands into the pockets of his jeans. "What did he say about your mom and me?"

"He said, he said..." She trailed off with reluctance.

"What?" he prompted, his heart thudding with dread.

"He said it's about time Mom found somebody."

Relief flooded over him like spring rain. Wade Jordan wouldn't be showing up to reclaim his family after all.

Julianne's face grew shrewd. "You were really scared for a minute, weren't you?"

"Naw," he said with a wry, revealing look.

Julianne nodded smugly. "You thought my dad might come back here after all this time."

Dillon grinned, raising two fingers an inch apart. "Maybe I was worried just a little bit."

"Dad hates the admiral," Julianne confided with fervor. "If he did have any ideas about checking out Mom to see what all the fuss is about, finding out about Grandpop's return squished it. Just because my father's a beach bum doesn't mean he likes to hear Grandpop call him one."

"I see. Did he have anything else to say?"

"He doesn't talk much. Never has."

They continued moving, stopping for a snow cone at a small stand.

"Cherry okay?" he asked, pulling his wallet out of his back pocket.

"Lime is my favorite."

Dillon shook his head with amusement, ordering a cone in each flavor.

"So you're afraid sometimes," she pondered as she

pressed her lips against the flavored cone of chipped ice, watching him out of the corner of her eye.

"No shame in it." Dillon sighed deeply. "Your mother is afraid sometimes, too."

"Mom?" Julianne shook her head with vehemence. "Give me a break. She's a doctor. She tells everybody what to do and how to do it."

"She's a concerned mother. She cares for you deeply."

"So what's she afraid of?" Julianne wondered. "I've turned out pretty good so far."

"She's afraid she might lose you to your father."

Julianne huffed in disgust between munches. "I'd never go away for good."

"You went away without saying goodbye."

"I came back!" she shot back.

"She's so glad you did," Dillon confided honestly. "And so am I."

"She really would've lit into you if I hadn't." Julianne chuckled knowingly. "I've been there. Whew!"

"Whew is right."

Dillon pulled a program out of his shirt pocket. "Let me check the time of the whale show. Wouldn't want to miss Shamu."

"You really are excited, aren't you?" she questioned in surprise.

"Sure," he exclaimed. "You're just jaded."

"What's 'jaded' mean?"

Dillon pinched her nose. "It means your mother's shown you a pretty good life. C'mon, we'd better hurry. According to this schedule, the show starts in ten minutes."

Julianne took him by the arm for the first time. "I'll show you the way."

They broke into a trot, weaving through the crowds of people clustered around the many exhibits.

"You don't have to worry about Dad," she said as they moved along, looking directly at him for a change. "He doesn't want me all the time."

"Are you sure?"

"I'm old enough to tell. Even if I can't vote! Besides, Mom's always been there for me. I'd never run off forever. Even though I'm very disappointed in her behavior," she added with a sniff.

Dillon smiled over her last remark, the timbre of her voice a good imitation of a parent's chiding.

"This whole thing isn't very funny, you know," she retorted.

"No, Julianne, it isn't. I'm smiling because we're getting along. Because I think you're beginning to understand my love for your mother."

"Do I have a choice?" she squawked, stopping in her tracks at a fork in the road. She lifted one skinny leg to rub her calf with her foot, reminding Dillon of one the park's pink flamingos. "I think it's this way," she decided, pulling him along.

"Certainly you have a choice," Dillon inserted smoothly. "No one can force you into cooperating. You're a mature young lady with ideas of her own. Not a three-year-old who doesn't want to eat her green beans."

Julianne straightened her spine, glowing over his praise. It obviously wasn't the answer she expected. "Here's the stadium."

Dillon took Julianne's hand and chose a spot in the steep bank of semicircular bleachers surrounding the huge glass-walled pool. Spectators were quickly filling the open spaces on the benches, and trainers in wet suits were moving around near the water. He cast a look at her neutral expression, wondering where he stood with her.

"Are we going to be okay, Julianne?"

"I can't help feeling let down, Dillon," she blurted out in a hurt tone close to his ear. "After all, I found you first. You made me feel so special when I called your show."

Dillon cringed, clasping his hands together in his lap. "I understand."

"Do you?"

"Oh, yes." How many lives had he profoundly touched with his show without realizing it? "The show wasn't real,

Julianne," he explained quietly. "I'm an entertainer, not a psychologist, not a father confessor."

"Was?" she gasped. "Have you quit the show? How could you? I've only been gone a few days?"

"No, I didn't quit. I just revamped my format."

Her face grew grim. "Mom made you."

"No, I wanted to."

"But your fans loved you the way you were. 'Dillon After Dark' is a romantic legend."

"With your mother's help, I've come to see that my show, whatever its format, should be nothing more than a performance. I used my fans as a crutch, Julianne. My listeners satisfied my ego, my needs."

She balked, flabbergasted. "So it's all over!"

"Not for you, Julianne," Dillon said softly. "Not if you want me in your life."

"You'd go away if I told you to?" Julianne asked, pointing at herself with openmouthed amazement.

Dillon cocked his head in thought. "In all honesty, probably not right away. But my relationship with Kris would deteriorate rather quickly if you fought it. You mean the world to her. We'd only pull her apart in a tug-of-war."

Julianne grew contrite. "Yeah, I see what you mean…"

"Which is why I wanted to speak to you alone," he explained intently. "Find out where we stand without putting your mother through any extra heartache."

"You make me sound pretty important," Julianne said in awe.

"Hasn't your mother always made you feel special?"

Julianne nodded. "Yeah, I guess she has."

"Can you understand that what I feel for you and your mother is different from the idle chitchat on my show? You won't be losing Dillon After Dark, you'll be gaining a real friend." Dillon watched her features slowly brighten.

"You haven't changed so much after all," she asserted with a twinkle in her eye.

"No?"

"You know exactly what to say to the girls."

"I've cut my list of ladies way, way down. You and your mother are the only ones left on it."

"So where is Mom?"

Dillon pointed up to the bleachers flanking the right side of the huge tank. "See the sunburned woman up there in the yellow sunsuit?"

"Where?" Squinting in the sunshine, Julianne scanned the bank of seats.

"Mom? Mom has a tan?"

Dillon raised his hand in the air. "A pinkish one. She's been frolicking on the beach, just like in the old days."

Julianne continued to gaze up at the figure, now waving at them.

"Isn't she incredible?" he declared with pride, watching her gracefully descend the concrete staircase.

"Incredible all right!" Julianne balled her fists. "She's wearing my clothes again!" She groaned in torture. "My brand-new sunsuit. She's going to stretch it out—like my dress—like my sneakers!"

"Take it easy," Dillon gently cautioned. "She's pretty nervous."

"Welcome home, honey," Kristina greeted, hugging her daughter as she slid onto the bench. "Everything all settled?"

"Mom." Julianne clutched Kristina's upper arms, their violet eyes merging in a direct mother-daughter line of communication. "I can understand why you want to get a new life. It's cool. But pleeeze... Get some of your own stuff to go with it."

Kristina's eyes widened in disappointment. "No more sharing?"

"I'm sharing him, aren't I?" Julianne tipped her head back at Dillon.

Kristina's face lit up with pleasure. "Seems you are."

Julianne gently shook her. "But not my clothes. Not my shoes..." She trailed off in thought as she eyed the older woman's tan. "And not my surfboard," she asserted suspiciously.

"Don't worry," Dillon interceded. "That's one gift your mother is going to get from me."

"Shall we go?" Kristina suggested as an announcer's voice blared out over the speakers.

"Yeah," Julianne agreed, popping up.

"No," Dillon objected, sitting still with his feet planted firmly beneath him. "I came to see the show."

"Let him have his fun," Kristina whispered.

"I guess we put him through enough for one day," Julianne agreed with a giggle.

Kristina reached across her daughter and patted his arm. "And it's only the beginning," she murmured to him with a wink.

"ARE YOU BUSY, MOM?"

Kristina looked up from the paperwork spread out before her on the desk as Julianne poked her head into the study the next morning. "Hi, kiddo. Just going over some casework."

"You're supposed to be on vacation," Julianne scolded, shaking a crimson-tipped finger at her.

"The week's almost over," Kristina pointed out. "I have to start preparing for Monday's grind."

"Hard to believe it's already Thursday."

"Yes, it is. I missed you a lot while you were away." Kristina rested her chin on steepled fingers, intently watching Julianne sidle up to her desk.

"Sorry I took off," Julianne apologized, nervously tugging at the cuffs of her white twill shorts.

"I know you are, honey. I hope your father's detached attitude doesn't upset you too much."

Julianne shrugged her narrow shoulders. "I didn't expect much help from him. Guess I just needed a place to run to."

"Next time, storm up to your bedroom, okay?"

"Okay." Julianne traced a finger over the polished surface of the desk. "You mad at Grandpop for helping me?"

"We...had words on the subject," Kristina admitted with a sigh. She leaned back in her chair, and tapped a pencil on the cover of her dictionary. "But," she added brightly, "we made some constructive headway during all the shouting."

Julianne grinned with relief. "There always seems to be some bad mixed with the good."

"Good mixed with the bad is what an optimist would say."

"Yeah, sure, Mom," Julianne agreed blandly. She picked

up the admiral's burl pen-and-pencil holder for closer inspection.

Kristina instantly recognized her daughter's roundabout method of getting to the point. She was lingering to pitch her latest notion. "So what's up?"

Julianne rested her hip against the desk, her eyes twinkling. "Lots of stuff."

Kristina rolled her eyes with humor. "Naturally."

Julianne's tone dropped to a confiding level as she leaned over the desk. "For one thing, I want to tell you I think I'm over Dillon."

"Oh?" Kristina tipped her chair forward with interest. "His little talk clear things up?"

"Yeah!" Julianne drew a breath of hesitation. "And his show last night helped me decide for sure. It was such a snore. Guess he is more your style."

Kristina gasped in objection. "He's not a snore!"

"Mom..." Julianne trailed off in a tolerant singsong. "His whole show is all messed up. Who's ever gotten a thrill out of listening to a man talk about consumer rip-offs?"

"Dillon's thrill-dealing days are over," Kristina informed her with pride. "He now intends to be informative and entertaining."

"Maybe Geraldo could pass the consumer-as-hero bit on an afternoon show. But Dillon's fans don't want to hear about laundry soap that doesn't make enough suds," she warned, her voice growing whimsical. "They want a charge from him. They want to tingle, Mom."

"Out of the mouths of babes..." Kristina mumbled under her breath.

Julianne's mouth gaped. "Huh?"

Kristina shook her head. "Nothing, kiddo. I just hope you're wrong."

Julianne nodded vigorously. "Me too. The last thing you need is an unemployed boyfriend."

Kristina buried her face in her hands. "Anything else for now?"

"Not really. Except that I'd like to go to the mall."

Kristina peeked at her, her expression brightening. "Say, it might be fun. I could use some new sportswear."

"Uh, Mom," she faltered, "I already have plans. I'm going with Cindy and Amy, and Angie."

"Oh."

"Please don't feel bad," she pleaded, twisting some of her black hair around her finger. "We can go another time. When I'm not so busy."

"Thank you, dear."

"I've been gone for four whole days," she said defensively. "I have to catch up on everything."

"Fine, Julianne. We'll make it another day."

Howard appeared in the doorway jingling his car keys. "All set up with your mother?"

"I was just telling her, Grandpop."

His face grew clouded at the sight of Kristina's drained expression. "If you don't want me to take the girls to the mall, Krissy, you only have to say the word. I don't want to step on any toes."

"No, no, Pop," Kristina said waving him off. "It's absolutely fine."

"I told her to check with you first," he assured her. "Your mother's the anchor of this house, I told her."

"I appreciate it, Pop," Kristina told him patiently, hoping his overcompensation for past sins would soon subside. "Believe me, I don't expect you to give up all your authority."

Howard winked at his granddaughter. "Don't 'spose an admiral could."

"As long as Julianne doesn't work us against each other, everything will be fine," Kristina said with a significant look at her daughter.

"I agree," he said magnanimously.

"Julianne is welcome to go to the mall. On the condition that she has set time of return and a ride home."

"Cindy's mom is picking us up. She's radical."

"Have a good time, then."

Julianne took a few steps and turned back. "Oh, Mom, I almost forgot. Can the girls spend the night?"

"You almost forgot?" Kristina repeated in wonder.

"You know how teenagers are," she said with a sheepish grin.

"Tonight?" Kristina questioned in surprise.

"Vacation's almost over and we can't talk about everything at the mall, Julianne claimed. "I almost invited them and Grandpop almost said yes."

"No, I didn't," Pop interceded with a small chuckle. "I'm a pop, not a pawn, remember?"

"Oh, yeah," Julianne reluctantly agreed. "I'm trying to change, honest. These things take time."

"I suppose the girls can stay," Kristina agreed.

"Awesome!" Julianne squealed. "I have to dash upstairs a minute, Grandpop. I need some extra money for a new Janet Jackson cassette for the party—just in case 'Dillon After Dark' fizzles out again tonight."

Kristina rose to her feet as Julianne raced past the admiral in a flurry. "Oh, Pop, what if I've destroyed Dillon's career with all my advice?"

Howard moved into the room, giving her shoulder a reassuring pat. "You didn't force Dillon into anything."

"I gave him kind of an ultimatum though," she admitted ruefully. "Drop the sweet talk or drop me."

"I think he just came to realize that a gal in the hand was worth two on the phone."

Kristina nodded with a wan smile. "I hope so."

"What's the worst that could happen?" Howard inquired reasonably.

Kristina tucked her glossy black hair behind her ears, her expression growing grim. "I'm not exactly certain yet, Pop. Dealing with the public has its risks."

"Do you have any change, Pop?" Kristina called from the darkness of the front porch later on that evening.

Howard muttered affirmatively above the giggly din inside the house. Seconds later a small outside light flicked on overhead and the admiral lumbered across the wooden-planked floor, favoring the pizza deliveryman standing on the step beside his daughter with a glare of military authority.

The young man in the uniform shifted from one foot to the other, nervously balancing the two pizza boxes.

"Don't they smell great, Pop?" Kristina chirped, taking the bills from her father's hands.

"Humph!" Howard grabbed the boxes and thumped back into the house, grumbling about how he could make them for fraction of the price.

"Don't mind him," Kristina whispered conspiratorially to the delivery boy. "This is his first slumber party."

The porch glider squeaked at the far end of the dark porch and Dillon's rich chuckle floated through the night air.

"His, ah, slumber party?" the delivery boy repeated skeptically, counting the money. Amazingly, the calculation of his tip brought a sudden, tolerant smile to his face. "Uh, yes, ma'am. Like I always say, anything goes in California."

Kristina reached inside the house to turn off the light Howard had turned on, then returned to her spot on the glider. "Poor Pop." With a sympathetic sigh, she molded her body back into the crook of Dillon's arm. "He can't accept ready-made food. If it isn't Navy, it better be Howard's."

"He certainly was worked up about it," Dillon observed, slipping his arm over Kristina's shoulders. "Maybe you girls should've let him tackle the pizza making."

Kristina regarded him with a dry look. "His pizza's on the level of his burgers and my pancakes."

Dillon surrendered in complete understanding. "You needn't say another word."

"I promised Julianne Buck's Pizza. And she promised me lights-out at midnight."

Dillon shrugged. "Sounds fair."

"Isn't this perfect, my darling." Kristina snuggled against his chest, tipping her head back to gaze at the stars. "All of us under one roof."

"Plus a few extra," Dillon remarked.

"There's never a dull moment with Julianne."

"So, what do we do now?" Dillon asked.

"Stay out of the way until the girls have their fill of pizza, cola, and cake in the kitchen. When the noise moves up to the second floor, we creep into the kitchen and gobble up all the leftovers."

"And until then?" Dillon uttered huskily.

"We improvise," Kristina whispered.

"Like the boy said, anything goes in California." The swing creaked back against an ancient vine-heavy trellis as Dillon pulled Kristina against this chest, seeking her mouth with his own. She emitted a soft moan, plowing her fingers through his soft blond hair.

"I think we'd better cool it," Kristina whispered, reluctantly pulling back, moving her fingers across his lips.

Dillon nipped at her finger. "I had no intention of losing control."

"Then you don't know much about making love on a porch swing," Kristina teased thickly.

"Just how far have you gone on this swing?" he demanded.

"Stick around long enough and you may just have the deluxe ride," she promised temptingly.

"I'll bring a can of oil with me for the big one," Dillon told her. "Can't have the admiral counting the creaks."

The small light fixture at the front door blinked on again. "It's all clear, kids," Howard announced, popping his head out the door. "The tornado has spun its way upstairs."

"Okay, Pop," Kristina called back.

Dillon glanced at this watch, then said with regret, "I'd like to come in, sweet cheeks, but I should be getting down to the station."

Kristina rose, following him across the porch. "I'll save you a slice of cake."

From inside the screen door, Howard made a gesture of clearing his throat.

Kristina paused to stare at him. "I won't, Pop?"

"Homemade fudge cake from your mother's favorite recipe is gone," he announced with a tinge of pride. "Plenty of store-bought pizza left though, Dillon. I could wrap you up a slice or two."

"No thanks, Howard. Your chili dinner will see me through the night."

"Good luck with the show," Kristina murmured, standing on tiptoe to kiss his cheek.

"Talk to you tomorrow," he promised. With a wave to Howard and a light kiss to Kristina's forehead, Dillon was off.

"YOU ARE TUNED TO the 'Dillon After Dark' show. It's half past twelve on the clock. And 103.9 on your FM dial. We're just sailing into our final thirty minutes of showtime. I want to thank those listeners who have called to discuss Dr. Herman's views on diet clinic programs. There is still time to speak to the doctor. We'd especially like to hear from listeners who have been to any of the local clinics—whether your experience was good or bad. You know the number.

"Hello, this is Dillon. You're on the air."

"Dillon, this is Claire."

"Yes, Claire. Do you have an anecdote to contribute?"

"Oh... I have a contribution, Dillon."

"You sound rather shaky. Are you all right?"

"No, I'm not!"

"Perhaps Dr. Herman could—"

"You're the problem, Dillon."

"Me?"

"Don't give me that innocent act."

"What are you talking about?"

"Your show! You! I thought you loved me!"

"I care about all my listeners, Claire, especially loyal ones like you."

"Then why did you change the show?"

"Because I found I could no longer do that sort of show. We all change, Claire. Change is natural. Personal growth is necessary."

"I—I thought at first it was a mistake. But you've continued with this new show night after night."

"I like the new format. I hoped my loyal listeners would be willing to conform."

"It isn't fair! You mean the world to me. I'm so lonely!"

"Believe me, Claire. I can't fill a void in your life. You're much better off turning to people who can give you something tangible in return. A voice on the radio cannot—"

"I can't go on without you!"

"Of course, you can, Claire."

"I can't stand this! I'm taking pills to forget you."

"Claire, I care about you as a human being. Don't do anything to harm yourself."

"I've taken some already."

"How many?"

"I—don't know."

"Claire. Where do you live?"

"The Palm Apartments."

"What is your address?"

"I'm too tired to talk anymore. Goodbye, Dillon."

DILLON INSERTED a long-playing cassette into the control board and pulled off his microphone. He turned to the doctor at his side with a harried apology.

"Sorry, Doctor."

The thin middle-aged man seated beside him in a baggy suit frowned in bewilderment. "Is it all over?"

"I hope not, sir!" Dillon lunged from his chair, yanking open the glass door leading to the adjoining studio.

"The poor woman," the doctor fretted. "What shall I do now?"

"Go home. Thank you very much."

"And thank you. I think."

Joe the technician handed him the telephone on the other side of the glass. "The lines are jammed," he reported. "Kristina Jordan is on line one."

"Thanks." Dillon picked up the receiver. "Clear a line and call the cops, Joe," he directed. "They can get the paramedics out to the apartment house."

"Right."

Dillon pushed the first button on the phone console with a jab. "Hello, Kris. It's me."

"Are you all right, Dillon?"

"Not really. I'm sending the police to check out the woman."

"Good move."

Dillon rubbed his jaw with a shaky hand. "Thanks for not saying it."

"Saying what?"

"I told you so."

"You're hard enough on yourself, Dillon. You don't need my help."

"I love you, honey."

"Do you want me to come to the station?"

"No. You've got your hands full with the girls."

"I can get away."

"It would serve no purpose. I'm going to wait here for word, then I'm going home try to get some sleep."

"This isn't your fault, you know."

"Isn't it?"

"No, Dillon!"

"I'm not too sure about anything right now."

"It's human to be upset. You're doing exactly the right thing by sending the police to check things out."

"I hope I'm doing right by her."

"You are. And remember you can always be sure of me."

"Okay, sweet cheeks."

"Call me when you hear something."

"Will do." Dillon hung up the phone and stared glumly at Joe.

"Can you believe screwy Claire?" Joe exclaimed.

Dillon shook his head ruefully. "No."

"You've really got the magic touch, man. Now they're even fallin' at your feet full of pills."

"Shut up, Joe."

The technician took one look at Dillon's desperate face and

raised his hands in a gesture of peace. "Okay, okay. You can't blame me for wonderin' just what makes a loner with shaggy hair and a grumpy disposition so attractive to women, can you?"

KRISTINA AWOKE Friday morning to discover she'd fallen asleep with her beside lamp on. She'd barely moved all night, or she was still snugly tucked inside her bedcovers, the novel she'd been reading still facedown on her stomach. Her thoughts swiftly shifted to Dillon. Had she been sleeping with him, the covers would've been on the floor. As for the book... The book never would've left the shelf in the first place!

The privacy and isolation she'd once enjoyed was now her lonely trap. Dillon wasn't the only one who had been hiding from serious romantic involvement. Waiting half the night for him to call had given her lots of time to think things over. She needed him as much as he needed her. Being comfortable wasn't all it was cracked up to be.

Kristina slipped out of bed, glancing at her clock radio as her feet hit the carpet. It was barely seven o'clock. It had been hours since Dillon's confrontation on the show with the desperate Claire. What on earth happened to the woman? Why hadn't he called her back? She'd told him to call!

Kristina reached over to shut off her lamp and pick up the receiver of her pale blue phone. She punched out his number with practiced motion, not certain what to say or how to say it.

What if the news was so bad he'd retreated into himself again?

Frustration and worry zapped the grogginess from her system. It would be so much simpler all the way around if he was in her bed every night. Taking his spot as the man of her house.

Kristina pushed some mussed black hair from her face, listening to the phone ring over and over again in her ear. With every passing day she needed him more and more, wanted him under her roof.

Kristina let it ring twenty times before crossing her thumb over the disconnect button. She had to find him. She'd shower and dress, them comb the entire state of California until she got some answers.

Kristina soon discovered she didn't have to search any farther than her own house. She entered the kitchen to the rumbling hum of male laughter. Seated at her table, wolfing down a huge plate of pancakes à la admiral was Dillon Danvers himself.

"I thought you were a shredded wheat man," she burst out in annoyance. A flood of relief spread through her at the mere sight of him, dressed in a fresh outfit of snug-fitting jeans and a spotless white T-shirt. His bleached hair was a mass of flyaway wisps, which softened his angular features nearly to boyishness. His eyes were a sparkling blue that could challenge the sky's brilliance on its best summer day.

He'd slept. He'd freshened up. He was just fine, she realized. His body and soul were intact.

Dillon sheepishly gazed at the slender woman standing over him in yellow-cuffed shorts and yellow-and-white polka-dot blouse, tapping a white sandaled toe on the linoleum. Oh, how he loved her in polka dots!

"Well, Dillon, what do you have to say for yourself?" she demanded despite her relief. "You never called me back last night. And to add insult to injury, you're eating his pancakes!" She thrust an accusing finger at her dumbfounded father.

Dillon swallowed his last bite of pancake in a guilty gulp. "They have a different flavor when the admiral makes them, honey. Less carbon—or something."

Kristina placed her palms on the tabletop, hovering over him in interrogation. "Why didn't you call me?"

"Because I didn't want to risk waking up the whole house." Dillon replied apologetically, lifting his juice glass to his lips for a long thirsty sip.

"Wait till you hear this, Krissy," Howard broke in, setting a place at the table for her. "You sit down and I'll get your breakfast."

Kristina took the chair beside Dillon, eyeing him expectantly. "What happened to the woman caller?"

"Well..."

"Another batch, Dillon?" Howard offered, hoisting the ceramic bowl of batter into the crook of his arm.

"Maybe one more round," Dillon replied. "If you have enough."

"We do," Howard assured him, ladling four circles of batter onto the griddle on the stove. "The girls were up half the night. I don't expect to see them until lunchtime."

"The woman, Dillon," Kristina prodded, digging her fingers into his sinewy arm.

"The whole pill thing was a hoax," he reported, his heavy blond eyebrows drawing a hard single line. "The lady's an actress. She was hoping I'd show up on her doorstep, anxious to placate her."

"It was a phony call for help?" Kristina drew back in her chair, her face set in shock.

"Her plan was seduction," Howard added, flipping his sizzling cakes.

"She was dressed in a negligee. Dressed for action. So they tell me," he added, when Kristina mouth opened in protest. "I didn't go over there myself."

"She actually lured you over there on false pretenses?" Kristina gasped in wonder. "Her life wasn't in danger?"

Dillon shrugged, then said dryly, "The place was full of lit candles which could have posed a fire hazard, I guess. She had a photographer on hand for publicity photos. Her plan was to be the woman who saved the 'Dillon After Dark' show with a night of passion for its reclusive host."

Kristina huffed angrily, accepting the coffee mug Howard handed her. "She was a regular listener, wasn't she?"

"Yeah," Dillon nodded soberly. "It was disappointing to accept that a regular would try to use me. She knew I'd be truly concerned for her well-being."

"You heard from management yet?"

"Roger Calhoun, the station owner, rushed down to the studio last night. He's been monitoring my new format, so he happened to be listing to the show live." Dillon leaned back as Howard filled his plate with four steaming pancakes. "You want a couple of these?" he asked politely, though his eyes held a possessive gleam.

"I'll wait for the next round," Kristina declined with a wave. "Make mine smaller, Pop."

"Aye, aye."

"So, what did Mr. Calhoun have to say?"

"I believe he was a bit overwhelmed by the entire ordeal," Dillon replied with a small smirk, dousing his cakes with maple syrup. "He's a shrewd businessman, but he's from the old school. Likes his women meek and obedient, like the good Mrs. Calhoun."

"Sounds charming," Kristina drawled sarcastically.

"He's okay. But rambunctious females are foreign territory to him."

"Then he should be behind your new format," Kristina reasoned.

Dillon face grew doubtful. "He may be a male chauvinist, but he's a businessman first. He wants a money-making show. A money-making show has to garner big sponsors. And big sponsors want high ratings."

Kristina sipped her coffee with concern. "So what happens now?"

"Calhoun was upset last night—didn't know what to do. So he called a meeting for this afternoon at twelve-thirty. I figure this will be the end my reign at WXNT, or a whole new beginning there."

"I'll go with you," she volunteered, accepting her plate of pancakes. "I'll wait outside to lend moral support."

"But you can't get away, can you?" Dillon protested half-heartedly.

"Sure she can," Howard inserted, pulling out a chair for himself. "If you want something around here, boy, you've got to ask for it in plain talk. It's the way shrinks run things, don't you know. Lots of plain talk."

"Right, Pop." Kristina flashed him a wry smile.

Howard stroked his jaw in thought. "I'll get those girls back to their houses when the giggling's over. And I'm sure Julianne can stay with one of 'em while I go over to Beacon House. Easy enough."

Kristina reached over the table and squeezed her father's hand. She had to give him credit. When he decided to root for someone, he pulled out all the stops. He was trying so hard to accept Kristina's life as it stood.

"Thanks, Howard," Dillon ventured. "For everything."

Howard shifted uncomfortably in his chair, inclining his head an inch or so to butter his pancakes. "Finish up your food, kids, and get the blazes out of my kitchen," he ordered with mock gruffness. "I've got to get lunch started pretty soon. Before those girls call the pizza man on me again!"

"WELL, HELLO THERE, big fella." The words were barely out of WXNT's receptionist when she realized Dillon was not alone. Her red lips froze in a pucker and her eyes widened in embarrassment.

"Hi, Ariel." Dillon paused at her desk, Kristina a step behind him. "Calhoun here yet?"

"Uh-huh." Ariel nodded, focusing curiously on Kristina. "And this is your agent?" she asked optmistically.

Dillon groaned impatiently. "I don't have an agent. I've never had an agent."

"You need an agent," Ariel finished firmly. "You shouldn't be negotiating with a wolf like Calhoun without an agent to look out for your interests."

"Thank you, Mother," Dillon returned impatiently.

"Ignore my advice," Ariel griped, propping her chin in her hand. "Go ahead and dole it out yourself six nights a week like so much fertilizer, then close your ears."

"Don't mind if I do," he tossed back eloquently, gesturing to Kristina. "This is Kristina Jordan, by the way."

"Oh?" Ariel's lips opened to a circle.

"She's going to wait for me out here," he explained.

Ariel stood up, tugged at her tight floral dress and nervously patted her spiked hair.

"Are you feeling all right?" Dillon demanded with concern.

"Sure," Ariel said in an odd voice, shifting her heavily made-up eyes to the left.

Dillon leaned forward across the desk. "Is there something in your eye? Let me have a look."

Ariel pushed his hands away from her face with a squawk. "Make yourself at home, Doctor," Ariel invited too brightly, stepping away from her desk. "We have some current magazines over there," she said, pointing over Kristina's shoulder.

Kristina turned to look at the small waiting area, then back to find Ariel tipping her head toward windowsill behind her desk.

"Ariel..." Dillon shook his head with puzzlement.

"You better get down to the conference room," Ariel finally said with defeat. "Arnie and Mr. Calhoun are waiting."

"I don't know how long it'll be," Dillon said, planting a kiss on Kristina's forehead.

"I'll be fine," Kristina assured him with a smile. "Ariel and I can get to know each other."

Ariel shifted nervously from one foot to the other.

Dillon started down the hall to the conference room only to be stopped by Kristina's cry of shock.

"My mum! You killed my beautiful mum plant!" Kristina rushed to the windowsill and held up the forlorn pot wrapped in crushed green foil. The petals were sagging and brown. "So this is what you're fidgeting about."

"I'm sorry, Doctor," Ariel murmured. "It's a curse. I kill plants and flowers with a quick glance. Living things don't have a chance with me." Ariel balled her fists in frustration. "I told Dillon not to leave it here. But he didn't know how to care for it, either."

"But he said you wanted to take care of it," Kristina as-

serted, pulling dead petals from the blossoms only to have
the whole thing fall apart in her hands.

"The big dumb oaf was passing the buck! I'm not to be
trusted, Doctor," Ariel confessed with genuine regret. "You
should've given him a frog like he wanted. The little creature
would've liked the sea air at his place..."

Kristina whirled to confront Dillon, but the door marked
Conference was just shutting with a solid thud.

"He wanted a frog?" Kristina repeated in awe, turning
back to the receptionist. "He actually said he wanted a frog,
instead?"

Ariel shrugged, spurting nervously, "You know how big
dumb oafs are!"

DILLON CLOSED the door to the conference room behind him,
keenly aware that the men had fallen silent upon his arrival.
Bad sign—Roger Calhoun conversing privately with his
nephew. Calhoun was seated in his usual spot at the head of
the long table. Arnold Rodale was seated at his right, his
plump face pinched, his fingers drumming on the tabletop.

"Gentleman." Dillon nodded at the pair, calmly taking a
chair beside Rodale.

"We had quite an adventure last night, didn't we?" Calhoun noted with a chuckle, which didn't quite reach a humorous level.

"We sure did, Uncle Roger," Rodale agreed, his head bobbing.

"You slept through the whole damn thing!" Calhoun chastised.

"I listen a lot," Rodale said defensively. "Somebody
could've called me," he added, frowning at Dillon.

"I had my hands full, Arnie," Dillon explained patiently.
"Roger showed up within minutes and took over. It *is* his
station."

Calhoun nodded. "I'm glad you remember my place in
line, Dillon."

Dillon watched the older man's mouth thin under his

moustache and tensed. The news Calhoun was about to deliver wasn't going to be the best.

"What's on your mind, sir?"

Calhoun opened a folded newspaper at his elbow. "This is the afternoon edition of the *San Diego Sun*. Have you seen it yet?"

"No," Dillon admitted. "I haven't seen any of the papers today."

"You made front-page news." Calhoun shoved the paper across the table at an angle.

Dillon grabbed the paper and grimly scanned the article, uttering a soft curse under his breath.

"I understand it's made the wire services," Calhoun informed him.

"Great," Dillon muttered grimly.

"It can be great, Dillon."

Dillon's eyes slowly rose from the printed page, his voice slow and deliberate as he weighed his words. "What do you mean, Roger?"

"He means showbiz, Dillon," Rodale jumped in eagerly. He glanced at his uncle, delighted to find that he wasn't going to be interrupted for a change. "We've been thinking, Dillon. This woman's publicity stunt can be used to enhance your career as well as hers. Just picture it," he proclaimed, raising his pudgy hands, "sultry actress draws Dillon back into the boudoir."

"Is this your attitude, Roger?" Dillon demanded.

"Yes, Dillon," he replied magnanimously. He intertwined his long gnarled fingers on the table. "You haven't seen this week's fan mail yet... It is fervently against your new format."

"I see. One week of experimentation and I'm back to square one."

"I would've given you more time," Calhoun admitted not without sympathy, "if this stunt hadn't brought you so clearly into the limelight. The world is watching WXNT right now. Showbiz is right now. The present is all that matters. A decision has to be made today."

"It's the perfect way to ease back into your old format," Rodale told him anxiously. "Kind of a way to save face after failing."

"I can't go back to the old format," Dillon announced adamantly.

"Your attitude is very disappointing," Calhoun muttered.

"I'm trying to be reasonable," Dillon stated simply. "My contract states that I have control over the contents of my show. It doesn't mention the format at all."

"It also states that I have final say on the format," Calhoun needlessly reminded him. "Which in plain terms means I cannot force you to follow the romantic theme, but I can stop you from following the topical one." Calhoun sat up straighter in his chair, his hawklike features growing sharper. "My position isn't up for negotiation. "If you do no wish to return to your romantic exhibition, we will be parting company. Today."

Dillon met Calhoun's gaze with equal force. "I believe goodbyes are in order, sir."

KRISTINA DROPPED the magazine in her hands when Dillon emerged from the conference room and stalked back down the hall. "Dillon?"

He moved into the reception area with the strides of a predator.

"You okay?" Ariel asked tensely.

Dillon rounded Ariel's desk and reached for the mum plant on the sill. "It's been nice, Ariel."

Her face grew stricken. "You've been canned?"

"By mutual consent," he replied curtly. Tucking the pot under his arm, he pulled Kristina to her feet. "Let's go, honey."

"You can't leave me alone with all these stuffed shirts!" Ariel cried after him as he pushed open the glass door leading to the street.

Dillon smiled fondly at the funky-looking girl, trailing behind in desperation. "Go through the studio later on and get my stuff together, will ya?"

"Okay," she relented with a pout. "I'll bring it by your house."

Dillon paused in protest. "You don't have my address. Let me—"

"Of course I have it!" she scoffed mildly. "You think I could work with a hunk like you for two years, much less two days without following you home just once?"

"Ah, simpleminded me." Dillon laughed softly, guiding Kristina out the door.

Kristina stopped on the sidewalk, giving his arm a reassuring pat.

"It'll be all right," he announced rather dubiously.

"Of course it will," Kristina agreed with more faith in her voice. "Tell you what, let's do lunch."

"Let's do rum and Cokes first. There's a place just down the street."

Kristina fell into step with his determined stride. "Dillon, I wanted to ask you about something..."

Dillon gripped the pot in his hand, his face set in granite. "Don't ask me about the frog. Not now."

Kristina sighed with submission. "Okay."

Dillon urged Kristina into a small tavern down the street from the station. Kristina blinked in the smoky darkness, nearly tripping over a small step near the bar. Dillon's hand swiftly captured hers, leading her through the maze of pinball machines and video games. Greeting the bartender with familiarity, he marched on to the back section of the room clustered with small square tables. He set the plant on the scarred surface of one and pulled out a cracked vinyl chair for her.

"I know this isn't the sort of pub you usually frequent," he half apologized, dropping into the chair opposite her.

Kristina raised a thin black eyebrow, her small mouth curving. "I admit the place has more of a nostalgic feel for me than a familiar one."

"This spot is very current to me," Dillon told her. "It's open late, so I can come here after the show for a nightcap. I sit at the bar and old Gus there tells me the facts of life. At least it used to happen that way," he amended soberly.

"Oh, Dillon." Kristina's face fell as he faced her with a defeated look in his eyes.

"Sit tight while I get the drinks," he said with forced brightness. "What's your pleasure?"

"The rum sounds good."

Kristina watched Dillon sidle up to the bar and place his order. He was a hulk of a man standing there with his ragged hairstyle and huge shoulders. So strong. Yet so vulnerable. She could already see the writing on the wall. He wouldn't want to make a commitment while he was out of work. And he was out of work because he'd made a commitment.

Kristina fingered the ailing mum plant with disappointment. He had been so close to giving himself to her completely. For always. Now what would happen?

"Here we are." He sat down again and slid her drink around the pot. "Don't know what I was worried about. Gus has just offered me a job here, waiting tables. How'd I do with your drink?"

"Oh, Dillon." Kristina smiled wanly across the table. "I feel so responsible."

Dillon took a gulp of laced Coke, closing his eyes as he swallowed appreciatively. "Why?"

"Because I forced you to choose! You know I did." Kristina's shoulders drooped.

"Perhaps you nudged me in the right direction, but I gave up my show for a lot of reasons." Dillon reached across the table and ran his finger down her creamy pink cheek. "You pried open doors inside me that have never even been knocked on before, sweet cheeks," he admitted huskily. "You were right about me from the beginning. I used the romantic chitchat to satisfy my need to be needed. I used the airwaves as my shield from the world. The show just didn't excite me anymore once I'd met you. The real thing is a whole lot better. Especially on a chilly California night."

"I told Pop it was spontaneous combustion," Kristina confided with a warm gaze.

"Exactly right." Dillon tipped his glass into hers in a toast. "Here's to ya, sweet cheeks."

"Please don't let what's happened today change our course," Kristina pleaded, her fingers tracing a line along his bare arm.

"Not a chance, he murmured huskily. "We're on proper course. And the daughter of an admiral shouldn't have to ask such a question in the first place."

15

"THIS PLACE IS AWESOME!" Julianne twirled around on Dillon's balcony Monday morning, the sea breezes picking up her long black hair.

Dillon leaned against the doorjamb, enjoying her childlike enthusiasm. "Thank you very much."

"If I lived here, I'd spend lots of time outside," she declared, her long thin body moving effortlessly in her terry cloth beach jacket.

"So would I, Muffin," Howard echoed from Dillon's kitchen. "So would I."

"Too bad Mom couldn't be here with us," Julianne lamented, slowing down to take a breath.

Dillon laughed mirthlessly, moving across the redwood planking. "Somebody in this motley crew has to bring home a paycheck."

"Are you sorry you quit your job, Dillon?" Julianne asked bluntly, her expression and tone resembling her mother's.

"No, not really."

"Some people I know are sort of disappointed," Julianne confided, resting her elbows on the railing, not quite meeting Dillon's gaze.

"Are you?"

"Not me," she pondered. "Not exactly..."

"Your sleepover friends, then?" he guessed.

Julianne shrugged her slender shoulders. "Sort of. They can't believe you gave up your super job. They want me to explain it to them."

"You could tell them that life is full of beginnings and endings."

"What are you going to do now?"

"Look for another job," he told her matter-of-factly. "Radio personalities bounce around a lot."

"So you're going to stay in radio?"

Dillon nodded. "It's what I do best."

Julianne's head bobbed in agreement. "You're excellent on the air. It's kind of funny really," she declared suddenly with a giggle. "Mom's been so careful about dating just the right men all these years, lecturing me about how to live. Then she goes and falls for a guy *I* find! He likes her in my dress, and gets her surfing on my board."

"So?" Dillon growled in confusion.

"So, I think Mom should listen to me and her heart a lot more often!"

"I wouldn't put it to your mother quite that way," Dillon advised ominously.

"Hey, I don't want to lose my allowance for a week. But let's face it, Dillon, if it wasn't for me, you two would never have gotten together. You were living on opposite ends of the earth!"

"May as well take credit for polio vaccine while you're at it, Muffin," Howard interrupted, poking his head out the sliding glass door. "Car just drove up, Dillon. Silver Charger."

"It must be the station's receptionist." Dillon tugged at Julianne's hair and moved into the house.

"We'll just get our things and head down for the beach," Howard said, picking up his straw hat from the kitchen counter.

Ariel was just emerging from her car as Dillon strode across the gravel driveway. "I am so glad you're home!" she called out, clutching her black dress against the gusty breezes.

"I'm so glad you're glad," Dillon returned with a grin, shoving his hands into the pockets of his cutoffs.

Ariel stood on tiptoe before him, scrutinizing his face. "You look okay. No hangover."

Dillon beamed with assurance. "I'm fine. Stuff in the trunk?"

"Right." Ariel handed him the keys.

With a burst of noise, Howard and Julianne appeared on the front doorstep.

Ariel shot the old man with the cooler and the girl with the hot-pink surfboard a surprised look. "I didn't realize you had company."

"I'm sure you'd like to meet the young lady," Dillon said, beckoning to Julianne.

"Who? Why?"

Julianne trotted across the gravel driveway, her surfboard hoisted high above her head.

"Ariel, this is Julianne Jordan, winner of the poetry contest. Ariel helped judge the contest, Julianne. She plucked your poem out of the slush pile."

"Nice to meet you," Julianne said with surprise, setting her surfboard in the nearby grass.

"It was a radical job," Ariel complimented, cocking her spiked head.

As the girls shook hands, Dillon couldn't help but notice the similarities in their lingo and appearance despite the five-year age difference. All of sudden he realized that Julianne would soon be old enough to drive, to date. In short, to behave like Ariel! How would they handle it? he wondered anxiously. He planned to be around after all!

"Why don't you and Howard head down to the beach," Dillon suggested a short time later once the small talk had diminished. "I'll be there in a minute."

"Okay!" Julianne took hold of her board and scampered off toward the trail.

"Nice kid," Ariel judged.

"Very nice."

Ariel's heavily made-up face grew pinched. "You going domestic on me, Danvers?"

Dillon stroked his stubbled jaw. "It's a strong possibility."

Ariel crowed in disbelief, then laughed. "I guess all things are possible."

"I'm believing in miracles these days," he confessed.

Ariel rolled her eyes skyward. "What romantic bunk! Your brain is getting too much sun or something."

"You should be so lucky," Dillon retorted with gruff humor. Jingling her keys, he rounded the Charger.

"Took an extra hour at lunch so I could come over," she told him in an agitated rush, right on his heels.

"Thanks, but you didn't have to." Dillon inserted the key and opened the trunk. "I could've waited."

"No, Dillon, you really couldn't have," she burst out excitedly.

Dillon gripped a brown sackful of his possessions and turned to regard Ariel with deeper interest. "What's up?"

"I've just come to change your whole life is all," she declared, beaming.

"WHAT DO YOU MEAN Dillon took off like a rocket?" Kristina confronted Howard and Julianne as she peeled off her gray suit jacket after work. She tossed the tailored garment over the back of a kitchen chair and pulled out the hairpins securing her hair, tugging it loose around her shoulders. Kristina had the Monday-after-vacation-blahs in a big-time way. Going from surfboards to desk had been a shock to the system.

"Well," she prodded. "Answer me!" When she received only a set of blank stares, she lost her cool. "I've just had a long hard day at the office, guys. I don't have much patience left for family games tonight."

Howard and Julianne looked to each other with hesitation.

"I told you she was going to say that, Grandpop," Julianne whispered nervously.

"And I told you we can't help it," Howard returned helplessly. "Is she always this way after a vacation?"

"Quit talking about me as if I'm not here!" Kristina ordered on the verge of exploding.

"We know you're here, Krissy," Howard empathetically assured his daughter.

"Boy, oh boy, do we know!" Julianne tossed in, rolling her violet eyes.

Kristina folded her arms across her chest and moved

closer to the fidgeting couple. "Come on, you two. Let's have it. I know you spent the day at Dillon's. Where is he?"

"We don't mean to let you down, Krissy," Howard placated. "We just don't have an adequate answer. Dillon's receptionist showed up sometime before lunch and Dillon never quite set foot on the ground again." He turned to Julianne for backup.

"It's true, Mom. We surfed, ate sandwiches, played some catch..." Julianne trailed off helplessly.

"He was with us, but he wasn't," Howard inserted. "Just seemed preoccupied."

Julianne rocked on the heels of her bare feet, shoving her hands into the pockets of her knit shorts. "When we were ready to leave, he just said to tell you he'd be out of touch for a few days."

"Don't call us, we'll call you," Howard finished with a shrug.

"Those were his exact words?" Kristina demanded in horror.

"No, of course not!" Howard amended, patting Kristina's shoulder consolingly. "You know Dillon turns a phrase like no one else." Howard paused in thought. "Come to think of it, he handled the entire thing quite cleverly. Didn't give us the message until we were in the car and I'd started the engine."

"But you two are nosy!" Kristina cried in frustration. "You leave no stone unturned when you want to find something out! How could you let this happen?"

"You aren't insecure about Dillon, are you?" Howard queried.

"No, I guess not." Kristina threw her hands in the air. "Why should I be? I pulled him out of his cave, steered his show into the dust. If he decides to crawl back into the depths for a little while, I should be totally understanding, right?"

"Right!" her family cheered in unison.

"Thanks a heap!" Kristina grabbed her jacket and stormed out of the kitchen and up the stairs to her room.

"Look, Mom, if Dillon wanted to dump you like yesterday's news, he'd do it out on the porch for free. He wouldn't blow a wad of cash at the Hotel Del Coronado on a Thursday night."

Kristina, who was sitting on the edge of her bed filing her nails, shook her head at her philosophical daughter leaning against the doorjamb. "You're growing more practical by the day, kiddo."

"It only makes sense," Julianne said, strolling over to her mother's dresser. "Why buy you dinner in one of the flashiest places in Coronado, then turn around and push aside his investment."

Kristina, who was sitting on the edge of the bed smoothing her stockings, balked in shock. "Push aside his investment?"

"Those were Grandpop's words," she confessed at the sound of her mother's disapproval.

"This certainly has turned into a family affair," Kristina grumbled good-naturedly, stepping into her strapless slip. She was admittedly happy that everyone was adjusting. Julianne was over her crush. In spite of Dillon's shaggy hair and unemployed status, the admiral was singing Dillon's praises. No longer did there seem to be tremendous barriers in their path. Even Dillon's job was out of the way. Aside from his three-day defection into nowhere without any explanation, things were moving along quite nicely.

"Do you think this is the big night, Mom?" Julianne broke into her mother's thoughts.

Kristina turned to confront her daughter, now primping before the dresser mirror with Kristina's pearl necklace looped around the crew neck of her striped T-shirt. "What do mean?"

Julianne grabbed a brush off the dresser and rushed to the bed. "Why, Doctor, I'm talking about the biggest night of a girl's life! Please, don't be shy," she said in a clipped, reporterlike tones, shoving the brush in her mother's face as if it were a microphone. "Speak up, Doc, and tell us if you are about to become Mrs. Dillon After Dark."

Kristina grinned with relief. It was good to know Julianne

considered a marriage proposal a girl's "biggest night." Kristina cleared her throat and took the brush. "Well, I can only say that such a proposal would be wonderful," she intoned with a toothy smile.

Julianne tipped her head over the brush. "And your answer to such a question, Doctor?"

Kristina struck an exaggerated pondering pose. "My answer?"

"Your audience is waiting," Julianne coaxed impatiently.

"I advise my audience to tune in again between eleven o'clock and midnight. I'll definitely be back by then because tomorrow's Friday, and I have early appointments."

"What if your audience can't wait up?"

Kristina drew back in disbelief. "I happen to know my audience has incredible stamina."

The interviewer's face drooped. "Aw, Mom..." Julianne stomped her foot and ran the brush through her hair as if it was just another handle with bristles. "You're no fun."

"Depends who you talk to," Kristina shot back airily.

"TO NEW BEGINNINGS." Dillon lifted his fluted champagne glass to Kristina in a toast.

"To fresh starts," she chimed in, tapping her glass against his.

They stood on the Hotel del Coronado's promenade deck together an hour later, arriving just in time to watch the sun set over the Pacific Ocean in a fiery orange blaze, gilding the surface of the shimmering waters in brilliant gold. The mood was festive, guests strolling around arm in arm, some seated at wrought-iron tables covered with red-and-white umbrellas. A four-piece band played music, its lively beat drifting over them and out to sea.

The evening was perfection, Kristina silently mused, resting her head against Dillon's arm.

"How did you know this was my favorite place?" she asked dreamily.

"Julianne told me."

"Ah, so it wasn't a fluke," Kristina realized.

Dillon's mouth curved invitingly in the lamplight. "Nothing left to chance tonight, sweet cheeks. This evening's far too special for risky restaurants."

Kristina nodded. "Mmm, yes. It must be special."

"You've seen through me, then?" Dillon clucked with disappointment.

"The suit's a dead giveaway," she replied merrily. "A surprise return engagement for the confining tuxedo."

Dillon gazed lovingly at Kristina, her blue-black hair a glossy tide on her bare shoulders, a man's fantasy in his favorite white-and-black polka-dot dress. "And you, cheeks, have me seeing spots again in that tempting excuse for a dress."

"It's not an official hand-me-down," Kristina told him. "Seems I've stretched it out and it no longer fits Julianne properly."

Dillon's eyes twinkled with mischief. "Inevitable under the circumstances. Was she angry?"

Kristina shook her head, sipping from her glass. "We struck a bargain, which included a new dress for her."

"I suppose I'd better come across with your surfboard, too," Dillon mused. "I promised Julianne you wouldn't use hers anymore."

"Promises mean a lot to children," Kristina concurred.

"Promises mean a lot to me," he intoned suggestively, pressing his lips against her hairline. Dillon hooked their empty glasses in his fingers and turned to set them on a nearby table. "There," he declared, raising his empty hands. "All the better to hold you with."

Kristina trembled as Dillon's hand moved up her spine to her exposed shoulder blades. She snuggled up against him, wrapping her arms around his waist. He smelled of fresh soap and suntan oil. A lovely blend, she'd come to discover.

"Dillon?"

"Mmm?"

"Where the hell have you been?" she asked flatly.

"Making plans."

"What sort of plans?" she demanded.

"Plans for the future. My tuxedo isn't the only part of me making an engagement," he rasped against her hair. "I want you to marry me, sweet cheeks."

Kristina lifted her face from his chest, a smile of acceptance splitting her face. "I'd like nothing better," she murmured.

Dillon reached into the pocket of his jacket and brought forth a diamond set in gold that made the sunset on the watery horizon pale in shame.

Kristina's heart tripped as Dillon took hold of her left hand and slipped the ring on her finger. The stone was huge. Outrageously so. Unemployment did the craziest things to the man.

"You...you went overboard," she chastised him without much vigor.

"I've been overboard since the moment I laid eyes on you," he rumbled dazedly, drawing her close for a kiss. Kristina melted into him, oblivious to the passersby. She had to be dreaming anyway, so what did they matter?

Kristina pulled her mouth from his, desiring much, much more. "Let's make it a quick ceremony," she proposed impulsively.

Dillon chuckled. "Can't wait to get me all to yourself, can you?"

"I'd like to move your stuff into my house tonight!" Kristina bubbled excitedly.

Dillon drew a hesitant breath. "Slow down, Kristina. We have to pause to discuss practical matters. My status of employment, for example."

"For once I don't want to be practical!" she protested, clutching his black lapels. "You'll find a job. I know you will."

"I already have," he announced proudly.

Kristina's eyes widened. "You think you're pretty damn tricky, don't you? Running off, buying a rock the size of a baseball, tracking down a new job, all without a word!"

"I wanted to make sure things were just right," Dillon explained, his shadowed features set soberly. "I had to have something tangible to offer you."

"So, are things just right?" Kristina sassily asked. "Another station decide to snatch you up?"

"Yes! Thank God."

"I'm so proud of you, Dillon. So glad you can pay for the ring," she added with a teasing smile.

Dillon cleared his throat, leaning back against the railing, which separated the promenade from the sand. "Kristina, my new job is in Santa Barbara."

"Santa Barbara?" she repeated. "Santa Barbara's nearly two hundred miles away!"

"Yes," he assented quietly. "Which is why I wanted to check it out without telling you." His eyes gleamed with excitement. "But as fate would have it, it's the chance of a lifetime. A midafternoon show."

"Oh?" Kristina asked softly, too stunned to react with little more than a feeble smile.

"KVSP is one of the area's top stations," Dillon continued, caught up in the reality of it all. "That woman's publicity stunt actually turned out to be a lucky break." He shook his head in wonder. "A representative from KVSP read about it and called me out of professional curiosity. Ariel fielded the call, and set up the interview."

"I see," Kristina said slowly. "So you've been in Santa Barbara."

"Yes. Got the V.I.P. treatment there, too," he reported with elation. "I had several meetings and interviews with station personnel. Got a grand tour of the operation. Oh, yes, you can rest easy about the format. The seduction production is out of service forever." Dillon searched her sober face in confusion. "Kris, this is the point where you're supposed to leap into my arms and tell me how happy you are about my daytime job, my proposal of marriage."

"Don't you realize what you're asking?" she whispered in panic.

"I'm asking you to be my bride, to move to the lovely seaside town of Santa Barbara." He did a double take at her frown. "Do you mean to say after all the adjustments I've made, you're not willing to move up the Coast?"

"Coronado's always been my home," she said softly. "I've been so comfortable here." She shook her head in bewilderment. "I thought you loved this area."

"I do!" Dillon said, struggling with his disappointment. "But a D.J.'s life seldom runs a steady course. I thought you'd appreciate my efforts to get a job in the vicinity. I may have ended up in Boston, or Chicago."

"Julianne will flip out," Kristina predicted, folding her arms against her chest over the sudden chill seeping through her.

"How do you know?" he shot back in a hurtful tone. "We've become good friends, she and I."

Kristina drew back in shock. "I know because I'm her mother! She has her friends here. She goes to a good school."

"There are good schools in Santa Barbara! There is plenty of office space for doctors," he asserted, his temper rising.

"You've assumed far too much," Kristina fumed.

"Kristina, this move was inevitable," he reasoned. "I've been a radio personality for years. I know the local market well enough to realize there is no job opening for me here. Even if there were, you know the people of this town view me as Dillon After Dark. I did my damnest to change their thinking about me—only to fail miserably."

"So you thought I'd just pull up stakes and follow you," Kristina reproached.

"You're a grown woman! I thought you'd be up to a move."

"You would've found out how I feel had you called me before you left."

"I didn't want to get your hopes up," he explained, smiling mirthlessly over the irony. "Imagine, I thought you'd be let down if I drove all the way up there only to be rejected."

"So this is all set in your mind?" she asked stiffly.

"The contract is signed. I'm leaving."

"Congratulations on your new job!"

Dillon grasped her arms, his voice laden with disappointment and bitterness. "I've made all the concessions I can for you, Kristina. It's your turn to bend some."

"Perhaps you would've been better off had I just let you alone," she lamented softly.

"No," he disagreed truthfully. "You've shown me I can open up, love one woman." Dillon inhaled sharply with hope, scanning her eyes. "Tell me you want to be that woman, Kris."

"I have to think..." she stammered, shaking free from his embrace.

"All right," he said curtly, dropping his arms to his sides. "You go back to your nest to 'think.' It's what you do best. Go and think in your comfortable home with your comfortable family. It's far easier if you don't feel. Take it from me. I'm an expert."

"I believe I'll return home in a cab," she announced, her chin held high, though her eyes shimmered with incipient tears.

"Fine," he said, his hooded gaze showing he was already gaining mental distance. "I've reserved a room here for the night and I intend to enjoy it."

Kristina tugged the diamond off her finger and set it in his hand. "Too impractical for me anyway!" she whispered chokingly.

"Oh, Kris..." Dillon growled in desperation.

Before Dillon could hook her arm, she was out of reach, into the stream of strolling people.

He shook his head, his face pinched in pain as he gazed down at the ring. How could something so right go so wrong? Was he mistaken to believe there was such a thing as a lasting relationship?

In all his years he'd never come so close, only to fall so hard. Was it really worth it, all the fuss made over total commitment? He closed his eyes, trying to hold back the skepticism, the sense of betrayal and abandonment that had haunted him since childhood. His inner self warred with visions of his habitual detachment and Kristina's lovely face.

He'd have plenty of time to mull things over. All night long.

16

"DIGGING TO CHINA, Krissy?" Howard ambled across the front lawn Saturday afternoon to the curbside garden where Kristina was hard at work turning up the soil.

Kristina stopped raking for a moment, wiping perspiration from her forehead with the back of her hand. "I've been meaning to replant this garden for a long time."

"I see."

"You're kind of dressed up for a Saturday," she noted, scanning him from head to toe.

"I know I promised to cut the lawn today," he began apologetically.

"It'll keep," Kristina assured him, sinking the rake back into the moist black dirt, combing it smooth with vigorous strokes. "Who knows, I may get to the grass myself before the day is through." She worked silently for a while, aware of her father's lingering presence.

"You got plans?" she asked conversationally.

"Thought I'd take Bernice Chambers over to the zoo."

Kristina's face expressed surprise, but she kept stroking the earth with a vengeance. "Nice idea. She can use a break."

"Can't we all." Howard shoved his hands into the pockets of his twill pants, casually looking over the cluster of colorful potted plants lined up on the grass. "You always did like growing things. Yes sir, you have quite the green thumb."

"Yeah," she said breathlessly.

"A green thumb, and a mean batter's swing," he added, eyeing the rapidly moving rake in her hands.

"I love tending plants," she shot back defensively. "It's...relaxing."

"Relaxing you say?" He stroked his jaw with a dubious look.

"Yes!" she snapped. Suddenly she realized she was nipping at an innocent bystander. "I'm sorry, Pop." With an exhausted sigh, she crumpled against the rake handle. "I've no right to take my anger out on you."

"Seems like your problem with Dillon is nothing that can't be ironed out," Howard ventured mildly. "If you really want him."

Kristina closed her eyes with a groan. "I don't know."

"Would moving up the Coast be so bad?" he quizzed.

"Julianne would have to start over, too," Kristina reminded him.

"She's a strong girl. And she likes Dillon. You talk to her about it?"

"Yes. She wasn't quite as negative as—"

"As you are."

"No! I was going to say she wasn't quite as negative as I thought she'd be," she reprimanded with blazing eyes.

"She's a good girl."

"I think so."

"So how about you, Krissy. How do you feel?"

Kristina shrugged, pulling her orange T-shirt away from her sticky skin. "Maybe I overreacted... But at the time, I was stunned. Dillon took me off guard with his announcement. You see, I'm accustomed to planning things very carefully. It's the system I've used all these years."

"I know. You've done a remarkable job with your life so far."

"There's this beautiful house to consider," Kristina pointed out, gesturing to the grand yellow Victorian structure behind them. "I see nothing wrong with loving your home and your job. Falling into a routine is natural!"

"Like Mrs. Fisker next door," Howard agreed, tipping his head to the gray two-story on the left. "She loves her house, too. Lived here in Coronado for as long as anyone can remember."

Kristina pointed a finger at him. "Right!"

Howard swatted at a fly on his arm. "Poor thing lost her husband in the Korean War as I remember."

"Yes," Kristina affirmed. "She's managed well enough. Always has a cheerful word for us."

Howard folded his arms across his chest, rocking on his heels. "She's always smilin'. Always inviting the postman in for coffee and chitchat. Loves to chitchat," he repeated with assurance.

"Always chatting to the birds in her yard, too, isn't she?" Kristina tossed in with a rueful look.

"And they chirpy-chirp right back," Howard returned with a benign smile. "She's never really alone, is she?"

"I am not desperate to marry anyone!" Kristina proclaimed.

"No, no," Howard genuinely agreed. "You've done fine on your own. I already said so."

"If I were a desperate manhunter, I'd have married years ago."

"No argument from your old man," Howard assured her.

"Marriage the second time around should be of the most spontaneous nature!"

"No contest, Krissy."

"Especially if I were forced to pull up stakes here and start over," she contended.

"A big step to be sure."

"It would take a passion of the utmost urgency, Pop!"

"Redundantly put," Howard agreed. "Dillon's a passionate man all right," he mused. "But he did expect a lot from you, on the spur of the moment. Seems sort of selfish on his part."

Kristina rested her chin on the top of the rake handle, pensively gazing down the tree-lined street. "I don't think he's intentionally self-absorbed, Pop. He's just accustomed to living alone, fending for himself."

"Could be," Howard deliberated.

"Why, sure," Kristina asserted confidently. "You know having a family teaches you patience and generosity."

"Maybe." Howard shook his head. "But this last-minute job thing..."

"He had to jump at the opportunity. He's hit a dead end here in San Diego and he has to work. He needs to work."

"But he didn't even consult you, honey."

"He was just trying to shield me from disappointment in case the deal fell through."

"He could've called long distance."

"Well, maybe... It seems to be his most grievous error though, Pop. Dillon sincerely didn't understand why I would protest so strongly to moving. He knows nothing about family roots, the nesting instinct to stay put in a cozy home. When a D.J.'s career runs dry in an area, I suppose the most logical thing to do is to move on. I suppose he figured I could work anywhere, being self-employed..."

"Sounds as if you've given this a lot of thought," Howard said gently.

Her violet eyes widened. "I can think of nothing else!"

"Well, you were right about the urgency thing, Krissy. No sense in pulling up stakes for just any man."

"Dillon's not just any man!" she exclaimed, tossing aside her rake. "He is the right man!" Kristina began to laugh as she locked in on her father's twinkling eyes. "But we both know that very well, don't we?"

"You've certainly told me so often enough," he quipped. "In no uncertain terms."

Kristina sniffed, resting against his shoulder. "Oh, Pop."

"So what is your next move?" he challenged.

Kristina shook her head with a sigh. "My next move? If I told you, Pop, you'd have me locked up in my room talking to the birdies from my second-story window."

"DILLON, I CAN'T FIND any newspapers to wrap your dishes in."

Dillon, stretched out on the sofa in his darkened living room, cracked open an eye at the sound of Ariel's impatient voice. "Huh?"

With a huff of indignation, Ariel marched across the room

and drew open the curtains with a snap. Midafternoon sun flooded the room with heated intensity.

"Ouch!" Dillon squeezed his eyes shut against the brightness.

Ariel stomped to the sofa, lifted his feet off the end cushion, and threw them to the floor. "C'mon, dark man, I've already donated most of my Saturday to this packing gig and you haven't lifted a finger to help me. You act as though you don't want to go!"

"Get me a beer out of the fridge, will ya?" he mumbled, struggling to sit up.

"Get your own crummy beer!" She reached down and shook his shoulder. "Dillon, get a grip on yourself."

He leaned back against the cushions, rubbing his heavily whiskered face with a growl.

"You had a call earlier."

Dillon's eyes snapped open alertly.

"Not her," she promptly reported. "The real estate agent you met with in Santa Barbara. He says he's got a couple of beachfront homes for you to investigate. Wants you to call him back today."

"Sure, sure."

"I left his number on the kitchen table."

"I'll call him."

"Will you?" she demanded doubtfully.

Dillon took a good look at Ariel for the first time all day, approving of her change in appearance. She looked like a whole new person dressed in a simple white blouse and blue shorts, her hair clean and soft, her face free of makeup. "You shouldn't paint up your face and gook up your hair all the time," he asserted suddenly.

"Hey, don't practice your father jazz on me, you big oaf," she scolded, though her eyes glimmered with humor. "I only go for the dull look when I'm packing for ungrateful guys."

"I appreciate all your support," he assured her, reaching up to tweak her cheek. "There's plenty of newspaper under the sink if you need more."

"Why don't you just go see her?" Ariel demanded in exasperation.

"Because," Dillon answered broodingly.

"It's been a couple of days. The dust has settled, hasn't it?"

"She just walked away," he complained.

"Is that all?" Ariel asked in openmouthed wonder. "She didn't kick you or spit at you, or even dump a dry martini on your head?"

"Would you do those things in the heat of anger?" he asked incredulously.

Ariel flashed a cocky grin. "I've had my fiery moments."

"Kristina isn't the type to resort to violence. Though she too has had her fiery moments..."

"Yeah, I'll bet you two really can get into it," Ariel crowed. Dillon shifted uncomfortably on the sofa.

"Don't worry, I can't read minds," she assured him.

"Then read my lips," he instructed. "Leave me alone."

Ariel stood her ground, totally unfazed by his hard-line attitude. "If you're too stubborn to zip over to Coronado, I'd start working on your lovesick mug. You're pathetic-looking!"

"What can I do?" he blurted out in helpless frustration. "Beg her not to reject me?" He sprang to his feet, restlessly roaming the room with a lost look.

"I can't believe you're the same man who can seduce women with the crook of your silver tongue!" Ariel protested. "Are you going to stand there and shatter every romantic dream I have left?"

"When your own mother rejects you twice in one lifetime, you approach women very cautiously."

"Kristina is a psychologist," Ariel pointed out anxiously. "She knows better than to push a mess like you over the deep end with another brush-off. Just keep that desperately sexy expression on your face and you'll be a hit for sure!"

Ariel picked up Dillon's key ring from the end table and stuffed it in the palm of his hand. "Go on over there. Get—"

The peal of the doorbell cut through the house.

Ariel swiftly moved to the door, Dillon on her heels.

"No one." Dillon frowned over Ariel's shoulder with disappointment.

"Why, here's something." Ariel picked a florist's box up off the stoop, quickly working off the bright red ribbon fastening if shut. "Looks as if it's long enough for roses," she said, peeling off the cover. "Eek!" She threw her hands in the air, the box dropping to the floor with a plop.

"What the hell?" Dillon gazed in sharp amazement from Ariel's horrified face down to the open box at her feet. With a crackle and a croak, a huge frog jumped out of the tissue wrapping.

Ariel took refuge on the nearest chair. "Get him, get him!"

"It's only a frog," Dillon consoled with amusement.

"Sure, sure, a symbol you told me," she cried, repeating his earlier description with a contorted expression. "A slimy, icky symbol! You people are crazy, Dillon. Crazier than I ever could be!"

With a hearty chuckle, Dillon scooped the frog back up in the box. "No wonder the cover has holes punched in it," he said, trapping the amphibian back inside. His heart jumped with elation. Kristina had to be nearby. "I'll be right back, Ariel."

"Don't you dare set that box down," she yelled from atop her chair.

"I'll release the little fellow outside," he promised.

"Not by my car, Dillon," she warned, waving her hands like a traffic cop caught in rush hour. "Go a mile down the road. Turn and go another mile!"

Dillon strode out the door with a chuckle, setting the frog loose in the sagebrush. With some quick investigating he found Kristina's car parked off the side of his garage. He stroked his stubbled chin, his mouth curving in a huge smile. So she was playing hide'n'seek with him. Toying with him. He launched into a run, toward the dirt path forged in the bluff. There was only one place his little sea siren could be.

Dillon jogged into the cove, stopping short at a heap of clothing. He reached down to the sand and picked up her mint-green sundress. Holding it in his hands, he scanned the horizon. There she was several yards out, swimming grace-fully through the cresting waters.

With his heart pumping wildly in his chest, Dillon tossed aside her dress, his own shorts, and rushed into the rushing waves to join her.

"What took you so long?" Kristina asked in a squeal as Dillon rose from the waters like a submarine to snag her in his arms.

"Why, I had to find a home for our slimy friend," Dillon said, kissing her face. "Couldn't have Ariel going into shock."

Kristina wound her arms around Dillon treading water at her side. "The frog's name is Albert. He's a he."

"Oh."

"Where'd you ever get the idea to skinny-dip in the light of day?" he demanded roughly, aware of her bare limbs moving under the water's surface.

"It doesn't have to be dark to be game time," she murmured breathlessly.

"No kidding."

"I'm sorry, Dillon. I shouldn't have walked out on you."

"I'm sorry I didn't handle the new job thing better. I should've included you from the ground up."

"Just be certain you do next time," she admonished.

Dillon's face brightened. "Does this mean you're coming with me?"

"Yes, darling."

Dillon captured her mouth with his, dragging her under-water as he kissed her deeply. Tugging at her waist, Dillon urged her toward shore.

"Look!" Kristina gasped, standing on tiptoe in the water. "Our clothes!"

"Ariel!" Dillon shouted above the ocean's roar.

Ariel waved cheerily at them, the bundle of clothing tucked neatly under her arm. She scurried across the sand to-ward the path.

"She'll get hers," Dillon growled. Grabbing Kristina's arm, he pulled her inland.

"But we're naked!"

"And we look pretty good, too," Dillon tossed back with pride. "C'mon, sweet cheeks."

A sudden sharp cry pierced the air as they scampered to the shore.

"What happened to her?" Kristina asked as she saw Ariel toss their clothes in the air and run off the bluff.

"Divine justice," Dillon chuckled, hands on hips.

"What?"

"Albert, of course."

"Oh," Kristina nodded with a giggle.

"Wait here, damsel." Dillon shot ahead up the bluff and returned to the cove with their clothing.

With slow, gentle care, he pulled Kristina's sundress over her head, molding the cotton fabric to her body.

"Oh, how I love you," she said softly, cupping his wet, whiskery face in her hands.

Dillon stepped into his shorts, then pressed her close for a long, luxuriant kiss. "So, is the Jordan wagon ready to roll?" he asked huskily.

"Yes," Kristina murmured. "We'll have to work things out of course. Julianne will want to finish out the school year in Coronado. I'll have to close my office. Refer my patients. "It'll probably be a weekend romance until summer."

"Sounds fair," he agreed. "Though I'm as anxious as a schoolboy to get hitched properly." He encircled Kristina's shoulders, and together they strolled across the cove to the path.

"Haven't you forgotten something, darling?" Kristina asked gently.

"Can't imagine what, cheeks."

"My ring," she explained intently. "I want my ring back."

"You do?"

"Of course!"

"I'll have to give the matter some consideration," he teased.

"You arrogant ass!"

Dillon's chest rumbled with a low chuckle. "Seems to me I've heard those words before."

"You're liable to hear them time and time again," she threatened.

Dillon paused on the path, thrusting her against him. "If you were wearing shoes, lady, you'd be losin' them just about now..."

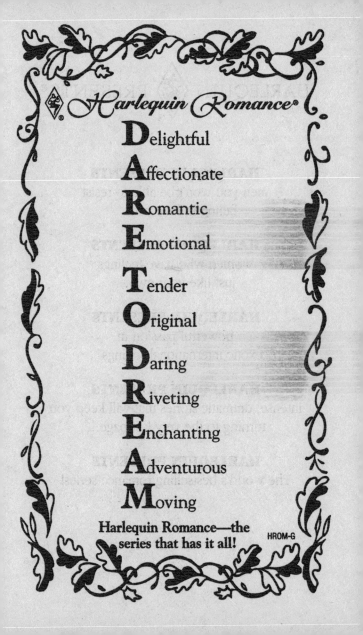

Harlequin Romance®

Delightful

Affectionate

Romantic

Emotional

Tender

Original

Daring

Riveting

Enchanting

Adventurous

Moving

Harlequin Romance—the
series that has it all!

HROM-G

HARLEQUIN PRESENTS

HARLEQUIN PRESENTS
men you won't be able to resist
falling in love with...

HARLEQUIN PRESENTS
women who have feelings
just like your own...

HARLEQUIN PRESENTS
powerful passion in
exotic international settings...

HARLEQUIN PRESENTS
intense, dramatic stories that will keep you
turning to the very last page...

HARLEQUIN PRESENTS
The world's bestselling romance series!

Harlequin®
Historical

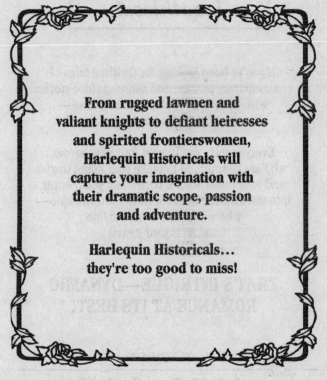

From rugged lawmen and
valiant knights to defiant heiresses
and spirited frontierswomen,
Harlequin Historicals will
capture your imagination with
their dramatic scope, passion
and adventure.

Harlequin Historicals...
they're too good to miss!

HARLEQUIN SUPERROMANCE®

...there's more to the story!

Superromance. A *big* satisfying read about unforget-
table characters. Each month we offer
four very different stories that range from family
drama to adventure and mystery, from highly emotional stories to romantic comedies—and
much more! Stories about people you'll
believe in and care about. Stories too
compelling to put down....

Our authors are among today's *best* romance writ-
ers. You'll find familiar names and
talented newcomers. Many of them are
award winners—and you'll see why!

If you want the biggest and best
in romance fiction, you'll get it
from Superromance!

Available wherever Harlequin books are sold.